"A powerful and moving experience."

—The *Washington Post*

"A lush, ambitious novel that offers a fascinating glimpse into the beauty and contradictions of Native Hawaiian culture."

—*Publishers Weekly*

"Davenport mines the depths of emotion…Readers who enjoy a Doctor Zhivago-like saga will appreciate the broad scope of this novel."

—*Library Journal*

SONG OF THE EXILE

"The strengths of this novel are many. Davenport is a superb storyteller!"

—*The Seattle Times*

"Deeply moving. …You can't read Kiana Davenport without being transformed."

—Alice Walker

"Her language is tender, lush, powerful. Unforgettable."

—The *Baltimore Sun*

SHARK DIALOGUES

"Great storytelling! An epic feminine saga...Davenport's prose is as sharp and shining as a sword. Her sense of poetry and love of nature permeate each line."

—Isabel Allende

"Torrid, yet intelligent...compares with Toni Morrison."

—*Glamour*

"Complex, resonant...handles the sweep of history and the nuance of the personal equally well."

—*San Francisco Chronicle*

Also by KIANA DAVENPORT

<u>Novels</u>

House of Many Gods

Song of the Exile

Shark Dialogues

<u>Short Story Collections</u>

House of Skin Prize-Winning Stories

Cannibal Nights Pacific Stories Vol. II

The Spy Lover

The Spy Lover

A NOVEL

KIANA DAVENPORT

Published by Thomas & Mercer
P.O. Box 400818
Las Vegas, NV 89140

ISBN-13: 9781612183411
ISBN-10: 1612183417

In Honor of

My brother, Braxton Rowan Davenport
My father, Braxton Bragg Davenport
My ancestor, Warren Davenport
My ancestor, John Tommy Kam

Heroes, who served in different wars

"Out beyond ideas of wrongdoing and rightdoing, there is a field. I will meet you there."

—Rumi

"Adieu, O soldier,
You of the rude campaigning...
The rapid march, the life of the camp,
The hot contention of opposing fronts, the long manoeuvre,
Red battles with their slaughter...
Spell of all brave and manly hearts, the trains of time through you and like of you all filled,
With war and war's expression."

—*Adieu to a Soldier*, Walt Whitman

"We speak of War and Conquest, and Begetting Heirs... Why do we not speak of Love?"

—The Journals of K'ang-Hsi
Emperor of China, 1661–1772

Johnny Tom

Prisoner of War Camp, April 1862

Each night his dreams begin with rice, the taste and texture of each grain aligned to parallel his hunger. But some nights his dreams are seized by Laughter and by Rain, two women so merged in his past they run together like mercury. In his sleep, he calls out to them in words that make no sense in English. At first light, he sits up and rests his weary head against his arm's hard cradle. Dawn lends a greenish cast to his sallow face, and in the cold his lips look mauve. Around him, wounded soldiers call out to their mothers; others lie still, so frail the weight of the air can scarcely be borne.

With stiffened fingers, Johnny scratches at the earth, lifts a small mound of dirt to his lips, and swallows, remembering how Raindance loved eating ashes from the fire. Thoughtfully, he pulls up blades of grass, arranging them to spell out the names of his wives. Laughter. Raindance. He presses each blade to his lips and thinks of his daughter, lost somewhere in the madness. *If she survives, will her half-Chinese womb be fruitful? Will she give me immortality?*

Wolves howl across the fogged Virginia mountains as a camp guard approaches, his face raw from the Piedmont cold. He kicks at a Federal prisoner who has been horribly shot up, then turns his attention to Johnny.

"Say something." He nudges him with his rifle butt. "G'wan! Say somethin'...I wanna hear what one o' you sounds like."

Johnny hesitates, then speaks in careful English. "You will...live...long, fruitful...life..."

The man guffaws and shouts to his friends. "Hear that, boys? Hear what the pigtail said?" He unbuttons his filthy pants and aims at Johnny's foot, pissing a steaming arc that instantly draws flies.

Johnny whispers after him. "Dog's vomit! Wild pigs will gorge on your liver."

Breathing in the acrid smell of sewage, he shudders, as throughout the stockade typhus spreads. There is no food, no fresh water for prisoners. Corpses lie unburied, slowly becoming their own moist graves. Men who try to bury them are shot. He crawls inside his ragged tent and pulls a cricket from his breast pocket, and chirps softly. The cricket chirps back. Its carapace is lovely, the color of chrysanthemum tea whose steam is blue. Its ferocious little face is shaped like a hatchet and the beady eyes shift like a gangster, making Johnny smile. The cricket has given him hours of pleasure and soon he will let it go. He is less kind to lice, snapping them between his teeth with a popping sound, swallowing them for nourishment.

He lies back, thinking how in his homeland great famines had spared him. Monsoons had clamored over him, bringing floods that washed whole villages away. *Why I was spared to end like this?* he wonders. *No one to mourn my death, no one to wail. No one to offer meats and fruits, or burn paper money at Ching Ming time so I not starve in the Afterlife.*

He rolls over, striking the earth softly with his forehead, his long queue bouncing down his back. *Be brave! Remember was born in Year of the Boar.* He thinks back on all that has befallen him and—always pleased to be amazed—feels almost grateful for this War, for having cured him of his childhood.

Is no worse than drought, which then brought clouds of locusts burying the land. He remembers how they swarmed to three feet deep, devouring crops, then harnesses on oxen, handles on farm tools. How they layered the walls of houses until each house collapsed, then crawled down the throats of humans and laid their eggs, smothering them to death in the tens, then hundreds, of thousands.

He remembers how the aftermath of locusts brought famine. *Which then brought madness, people eating their elders, their dead children, while Emperor smoked opium in jade-lined rooms.* It had been rumored by the Emperor's enemies that when his eunuchs told him of the famine, millions dead, he dreamily replied, "*Jan Yeh, Jan Yeh.*" *So it is.* His eunuchs had smiled indulgently, and resumed decoding the secret life of chopsticks.

And war is no worse than bandits, armies of them growing in famine's wake.

From one catastrophe to the next, one generation to the next, his people had grown to hold their lives as worthless. That part of China deep in the province of Shensi became so destitute and ravaged it robbed their lives of all meaning. Johnny's village, a collection of weed-and-mud huts in the backwater swamps of the great Yellow River, no longer attracted rain and so their fields did not come to fruition. Water became so rare, a mere bucketful was traded for precious flint and iron with which men had created flames. Without water or fire, their village began to die.

When there was no dead flesh left to consume, people ate dirt. Johnny's mother grew dreadfully thin and yet her stomach swelled. One day, his father put his fingers down her throat and pulled out a worm, twisting and twisting until the ball of the thing was as big as a fist. Fascinated, Johnny and his younger brother, Ah Fat, watched as their mother deflated and the ball of worm grew big as a melon, until finally their father pulled out the head, wide as his thumb with eyes and a mouth. While their mother expired, villagers stretched the worm from end to end of the village, then hacked it in sections to be shared.

Their father looked down at the swelling stomachs of his sons and whispered, "Run! So you not become worm-dumplings."

The brothers had fled. After months of foraging and thieving their way through squalid villages, they came upon a parklike town called *Po Lin*, Precious Lotus, outside the great city of Chiangnan, where scholars and merchants had built summer homes. In Po Lin, the two boys had squatted in the shadows, watching people languidly repose, eat sugared lotus seeds, and bathe in scented waters. Even the lowliest citizens spoke in the scholarly tongue of Mandarin, and even the thieves comported themselves with dignity.

It was such a wondrously civilized town that Imperial Censors and District Magistrates from Chiangnan stopped their *palanquins* outside the town gates while retainers trimmed their ear hairs and nose hairs, clipped their toe-nails and fingernails, and scented their sleeves before they entered. Though they were swiftly run out of town as famine refugees, it was Po Lin that taught the brothers to dream, to imagine that one day they could become prosperous and admired. Looking back, Johnny sees that though his life has been eventful, he never quite achieved these goals. *Yet, I am prisoner of war. Is that not honorable thing to be?*

* * *

He looks round the filthy stockade at prisoners huddled together, their expressions those of old children waiting to die. The Battle at Kernstown, in Jackson's Valley Campaign, had been disastrous for Union forces. Ashamed of their defeat and capture, a boy gone mad has hanged himself.

But we will soon win, Johnny thinks. *In Christian God's eyes, Union Army is right, Confederates wrong.* He wonders if in fact this Christian God has eyes. Does he have a generous American nose? He cannot imagine such a being; in China one worshipped only the Emperor. But now Johnny is here, fighting for the Union, and he has been told that when the Union wins, he will become an American citizen.

His comrades tell him that to achieve citizenship it is important to know the Christian Bible that so many soldiers quote from and sleep with, and carry into battle. Hoping to barter for such a book, with a sharpened stone he whittles away at branches, bird skulls, and rat skulls, fashioning little brooches and whatnots. Focused on his carvings, he is not fully aware of how his comrades regard him—some with lazy curiosity, others with outright hostility. A slender but wiry little man with smooth yellow skin, a shaven foreskull, and long black pigtail, he looks alternately playful and threatening.

His command of spoken English is fair, but when confused or tense he drops his articles, barks out made-up words that sound like hat tricks. Most irksome to the prison guards is how relentlessly he smiles, especially when sad or frightened or embarrassed. Just now he thinks of his wife and daughter, wondering if they have survived. He whittles at a branch and smiles.

At first, his comrades had interpreted Johnny's smile as craftiness; he had defected from the Other Side, perhaps a spy. Then they saw how ferocious he was in skirmishes with the enemy. And he was sly, with the movements of a cat. Sometimes he moved so fast he appeared to be there, and not there. They had seen him drive a sharpened branch straight through a Rebel's eardrums, after which he dangled the corpse by the branch like something hanging from a clothesline. They had watched him strangulate a man, leap from behind and slash his jugular so swiftly he went down with a sigh. He once showed them how to render a man a eunuch with their teeth, a practice swiftly banned by the company commander.

Still, seasoned troopers are wary of him, his broken English, his sallow skin, the way he slides his glances along without moving his head. But they are prisoners and desperate, and younger men begin to look to him, sharing meals of grilled rat he has trapped. And when there is only grass to chew, they sit close and listen to Johnny's stories that sometimes resemble Scriptures from the Bible. He is generous with his memories, knowing it will be the talking and listening that saves them.

"Busy tongue," he tells them, "keeps fear in shadows, hope alive."

But often he sits alone. Because of his modest grasp of English, he cannot join in discussions with men who speak a slangy shorthand; he cannot joke with them like brothers. After years in America, he has begun to feel nowhere and half-where, a man who still speaks English like a child, and speaks his Mother Tongue with half a tongue. In his desire to become American, he has begun to squeeze Chinese from his brain.

One day he strikes a bargain. In return for his stories, a boy will loan him his Bible for an hour every day. And so each day at the appointed time, Johnny hunches over the Good Book and follows words discreetly with his finger. *Leviticus. Deuteronomy.* Words that threaten to deform his jaw. When he attempts to pronounce them aloud, his mouth feels as if it will fall off in his hands. Still, he perseveres.

Later, he gathers boys hungry to the point of death and recounts earlier times of hunger in his life: two brothers in rag shoes, foraging for food while winds harvested their icicled brows. He and Ah Fat had finally arrived in Yangchow on the Yangtze River, but so had millions of beggars, and bamboo yokes nearly broke their slender shoulders as they carried gourds and roots, begging folks to buy. When no one bought, they stalked old men, knocking them down for rice balls.

"One day, we see public execution of man who sell his queue. Bald heads against Emperor's edict. So! Ax flies, man's head roll between my legs. Then family of executed man rush forward waving thread and needles, join head and body back together so his spirit be whole in Afterlife, so he not wander in little pieces. Even execution have happy ending."

Their lives vacillating between starvation and the executioner's ax, one day the two boys had stood on the docks of Yangchow, gaping at big American ships and their well-fed crews. Cautiously, they approached a ship where long-nosed men with ruddy faces signed on a crew. They walked up the gangway to beckoning sailors, but before they could ask about wages, canvas sacks were thrown over them and they were rolled down to the galleys with a thousand other kidnapped Chinese.

While Johnny "talks story" he adds little asides and footnotes, believing that they give bones and gristle to a tale.

"Only Chinese *tongsee*...sugarmasters...treated well as part of crew. Old experts in sugar refining, they badly needed all over world wherever was sugar plantations."

Thus, he and his brother, Ah Fat, had arrived in the Hawaiian Isles far across the Pacific Ocean.

"After many months at sea, ho! First gulp of island air so clean, flowers so perfume it make us sick for days."

And it was here at Honolulu Immigrations that his name had been changed to Johnny. "My real name Zhong Yi, Needle Master, for my fingers shaped like such masters who cure illness by pushing needles into flesh. My poor mama dream one day I become such revered needle man."

He holds out his hands, showing long, slender fingers, so incongruous to his wiry, cunning body.

"Immigration man cannot make tongue say 'Zhong Yi,' so change name to Johnny!"

A boy with gangrened feet leans forward. "What happened next? Did you meet cannibals in those islands?"

"No cannibals. We taken to outer island so large was called *Moku Nui*, Big Island. Here I meet brown-shouldered girl, Mahealani Hanohano. Her name so ha-full I give up! I call her Laughter."

His eyes close, he drifts, hearing her laughter like temple bells, while he recalls how he and mobs of Chinese were trucked to sugar plantations as forced labor, and how in time he and the girl had found each other. Still, Johnny grew to detest the crippling work of cutting cane—machete wounds, infections, food that left them a hair's breadth from starvation—and white plantation owners with their vicious *luna* foremen.

They had been forced to sign labor contracts for three years, or be returned to China where they would be swiftly executed. No matter that they had been kidnapped; the Emperor had not granted them exit favors.

"No choice but work like slaves or die. In first year, eighteen men hang themselves."

Still, when Johnny lay with Laughter the lion of contentment stretched its paw across his chest. But then the girl broke his heart and disappeared. He began to hear rumors of California, how streets were paved with gold. He began looking toward the sea. One day, Laughter's father hacked his way through the cane fields, threatening to cut off Johnny's testicles for giving his daughter a "yellow monkey" baby.

Fearing for his manhood, he gambled his wages for passage on a ship and sailed for San Francisco. The day he departed, Laughter appeared at the dock, holding their child, and as she frantically waved her uplifted arm, so slender and defenseless, it touched his heart. He pleaded with the captain to drop anchor, allow him to rescue his wife and child, and take them with him. The captain laughed. The ship sailed on.

A boy with a helmet of head lice moves closer, gums gone black, his teeth a rich, rice-paddy green. "What happened next, Johnny? Did you get to San Francisco?"

He nods his head, exhausted. "A tale for tomorrow's ears."

Dark now, and cold. Prisoners, pressed together for warmth, snore fitfully. He wanders to his tent, but it is someone else's hour in the tent. He lies down and hunches up, pulls his long queue over his shoulder, and thinks of Second Wife, Raindance. He has been gone almost a year, his letters not answered. Perhaps she thinks he deserted her. Perhaps she thinks he is dead.

Pencils have no purpose here. Paper has become a source of food; men are eating their Bibles. As boys, he and Ah Fat had grown their pinky fingernails to long, sharp points, ideal for snapping lice in half and for digging insects out of ears. Lately, he had adopted a more urgent application for his extended fingernail—penning letters to Raindance on the palm of his hand.

Each day he "writes in his journal," pressing down hard with his pointed nail so that the letter of each word is briefly visible on his palm. A process slow and laborious, so the words have come to feel engraved like scars. In this way, he memorizes each word he writes: each rice-ball belly of a C, each listing chopstick of an M, imprinted upon his brain. Thus he is able to read his letters over and over in his head.

"My honorable and cherished Raindance,

To continue with my story...We fought hard at Kernstown in Shenandoah Valley. Ah, but even so, they bested us. Speed of our defeat astounding, hundreds our soldiers turn and ran. Now prisoners, we are dead weary, dog hungry. Much death before and after dark.

Still I slaughter many enemy, make many children orphans. For this my dreams are haunted. In battle I run over dead like logs. Run over many faces. White, red, even Russian, French. See many hundreds stomachs burst. Strange skins of many hues, but intestines all same color!"

Now and then, while Johnny writes, he pauses, searching for a word.

"We die for clean water. Here is only sewage. So, are forced to drink our ruin. At first men turn away, disgusted. I tell them is old Chinese custom in famine and drought. They watch silent when I drink my ruin. When I not die, they drink their ruin too.

Most uncomfortable news. Chinese boy from Kentucky in our brigade, caught as spy for Rebels. Soldiers pour gasoline down his throat, then light match and stick up nose. He explode, float down in little rags. Even so, I wonder, would they do such thing to Rebel spy with white skin?"

He stops writing and flexes his hand, softly repeating what he has written, trying to memorize each word. Then he begins the hard part—deleting in his mind what is not essential. He scribbles in his palm again, frowning with concentration.

"How I will remember everything? Am living so many lives my brain become a stone sinking to forgetful depths. Will you believe such tales I write? Will our daughter? Is fitting for young girl to know such things?"

His daughter is sixteen now, or eighteen. The war has done strange things to his mind. *Is she still beautiful?* he wonders. *Does she still have special love for books? And does she read to Raindance?*

He moans softly, recalling his wife's scent, honeysuckle, wildcat hide, the glow of her copper-colored breasts. Then he returns to his writing, fingernail busy scratching at his palm, practicing words whose spelling gives him trouble. *Urine. Ruin.*

* * *

Captain Jenson from his regiment approaches, a young man so weary and gaunt his head seems too large for his frame. "How are you keeping, Private Tom?"

Johnny jumps to his feet and salutes. "OK, sir! Everything OK."

"At ease, man. I want to commend you for keeping up morale, cheering the boys with your stories. And I don't want you thinking on that Chinese boy, Elijah Low. He was a spy and got what he deserved."

He straightens up, tightening a filthy bandage made into an arm sling. "I've watched you on the battlefield. You're one of the bravest men in our regiment. I'm proud to have you serving under me."

Embarrassed, Johnny nods repeatedly and smiles.

Jenson hesitates, then offers something hidden in his fist. "Take it. I'm tired of seeing you whittle with that hunk of stone."

Johnny stares at a small bone-handled object with a button at one end. When he presses it, the blade snaps out like a small, slender fish caught in a sheaf of sunlight. He strokes the blade, remembering a similar knife he had given his daughter because it was delicate like her. He folds the blade and slips the knife into his shoe.

For weeks, he spies on the captain while he forages for roots with other prisoners, and while he lectures them to

keep their courage up. He spies on Jenson when he defe-
cates, and squats beside him while he sleeps, feeling forever
attached to this young man because he has given Johnny
something infinitely more precious than a knife: the faint
hope of acceptance, of acknowledgment that he is human
and brave, and therefore significant.

He has observed the confidence of Americans: that of
accepting their lives completely, never wishing they were
anyone else, or that they were born anywhere else, or raised
in any other way. Just now, they may be wounded and starving, but they are secure in a way a Chinese could never be.
Captain Jenson's pride in Johnny fills him with confidence,
the sense that he is becoming more like them, that he is becoming, incontrovertibly, *one of them*. And so his spirits lift.

He presses on through months of near starvation, of
whippings by prison guards, of gangrene and typhus that
take more than half the prisoners. He presses on because
he believes this time will pass. America is so large and generous it will never abandon or betray him. He has offered up
his life for it, and one day it will reward him by welcoming
him as a citizen. He moves through each day with burgeon-
ing pride, almost with arrogance, as if his feet had turned to
dragon claws.

But on the day of his release, lined up with fellow prisoners awaiting the exchange, Johnny sees crows darting overhead in a floating and shifting calligraphy. Hearing their
garrulous and raucous cries, he looks up again and sees they
have formed the Chinese character for death.

ERA

Field Hospital, Near Corinth, Mississippi, April 1862

Even the sunlight here is old. It falls exhausted through dead leaves and rests on the face of a boy so frail he looks transparent. It has rained all night and the downpour has gently exhumed the dead. Across the fields, their bones rise up unbidden.

A young nurse stands at the upraised flaps of a hospital tent, unable to see the dead but knowing they are out there. In here the air is so close she reels with faintness. Still, with the coming of light she lifts her arms, midwifing the dawn as if it were trumpeting a new age, not one of slaughter.

At the call for reveille, she watches Confederate boys crawl from their tents, numb from the recent engagement and from the creeping squalor of camp life—rancid food, crippling dysentery, the dull, grinding rasp of the field surgeon's saw. They stretch and stare blankly at a landscape stripped of vegetation, at buzzards in the distance swooning over corpses of horses and mules.

Slipping a hand inside her pocket, the nurse rubs a smooth knob of bone, a talisman, then turns to patients in the tent behind her, many so young they do not shave. Nine will be dead by sunset. It has been another sleepless night, so her movements are slow and measured. When she speaks, even her words will sound stretched out.

Just now, she feels no patience for the wounded little drummer, or for the quiet one who sits on his cot and tries to sketch. Sometimes he sketches in the dark by candlelight, struggling with his left hand as if learning the rudiments of ciphering. It has been several weeks since his surgery. He does not remember that time, and she cannot forget it. How they carried him half-conscious from the field, his body blood-soaked, the shattered, splintered arm.

She remembers forcing whiskey down his throat, then pressing a chloroformed rag to his face while attendants held him down. She remembers the surgeon's blood-splattered coat, his saw flocked red from earlier amputations, the weary way he rinsed the saw in a pail of filthy water, then paused, puffed his cigar, and placed it on the edge of a table before applying himself to the trooper's arm. The arm would be gone before the ashes hit the ground. It was the first amputation with which she had been allowed to assist, and she remembers her face suddenly speckled red.

After she applied briefly rinsed sponges to the raw stump, the surgeon had attempted to join the flaps of skin but, thoroughly exhausted, he could not properly align needle and thread. He vehemently cursed, then asked her to moisten the thread with her saliva, after which he rolled it between his filthy fingers into a point that slid easily through the needle. While he sutured, his hands shook so badly she looked away. Later, she dressed the stump with musty sheets torn into strips.

Each night, while the soldier lay feverish and drugged on morphine, she had changed his dressing, looking for signs of pyemia, the infection that killed most amputees. Secretions from the womb were healthy and, though he grew morbidly thin, she eventually saw that the union of skinflap had begun. He had been carried from the field with no identification, and so he was known as Patient in Cot 9.

One day troopers came, all jangling spurs and sabers. She knew from their leathery faces and their swagger that they were cavalry, and she had stepped back from them, keeping her distance as she spoke.

"He's lost his arm. There is no infection. I expect he will live."

Relieved, they hung their heads. Then one of them stepped forward and spoke with a prideful drawl.

"For the record, ma'am, our unit is the Prattville Dragoons, attached to Company H of the Third Alabama Cavalry. And, by God, he's the best of us."

"What did you say his name was?"

"Petticomb. Warren Rowan Petticomb." The trooper smiled. "Fella once called him 'Petticoat.' He shot the saphead's coffee tin out of his hand 'afore it reached his lips!"

"And what hand was that he shot with?"

"His right! Always his right."

She spoke softly then. "Well, I'm afraid it's gone."

For weeks he was sublime on morphine. When morphine ran out, she was there with whiskey meant for officers and herbs that dulled the pain. Slowly, he gained hold of the whipcord of time. He began to respond to questions, and to turn his head when his troops sortied out—leaning in to the jangling of their accoutrements—in a way that suggested he might want to live again, and fight again. One day, he had asked for pencil and paper, and sat hunched over for hours. Now he sketches unceasingly, sometimes through the night. *Perhaps*, she thinks, *that is his way of screaming*.

She has been drawn to him because of the arm, and the way sunlight plays on his blond, water-parted hair, and because he seems a man uncommonly suited to stillness. His stillness has an odd effect on people—when he sketches them he imparts character to them. They, too, fall still. Yet when she pauses near him, she senses something inside him move and stand off at a distance.

* * *

The skittering of rats as they burrow through a heap of amputated limbs in a wagon outside the hospital tent. Steeling herself, Era steps outside and lifts the canvas covering the wagon. Some nights she dreams of begging hands, gray legs, feet with their blackened toenails. These limbs are so fresh some of them resemble marble, rose-white, ivory, eerily beautiful in murky light. She moves close and places her hand on the arch of a foot, as if placing a comforting hand on a forehead. She shuts her eyes, wondering if she is going mad.

After a while, she retreats inside and ministers to a boy dying of typhoid. He calls out for his mother and she leans down and comforts him, wisps of her dark hair soft as first grasses on his cheek. He is nothing now, only a soul trapped in this weary sling of bones.

So the day begins, sunlight warming the campgrounds to a grim and moving tapestry. Overhead, Confederate flags fly, ragged, proud. Soldiers squat before their tents, frowning at cups of overboiled coffee. Some hold bread over fires, wistfully watching flames paint slices an uneven brown. In their paddocks, cavalry mounts whinny and lift their muzzles to the light.

And in a distant tent, an artillery officer lifts his head from a map over which he has fallen asleep while devising new strategies. One month after Shiloh, a loss of thousands, the war is no longer perceived as a novelty. In larger, private tents where black men serve collations, officers with their West Point English and soft Southern cadence sit mournfully and disgustedly recounting Shiloh, that recent misbegotten battle, wondering by what strategic shortcomings their divisions were defeated. Entire regiments slaughtered.

Their major general, Braxton Bragg, sits alone at his headquarters fully aware that he is hated, the butt of jokes. A thin, feral-faced man with wild, Mephistophelian eye-

brows, he is wracked with the constant pain of hemor-
rhoids and malarial agues. A man of general irritability and
vacillation—some say incompetence—in battle, Bragg
shuns his officers and infantry alike, and worse, he does not
pursue the enemy when victory is in sight. Something inside him lacks the will to win.

Still, boys wait for the next call to arms, wondering,
When? When? For waiting is a crucifixion. And even as
there are rumors of the next campaign, the weather turns
filthy. The good snows that brought a reprieve from fighting in Mississippi have come and gone and now it is just
sleet and rain, and it will hold. Tents become freezing cata-
racts. Healthy boys begin to smell rotted out; only the heat
in their young bodies preserves them. Soon cooking meat
will freeze and grow rancid.

And in the "great hush," the numbing lull of weeks and
months between battles, every man is made to drill and they
are drilled prodigiously, hour after hour, day after day. In
sleet and ice, in abominable mud, they march, at first with
a stubborn show of valor that after weeks becomes a kind
of marching stupor. The war seems far off now, almost im-
plausible. All fighting has moved to the Eastern Theater in
far-off Virginia.

Era walks briskly through the camp, instructing laundry girls and sewing girls, inquiring about shipments of
medicines from the quartermaster. A colonel passes her and
frowns, for in spite of her unseemly black dress and old-
maid bun she is slim and fetching, a thing uncommon in the
camps. It is decidedly plain women who are sought out to
serve as nurses, laundresses, even scullery girls. Loveliness
of feature is too heartbreaking: it turns men sentimental and
has no place here.

The colonel glances back at her, her skin color a puzzle.
Pale yellow as chamois but in sunlight a trace of something

else, a copper undertone. The strange coloring and her golden, slanted eyes unsettle him. In suitable clothes, she would be reckoned a beauty. He shakes his head. *Another mix-blood to distract and confound my men.*

She moves quickly down the path dividing rows of hospital tents and pauses at a fenced corral, relishing the high-blooded smell of the horses. They lift their heads and come to her, prancing and tossing manes, a divine poetry in the flexed muscles of their polished flanks. She suspects that one day this will be all that will save her. A horse to ride, a gun. It may be the only way she will get out.

Again, she slides her hand into her pocket, rubbing the smooth, knobby thing that helps her to remember. Most often, she does not want to remember, but not wanting to remember is the same as forgetting, and she must not forget. How she was mauled and buffeted, the stain of her mother's blood across her cheeks, the smell of her burnt flesh. She backs away, shaking her head, but her mind fastidiously clutches at memories.

She curses and shakes her head again. Yet, each night in sleep, a copper-colored arm with a long-fingered hand drifts down and touches her and whispers, *"Daughter."* And she remembers what her mission is, her purpose. She grows more attentive to idle gossip, to officers exchanging drolleries over chessboards. Information is a thing to be sifted from the merest comment, a gift to be hoarded.

* * *

One morning the sketcher sits up, arranges his pencils in a row on a tiny, makeshift table, then stands and slowly moves between rows of sleeping patients. The first time he has walked about unaided. She sees how tall and lean he is, and carefully approaches.

"Be wary of the damp. Although it is less killing than the rank air of those fever-ridden city hospitals."

Since Lincoln issued the Neutrality Act—allowing medical staffs to move unhindered back and forth between the lines—she has seen the charnel houses of Corinth and Memphis, has spent time there nursing boys of both armies forced to lie for weeks in filthy, bloody uniforms, the wards so overcrowded they were packed together on floors swarming with rats. She has seen ambulance wagons jostling boys with half their skulls gone. And transport trains—thousands of soldiers lying in open-platform cars in the bitter cold, most of whom arrived as corpses.

She moves closer, for he seems unsteady on his feet. "I understand you refused to be put on a transport train to Corinth, where you might have been given a furlough. Is that true?"

He stares out at the landscape. "I honestly...don't know... what the truth is anymore."

His eyes are gray, eerily pale, a sharpshooter's eyes. He had the loose-limbed stance of a horseman. But it is his hand that draws her, long tapered fingers like a pianist, the tips smudged with lead from his pencils. In that moment, she longs to see the missing hand, to see them at rest side by side. The beauty of it. At the entrance to the tent he hesitates, then moves back to his cot.

The next day, in sleet and cold, she sees him outside, lifting the canvas on the wagon cart of limbs. He reaches out, touching the blue fingers of a hand, studying a forearm stiff as a log on which blood has frozen black. He moves slowly round the wagon, his hand reaching out, then falling to his side, and she understands that he is searching for his arm. Time and again she sees him out there, searching.

Sleet skirmishes with rain, then warm winds come, softening the earth. Through morning mist, a detail of limers passes with heavy buckets, headed for pits beside which rows of the dead wait to be buried. Warren gazes after them, wipes mildew from a page, and begins to sketch their weary black faces, shoulders slumped by the weight of their task.

She moves close, watching figures on the page take shape. "It is a very good likeness."

"I sometimes...have the measure of it."

He casts his eyes down. If he raises them, they will be gazing at the place where her body joins at the center. If he looks up at her face, she might begin a conversation—all the plethora and generality of words. Instead, she moves off, leaving a hint of lavender that causes a skittering in his bones. She moves quickly, getting her distance, for neither does she wish conversation.

She has become dangerously aware of how words have a way of unraveling into confidences. One confidence is liable to be revealed in the place of another that is harder to tell, and the substitute confidence might be more incriminating. She is so cautious and distant other nurses avoid her. This suits her, for she has nothing in common with them; her personal history would shock them.

Dusk gathers. Across the campgrounds someone fiddles, then the lowing of a coronet. Union picket lines are not far distant and soon there is the lowing of an answering coronet. The camp falls still and listens. Now soldiers play in turn, enemy to enemy, taunting then soothing each other, making boys weep with the wonder of it.

"Why are we fighting them? They just boys like us!"

Exhausted, she sits at the nurse's station huddled in a shawl, thinking, *These are the ancient days. Rebel or Yank, only the very old will come out of this.* A sheet of paper floats in the air, then settles to the ground. She stares at it, then glances down the rows of cots to Warren, dozing in his chair. She bends, retrieving the sketch: eight soldiers at their tasks, as focused as children, each boy sewing a slip of paper with his name onto his jacket. When he is killed, his corpse can be identified. She has seen such "tasking" a thousand times.

She lets the sketch rest in her lap, remembering clouds rolling by before the Battle of Pea Ridge. The sun jumping out, touching soldiers' heads in passing. She remembers regiments lined up, mounted officers aligned with sabers raised. The infantry staring up at them, at the ready. Then their steady advance across the land, the order to "Charge!"

She remembers the thunder of horses' hooves shaking the very earth, the clattering of sabers. A cannon's roar. A scene of martial beauty that laid the way for massive death. And it prepared her for the larger horror one month later: the Battle of Shiloh. One hundred thousand Confederates and Federals battling across a three-mile front. Boys fresh from recruiting camps, unpracticed and unseasoned—not knowing north from south or east from west, and never having seen a map—pressed into an engagement that would end in a massacre on both sides.

But the Federals possessed the "long purses"—the Northern industrialists—who assured their recovery. Whereas at the end of two days over ten thousand Confederate boys were dead, wounded, or missing, a loss from which they might never quite recover. Sometimes Era starts to grieve for them, then strikes her chest softly with her fist, reminding herself why she is here. What brought her here.

She allows the sketch, the interesting hell of war, to slip from her lap and yet the dozing man named Warren draws her eyes. The first time she saw him sketching, all she had seen from the back was the silhouette of his hunched shoulders, the bandages, the missing arm. There must have been continuing pain, unutterable shock, yet he sketched steadily, almost studiously, only his hand moving, the rest of his body caught in stillness.

In her life she knew only one other man with this gift for stillness, the movement of his finger serene across a page. Her father, engaged in decoding English words, straining to decipher their meanings, to master their sound. And thus in that moment of first watching him, his stillness, she had loved the sketcher; for an instant he replaced someone she fears she has lost. Even now, sometimes she moves close, wanting to partner his stillness, then quickly moves away.

But as she passes day to day, she sees on his makeshift table his three pencils worn to nubs. Impulsively, she takes a small knife from her pocket and carefully sharpens each pencil to a point, its shavings curling and dancing in the air. That night she helps administer to a boy with tetanus held down by two attendants. Death comes within hours, a hideous sight. Utterly spent, she moves down the row of cots toward the nurses' tent.

In the dimness, she sees Warren staring at his pencils lined up in a row, carefully touching their sharp, fine points. He lifts his head and looks down the aisle to where she stands. She hesitates, then rouses herself and approaches, pulling from her pocket a small bone-handled knife.

"Keep this awhile," she whispers. "To sharpen your pencils. Tomorrow I will show you how to do it with one hand. A trick my father taught me."

WARREN

Near Corinth, Mississippi, May 1862

Dear Mother and Father,

After long silence I embrace the opportunity to write you. Thank you for the socks knitted shawl and news from Prattville. I am sorry to tell you McGruders boy Hazard was taken with the typhoid worse case I ever saw.

They still feed us tolerably well beef about every day but wormy. We are running short of coffee and make it out of any way we can. Excuse my writing was wounded in the arm. Dont fret am healing fine and no wounds in my internalments. It was a long hard battle name of Shiloh on the Tennesee Misisippi border. Plenty men killed both sides. I took a bullet but verily took down my share of Yanks.

Am learning to write left hand. I like how it slows me down makes me think if what I have to say has weight or merely paltry. Am learning to sketch left hand too. Weather is mighty disagreeable rain sleet mud so there is precious else to do.

A preacher comes twice a week to spread the Word and sing the Doxology. Prayer meetings bout every night more boys offering themselves up to be dipped. Tell the truth since Shiloh I feel much more soldier much less Christian. Cant describe what all I saw 100,000 boys slamming at each other. Used to be I thought it took ten Yanks to beat one Reb. Well father I seen the monkey show and I guess I don't think that anymore. Such thoughts is odd caprice as

Yanks are tough and brave like us. Our picket lines meet up with theirs swap tobacco and the news. They ask what we are fighting for. No one is sure as none of us owns slaves.

The smallpox is getting common. Also measles scurvy and suchlike debilitas. After some demurral I got the vaxination. Do you have any money left should I send more. Sorry for no furlough home my wound is slight and merits naught but rest. Plenty boys worse off then me.

I miss my Prattville boys to weeping. It hurts when they ride out to skirmish I am left behind. They are good pards and visit when they can. Our supply boats are regularly attacked and nurses running out of needles morphine and such. For pain they hand out strange decoctions we call bulls eyes raw opium tucked inside little wads of bread. Also disposed to stop the diahrea so common now.

Well again to tell you I am fine except the minor arm wound. I sorely need an overcoat will have to take one from a Yank. We strip their dead near clean— shoes coats weapons even longjohns. It brings a staidness of demeanor to see a hundred naked corpses in a row. Don't fret they are the enemy.

Mother I thank you for teaching me reading and writing. It serves me well. I read letters for boys and help them write letters home omitting their wild vagaries. I do not lack for friends. I trust you like my drawings. Kiss little Annabelle for me, the sweetest sister in the world. I send you love and pray you rest yourselves contented I am well. Your devoted son untell death.

W.R. Petticomb

Some nights a half-finished letter slides from his lap as he dozes, recalling his father walking him to the Prattville Courthouse to swear him in two days after Alabama seceded from the Union. He remembers the dusty streets of his little town, boys banging out tunes on peach tins, and cotton fields sprawling, shaping themselves to the curve of his eye.

He remembers his protestations. "But, father, I'm not a fighter."

"Nonsense!" His father was a man who saw caution as a character failing. "You can ride and you can shoot. You were born with the eye of a marksman. G'wan now, be a hero! Find your place in the firmament."

It was April 1861. He and his friends—startlingly young and beardless—sat high in their fine wool uniforms sewn by the Ladies' Aid Society as they were officially named the Prattville Dragoons, a volunteer unit of horse soldiers sworn to the Confederacy. Their mounts were eager, their saddles polished, guns oiled and ready—all donated by Daniel Pratt, wealthy founder of the town.

They bent down to kiss their mothers' cheeks, then shook hands with their fathers. The band played "Dixie" as they waved and proudly trotted off in formation. Then, rounding a bend, they broke into a gallop, giving out the Rebel yell. And away with them into the future! The world waiting, all brand new. He rode off keen as the horse beneath him, a boy of seventeen.

They had ridden thirty miles to Montgomery, then trained down to Pensacola, Florida, where they would become part of the Confederate Army under Generals Pierre Beauregard and Braxton Bragg—months of unrelenting training in riflery and horsemanship, in jousting with short swords, and galloping toward melons on pikes with pointed sabers.

Since his boyhood in Alabama cotton gin mills, separating cottonseed from lint, Warren had always been a sketcher, given to scribbling and shading, trying to take the measure of life's creatures. Annabelle running through fields of timothy and vetch, mule skinners frozen in their armor of dried blood, his father's profile handsome as a hawk. In those long, exhausting months of combat training he never put pencil to paper, but once they were entrained from Pensacola up to Chattanooga he began perforce to sketch again. Mostly the eager faces of his friends impatient to meet up with the *bluecoats*, to test their skills in battle.

At night they lay sleepless, watching the world pass by. Years later, recalling those nights, Warren would understand that it was youth that was passing, that their self-centered childhood was over. Some nights they sat with their legs hanging out of open boxcars, watching sparks from the wheels on the rails fly out behind them as rose-red cinders turned to ash. Houses far back in the hills resonated with candlelight like tiny stars, the very families they were going to defend! They whooped and shouted, incipient heroes joking and larking in the moonlight. He would recall those nights with searing clarity; he would remember each boy's name.

In the mornings as the train slowed, passing through small towns, he had sketched women in hoopskirts swaying under trees, pulling down swags of Spanish moss with which to make ropes for their soldiers. In other towns, long lines of women stood holding bottles that glinted in sunlight so they seemed to be holding diamonds. A sergeant explained that, with the Union embargo of Confederate supply ships, Southern women were collecting urine from which to distill niter for gunpowder.

"They're growing poppies too. Making opium and morphine for our wounded boys."

In spite of his shock, the women briefly slipped his mind. He was seeing his country for the first time and was lost in the effort of not missing a thing. But through the coming months of being assigned a company and regiment, and brief scouting and skirmishing forays, Warren saw more and more women engaged in the Cause. They poured into towns, collecting clothes and money. They enlivened Army encampments—Bible thumpers and seamstresses, cooks, laundresses and whores. And later, nurses near the battle-fields.

He trained with the fervor of a natural warrior, grew swiftly conversant in cavalry tactics, thus impatient for combat. Not the notion of killing and maiming, but the sober acts of perfectly planned and executed strategies. The thoughtful advance, flying colors, the enemy surging forward, the glinting sabers, then the roar, the full en-gagement. Afterward, victory, his generals erect in their saddles.

He would enter the war and gallop straight to the heart of it, resolved to always look outward beyond bleeding land-scapes, to focus his attention on the distance where Union commanders turned their horses back, defeated. And after-ward, lying on summer grasses, his head propped against his saddle, he would reflect on their strategy, their tactical maneuvers, how the Confederacy had been able to surprise, overwhelm, and defeat the invaders.

* * *

When he first became aware of the nurse—when he was able to focus beyond his horror—he had felt like a sojourner in a foreign place. For she was instantly foreign to him, a female, and one whose skin color varied like a mood—a yellow, walnut hue that could change to near-ocher. Her coloring and her unbecoming clothes all betokened the cause of his discomfort. Her dark hair was pulled back in a bun beneath a hairnet that called to mind old spiderwebs. Her dress was the common nurse uniform, voluminous and mournfully black.

The first time she had touched his stump, slowly un-winding the dressing, he thought he would faint. From pain, and because in his life a strange woman had never touched him. As she sits night after night changing his dressing, small exhalations escape him, perhaps from the morphine limning his veins, or the sound of her breathing, so different from a man's. Or her light touch that makes him feel naked and childlike.

Now, as Warren turns away, she takes his chin and gently turns it back. "Give thanks for what you kept. Others have lost much more."

No one has ever talked to him like that. He wants to ask her something, a question that will shock her into compassion, or at the least distract her. What is her name? Her age? She looks too young to be here. Curiosity and shyness swirl in concert and he retreats into his dreams.

...Snow and sleet in Chattanooga...joining up with other divisions as part of the Army of Tennessee...then on the move to someplace called Corinth...setting up camp...no wood, no fires, no food...

The climate change from Pensacola had been drastic. Sickness and disease grew common and they learned that Federal regiments were closing in, encamped only eighteen miles away. One night, he was part of a mounted detail organized to scout the enemy's position. As fifteen of them thundered down the road, their captain had leaned back and shouted.

"Remember...every skirmish is a battle to be won. You're cavalrymen! Drive on!"

Ten miles down the road they had spotted a *bluecoat* on picket who took off through the woods, sounding the alarm. Within minutes, a troop of Federals had borne down, at least fifty, armed with Spencers.

Reins in my mouth and biting down, saber thrust out in my left hand, Colt navy pistol in my right...blindly spurring my horse on...

Seeing Rebels on the gallop, the Union troops had faltered. Instead of pushing forward in their charge, they dismounted and took position in a grove of trees. A moment's hesitation, then Warren's commander had let loose that high-falsetto Rebel yell and his detail went berserk—charging into the woods, crushing the skulls of the enemy with their horses' hooves. But the Federals had superior arms and bright moonlight on their side and Warren had watched in horror as his friends died.

Seth Roper...Remus Fitzhugh shot in the face...dragged through the woods with their feet still in their stirrups...

Feeling the *Thtt! Thtt!* of bullets whizzing past his head, he had leaned down and thrust with his saber, brought up a speared enemy by his chest, and used him as a shield as he galloped on. Eventually, they ran the Federals off and were left with thirty enemy dead, nine dead or wounded of their own.

Limbs, innards flung everywhere...bits of flesh stuck to my arm and to my face...leaning over and vomiting from my saddle.

His first engagement with the enemy. No time for wonderment or prayer, or the conscious acceptance that he might die. Skirmishes would continue for months, ceaseless rounds of raiding, sabotage, slaughter. He stood over dead men, stupefied, his pistol smoking in his hand. All this, while Ulysses S. Grant built up the Federal Army near a place called Shiloh.

Warren would always fall silent at that word. A strange and melancholy sounding word, the first great, bloody battle of the War. In two days of unfathomable slaughter—bodies carpeting the fields for miles, blood so deep that wounded soldiers drowned—boys had touched their own faces, knowing they had changed perceptibly. Those who survived down the years would be quiet men. Now and then they would remember the face of a dead boy and weep, as if that boy had been their child. For many of them, after Shiloh there would be no greed for life, no ambition. That single battle would be their youth, their age, their death.

Yet he would ever remember the grandeur as they prepared to charge. Companies and regiments, brigades and divisions almost fifty thousand strong—long, mottled lines of infantry emerging across the plain in perfect order, their colors flying, bayonets gleaming. Hearing the brace of fifers, the measured cadence of the drums, Warren had wondered, *How can God let such beauty be destroyed?* While courier battalions cantered back and forth, their mounts already lathered, a bugle boy looked up at him for courage. Warren had reined in his horse so close a fleck of foam hit the boy's cheek and he had winked at him, hoping that it made him feel a man.

Then the order of "Forward! Quick time!" The order to "March!" To keep their ranks closed tight. The order to shoulder arms as forward brigades were swallowed in smoke. He had watched the infantry step out smartly as cavalry troops pressed forward alongside them, sabers raised. The deafening BOOM! of cannons, the sky alive with shot and shell.

The drummers drumming, the sudden advancing horizon of Federal *bluecoats.* Warren had tightened his horse's reins, nodded at a fellow trooper, and spurred his mount, his pistol aimed. Then their Rebel yell, a thousand banshee screams, and they rode into battle while cannons from Federal gunboats on the Tennessee River shelled their flanks.

The enemy had leapt at them. He shot one point-blank in the eyes, then swung his saber left and right, slashing savagely, shooting blindly for hours it seemed, not feeling the graze of bullets until he heard that their general, Albert Sidney Johnston, had been shot and bled to death. It took the breath out of him, out of all of them. The sun sank slowly, as their Army had run out of steam.

A stormy night, no one had slept. Bivouacked boys lay stunned at what they had witnessed, what they had committed. At dawn they rose, loaded their muskets, sharpened their sabers, and once again marched out to the killing grounds. He would not clearly remember the second day. Would any of them? Time no longer existed as they had known it. It was now measured by the number of humans they took down, and by the slippery thickness of blood that slowed their horses.

Mid-battle, and midst the oft-voiced commands of their generals to "Charge!," they heard the sudden orders to withdraw. Boys had looked at one another, incredulous. After the monumental slaughter, for which there was no precedent in this War, there would be no victory for either side, only a ghastly winding down. But killing was in them now, Yank and Rebel. Ignoring the orders to withdraw, each ragged Army pushed on, utterly insane.

Warren suddenly came face-to-face with a pair of barrel sights, a *bluecoat* aiming smartly, and he had smiled, thinking, *This is the one who will kill me.* His horse reared up, hooves raking the air, then went down in slow motion, and in that moment Warren flew, his arm a burning wing. He woke with his blood pouring out of him and dreamily gazed out at the landscape, wondering what last vision he would take with him into death.

The freckled face of the redhead from the Calhoun Beauregards? A face angelic, though below his shoulders his body was gone. Or would it be the boy from the Gadsden Light Guards bayoneted to a tree? Or the cinnamon fingers of a severed hand, that of a scout from the Choctawhatchee Rangers? Or would it be all of them? An endless palisades of gut and limb, each corpse a youth whose shortness of life challenged credibility.

The sun had slowly set, shadowing fields and trenches. He watched it slip into the pockets of the dead. Only inches from his face he saw a large, splendidly patterned butterfly— a creature of astonishing and evanescent beauty—alight on a soldier's blown-apart skull. Fluttering its wings, it picked its way delicately across the moist, gray brain. In that fleeting moment of consciousness, which he imagined was his last, this was the image Warren clung to that would forever call forth the Battle of Shiloh.

* * *

Some nights in a semi-dream he sits up, lights a candle, and begins to sketch. The flying limbs. Random meat. He sketches fire. Faces of boys caught in a forest of flaming underbrush. Here is a soldier urging his mount forward into the flames to save a friend. His horse pawing the air, refusing. Warren moans, reliving it: his best friend screaming as flames snake up his body, then cocking his pistol and blowing his head off.

His trembling hand covers his eyes. He tries to erase the memories, but some are too persistent, and he is forced to confront the most indelible memory of all. A thing he cannot sketch, will never sketch. Huge, feral hogs forming out of the mist. The way they placed their forefeet on the dead boys' chests, their heads depressed and busy. The sounds of their slobbering, greedily nudging the bodies with their snouts. A dying boy grappling with forked hooves.

He sits paralyzed till the nightmare exhausts itself, then begins sketching boys from the Prattville Dragoons as he remembers them. Long, hard limbs of the American backwoods now gaunted and filthy, their faces saber-scarred. He smiles, recalling how they had strolled through the camp like princes. How they lounged back on their elbows, pipes clenched between their teeth, and gazed at lowly infantry boys with belligerent casualness. Superior horsemen and marksmen, they had long surpassed the fear of death, which now rendered them arrogant and lawless.

He looks up from his sketching and sees how those cavaliers who have survived are closer now, zealously protective of each other. Predatory yet discreet, when they walk through the camp no one hears their footsteps. Heading out on raids, their eyes are cold, they seem to turn inward, and when they finally confront the enemy there is a collective sigh among them, an impatience to be done with it.

Warren recollects how he himself had been one of them, the *chosen*. How he had seldom looked back at a man at whom he had fired, and for whom he had had a marksman's intuitive sense of having hit. He flexes the fingers of his left hand and wonders, *Can I be that again*? The fingers lengthen and go rigid, then the hand starts to shake, not out of fear but some musing reflex of the hand alone. And it is only when he studies the left hand does he feel the itching of the phantom right. He looks down at his bandaged stump, perplexed.

She watches him with listening deliberation. Having seen his flickering candle, she has come from her tent and stands shivering in her shawl. This is the one who worries her. He belongs to her in a way none of the others can. He was her first, she was his witness. Even under chloroform he had heard each rasp of the saw as it cut bone. She helped hold him while he screamed. She held him when he fainted. And when he woke and saw what they had done, she held him through his tremors.

For a while she had thought he might die. For weeks he lay under morphine, and when they staggered the drug, he lay wide-eyed, his body morbidly thin and childlike. Where had the muscles gone? She watched his expression grow deathly, like an old man waiting for the Reaper. When he sat up, struggling for breath, she held his head.

Sometimes he had raved, feeling crawly things on his arm, the one sawed off six inches above the elbow. He swore that the fingers of his right hand felt sore and stiff, the wrist itched terribly. When morphine ran short, she gave him opium "bull's eyes" to soothe him. In time, the joined flesh began to take, and his color returned. He began to look at food again. He no longer raved.

Now, in the dark she comes forward with that air of consolation. "How are you? Is there much pain?"

Her voice is soft with the Southern cadence, but her words come more slowly than most folks', giving them an added weight.

"No, ma'am, but sometimes…sleep is hard to come by."

She thinks of a bull's eye but hesitates, knowing what addiction does. "Would you like me to read to you?"

"Why, yes. But could I ask you, ma'am…What is your name?"

"My name is Era. But you must address me as 'Nurse.'"

He nods and lies back in his cot as she draws a book of verse from her pocket, sits down, and begins to read softly, almost carefully, as if her full voice would give away too much of her history. Occasionally when she looks up, he stirs under her scrutiny, wondering why she bothers with this forlorn, butchered thing of a man.

Then he closes his eyes and thinks about her name, and wonders what it means, where it comes from. It's like a tree blocking his way. Era. He keeps walking round her name. All these weeks of her bathing him, feeding him, watching him sleep, and he knows nothing about her. Where is she from? How did she come here? He is not even sure he thinks she's pretty. Her eyelids have such a startling angle, when she raises them her pupils slant upward. And the irises, eerie amber-gold. Sometimes they seem to disappear in the strange, changing tones of her skin.

Still, she has such knowledge of him, he would like to know something of her, something to defend himself. He thinks to ask about her books; she reads and quotes a lot. Shakespeare and Thackeray.

"You are educated...are you not?" he asks.

She looks up surprised. "Not formally. But I am fond of books."

"You seem...to know so much."

"In truth, I know very little."

Candlelight flickering on her face, the soft way it strokes her skin, robs him of composure. "Well, I know this. I'm now a freak. No girl will ever look at me. I can't hardly stand to look upon myself."

Her voice remains soft, but again her lack of compassion shocks him.

"Why, sir, do you think *anyone* will come out of this War and be able to look upon ourselves? To verily *face* ourselves?" She stands and slides her book into her pocket. "Hush, now. Try to sleep."

Walking back to the nurses' tent, she pauses to gaze upward, to stretch and comfort the tight ropes of her muscles. A breeze lifts strands of her loosened hair, and somewhere a soldier curses at the shortage of paper and wipes his rear with damp grasses. Passing long rows of hospital tents, she thinks of the boys inside them, and of acts she has vowed to never commit. *Purloin a surgeon's instruments. Refuse dying patients morphine.*

These small, persistent aches of conscience are like poignant flaws, signs of a lingering morality. But other of her thoughts are deadly. Inside, she is a living rage. A woman with nothing left but the tasks of each day. That and the gathering of small gifts—a snatch of hearsay, dropped hints, overheard bits of conversation.

Lately a few nurses have turned to her, seeking advice, consolation. She discourages them for they are too fragile, too pink-skinned and earnest, and do not have the long continuance of calm and strength other women have. Yet she avoids these other women too. Negroes, Indians, mixed-bloods. They might ask questions she would have to lie to answer, and history has already damaged them with lies. She stays alone, with only one goal to sustain her.

But sometimes she is drawn to the laundresses, to their tired waltz as they pull linens from the lines—the way they hold sheets out and step to each other in an odd duet of matching corners, then step away to carefully fold the sheets and arrange them in piles. Or, she watches the whores who follow the Army, offering up their weary flesh. And she wonders, *Who is really the laundress? Who is really the whore? And who the spy?*

Johnny Tom

Belle Isle Prison Camp, Autumn 1862

Everyone around him looks wounded. It seems only he has not been shot; Johnny is not sure he has even been shot *at.* His only wound was sustained in June, the Seven Days Battle of Richmond, when a bit of shrapnel sliced through his shoe and cut into his heel, an injury so minor it drew white eyeballs of indifference. Still, for weeks he skipped a little, favoring the heel, which prompted smiles from his comrades, for the skipping gave him a rather playful air that seemed to match his pigtail.

Slowed down by his heel, during skirmishes Johnny reverted to ancient Chinese tactics employed in the art of attack and self-defense, which he had learned as a boy. Unable to rush the enemy, he flew feet-first, smashing the man's face, a leap called "Phoenix Bird Spreading Its Wings." While Rebel soldiers paused, gaping at this "pigtailed monkey," he crouched in a wrestler's stance, then, rifle butt extended, hurled himself forward, aiming a crushing blow at the soldier's ribcage.

In a leap called "Tiger Clawing at Sheep," he approached a Rebel from behind, jockeyed his back while he clawed his eyes, then quickly slit his throat. Sometimes he flew from a tree or rock, landing noiselessly behind a *graycoat*, the leap called "Butterfly Alighting on Flower," then dispatched him weaponless, as if by sleight of hand.

But recently, during the Second Battle of Bull Run at Manassas, he has been captured again while dragging a wounded boy to safety. Belle Isle Prison is a barren island in the James River near Richmond. A compound built to hold two thousand prisoners, it now holds twelve thousand grievously wounded and starving Union boys.

Still favoring his heel, Johnny skips slightly, bouncing his pigtail like a girl while gathering weeds and dandelion for tea, and setting traps for rats and frogs. These he shares with comrades while once again hoarding the skulls for whittling; when he skips past, men hear the rattling of tiny bones. He slyly eavesdrops with a pickpocket mind, and it opens a fan of possibilities. He learns where guards throw their garbage, which he scavenges at midnight, and the location of their latrines, which ferries him back to boyhood when human excrement was prized as fuel. He is ingenious in keeping himself and his friends alive.

But feeling cold weather approach, *Yang* forces in ascendance, Johnny begins to know fatigue, much worse than his first camp experience. The war is older now, the enemy less human. Or is it that so much killing and maiming have begun to weaken him? At night he gently taps his forehead against the ground, *kowtowing* to the gods, imploring them for strength.

Guards call him "Yellow Monkey." "Pigtail Girl." A foreigner, a double-invader, they hate him with double intensity and poke their rifles at his legs, jeering and making him do "monkey tricks." He juggles balls. Spins an unsheathed sword on the soles of his feet while lying on his back. He performs a coy handkerchief dance during which they command him to sway his hips like a woman. Lewd things are shouted at him that he will never grasp. Things he does not need to know.

Most of these Rebels are illiterate farm boys. But Johnny knows from having fought with them before defecting to the Federals—and from having lived on the fringe of their lives with Raindance—that Southerners are smarter and deeper than they look. They are loyal and wily and often better fighters. But now they are the enemy and must be outsmarted.

One day, a guard strolls toward him brandishing a knife, announcing that he is going to cut off Johnny's pigtail because of spreading lice. Guards in the background egg him on. Johnny stands momentarily confused. *Did guard say cut off pigtail? Or other thing? Why he is staring at my crotch?* He has heard that they take Union scalps. That they cut off men's private parts.

A buzzing in his head. He suddenly grins, but only his mouth is playful. His dark eyes grow large and fiery. He snaps his head back, angrily tossing his queue so it flies out like a whip. The prison compound falls silent. The guard moves forward with his knife. Johnny spreads his feet and bends his knees, arms raised before his face, hands held stiff and edgewise like two blades.

Grinning broadly now, he beckons the man forward with his head, each muscle in his body tensed, the veins in his neck and legs jumping out like ropes. Perhaps it is his suddenly bared teeth or the aggressive brightness in his eyes that show, not fear, but eagerness. The guard hesitates, looks back at his friends, then spits a plug of chaw and contemplates his knife. Finally, he shakes his head and backs away, cursing the "filthy Chinee" as not worth the effort.

"I'll git you," he says. "When I'm good and ready."

The explosions of his beating heart threaten to pop his eardrums, and in a daze, Johnny turns back to his tent. His comrades are waiting, hands clasped over their heads in victory, tears runneling their ravaged cheeks. One gives him a ratty head warmer knitted like a sock with holes for eyes and nose. Another offers a greasy slouch hat. He draws them on at night and, to be sure, tucks his queue inside his collar, curling it beneath his arm. His friends pile broken glass around his tent and while he sleeps they take turns keeping watch, for his queue has become their mascot, a symbol of audacity and pride.

In return, Johnny carves little charms for them, bone brooches for their sweethearts, lacey thimbles from acorns. He guides the hand of an Irish lad, showing how to write the Chinese character for *mother*. A blinded boy proffers a Bible, asking for Isaiah. Johnny reads slowly, painstakingly, until the boy sleeps, then looks for someone else to cheer while hiding his own sorrow.

All this time, still no word from Raindance. At mail call, his scalp tightens, his chest constricts. He studies boys like him whose names are never called, those with no family and no sweethearts. Yet he sees them writing on paper scraps, acknowledging, if only to themselves, the hurt that has been done to them, the need to set it down. Those with families find their letters coming back inked out, cut up in tatters by prison censors. They have no paper left on which to rewrite letters, and clasp their heads and weep. Some give up. It will linger as a mystery how a boy with shot-off arms has hanged himself.

* * *

Autumn now. Their words come out in little clouds. Men take turns sleeping in ragged tents alive with lice and mold. Mostly, they sleep huddled on the ground in scraps of blankets, holding each other for warmth. Some are found frozen together like statues. It is only frost, not winter snows, but they are so weak a chill can take them. The hardiest sit groping in their armpits and groins for handsful of lice, which they stuff into their mouths while their pants fill with frozen blood and mucus.

Johnny dredges up pieces of his life for them, offering memories astonishing as fables. Sometimes he talks for hours until he starts to doze. They tie his pigtail to a hanging branch with which to hold his head up, afraid if he stops talking they will die. He describes his beautiful Raindance, how he first saw her and how, when they are reunited, he will tell her he loves her each day for the first ten thousand years.

A boy asks how he, a Chinese, had married a Creek Indian girl. Once more Johnny tells of leaving China, then running from the cane fields of the Hawaiian Isles and finally arriving in San Francisco. Though folks were rich from gold finds there, they were also full of hate. Posses with rifles kept him from mining gold because he was a *coolie*, a lesser species imported strictly for cheap labor.

"So, with thousands other Chinese, I build road, levee, lay track for railroad. When jobs finished they tell us, 'Now go back to China!' where we know we starve to death."

He had joined mobs of resisting Chinese, who competed with Irish immigrants for jobs, and incited them by taking lower wages.

"This how massacres begin. Irish ambush us, set us on fire, tie Chinese to running horses till Chinese heads fall off. Hang from lampposts till necks break."

For almost a year he had laid low, scavenging and working odd jobs, hoping to make his fare back to Ah Fat and to Laughter and their child. Ah Fat's letter reached him through a brother of the *tong*.

"…So sad to tell you…Laughter died. She took her child in right hand, her shame in left hand, and walked into the sea…"

Heartbroken, Johnny had roamed the streets, still hiding out from lynch mobs. Then ships appeared at San Francisco's docks, advertising in Chinese for laborers to work cotton plantations in the South, far removed from the bloodthirsty Irish. Contracts were offered for three years, the yearly pay a staggering three hundred American dollars guaranteed in writing.

"I am desperate," Johnny explains. "Also greedy for adventure and American dollars. So! I sign contract and find myself on hell ship."

He had unwittingly surrendered himself to men supplying a new kind of slave for the American South. Speculators who found the Chinese much cheaper to purchase than Negro slaves, a race whose lives were considered less valuable. Much later he learned he was on one of the most notorious slave ships out of San Francisco, bound for a city famous for its human auction blocks. Before they had signed their X's on the contract, Chinese in the thousands were handcuffed, dragged down to the galleys, and pressed together like seaweed. By the time the ship arrived in New Orleans, half of them were dead from suffocation.

Johnny shakes his head, remembering. "I am thrown into stone cell, floor slippery with blood and fresh manure of humans. Each night I sleep shackled to stone wall. Each day they bring me out in chains, strip naked, hose down, disinfect. Then shove me up on auction block like goat, half-starved, running with scabies. I stand and shake with terror…

"Pink-skinned men with handkerchiefs to nose pinch me on cheeks, arms, look my teeth, lift my privates with sticks, then shake heads no. This Chinaman too scrawny, weak…Guards throw me back in cell. Now I shake with hopelessness."

He tells how this went on for weeks while dozens of Chinese perished in the holding cells. He bided his time, struggling to survive on fantasies of pork cheeks and fish heads, and to draw strength from the memories of outrunning famines, locusts, cannibals.

"Compared to such things, these human auction blocks like child's play! A game to win, if not first starve to death."

But in his heart, Johnny had leaned across the years, remembering two boys bartering half cups of their blood for bowls of rice or for little brass bells that shivered when they ran. In his heart, he had feared he would die far from his brother and his homeland. His soul would be damned by the gods as a wandering *change-face*.

Eventually his wrists grew so thin his hands slipped through their shackles. One day, while guards carried out corpses, he and another man leapt behind them, snapped their windpipes with their chains, and ran. Bullets whizzed past them, the sobbing of bloodhounds while they zig-zagged through miles of wharves, losing themselves in the maze of ships.

"For days we live in shallows of muddy Mississippi, hiding in rushes, breathing through reeds for air."

At night, they crawled up on the levee in search of food, their bodies rank with the smell of creosote and bait, and in time his friend succumbed to fever. One day, a whiff of cheap perfume, women from a bawdy house promenading along the river. One of them looked down and saw his face among the reeds, a little straw of fate. They found Johnny beautiful, his face doll-like and radiant as jasper.

"They take me home, feed, and bathe me, try drown me in absinthe to kill lingering bait breath."

So he came to live in a bordello with girls of many races, ages, and persuasions. He was eighteen and strong, small but muscular in arms and legs. The fancy girls loved stroking his smooth, hairless skin, making up his eyes, brushing his long, black hair, and braiding it to a pigtail. But each time they offered themselves he demurred, faithful to the memory of Laughter. Still, he came to love their painted faces, their red monkey-bottom lips and garish gowns, which brought back memories of China: the bright, painted screens round night-soil troughs.

He washed their linens, mended their stockings, walked on their tired backs for them. He cooked and entertained them with shadow dances and songs from Chinese operas. In return, they allowed him to watch them with customers through peepholes, and in this way he learned the whole cornucopia of "female ecstasies."

"So, in my horrorful adventures across this land, I am reminded of precious woman-things, softness and playfulness and passion. And I am seized again by memories of my beautiful, perished First Wife. Night after night, my longing for Laughter summons greater need to weep."

He lived in the bawdy house for months until he grew restless, ambitious for the new. It was 1842, and Johnny was quickly absorbed into an ever-changing human tide of races, bloods and mix-bloods—Creole, French, Spanish, Chinese, Cuban, West Indian. The huge port of New Orleans was a melting pot thronged with foreign ships, the streets gay and noisy cavalcades. A city of plentitude, lucky occurrences, endless opportunities.

He found work hawking shrimp and crayfish, then straightening nails for blacksmiths. He learned to wrap cigars. But the best paying jobs were on the shipping docks, hoisting cargo with big, husky Creoles and half-breeds. He grew tanned and muscled, learned to swing his crate hook savagely, and no slaver bothered him again.

"But in time I feel the same-same loneliness. In my bunk at night in Chinatown I see nothing auspicious in my future."

He consulted a diviner who saw only bad auguries because he had no wife or children. "Man without family is only ashes in stove. Family give you purpose, bring you close to gods."

He gave Johnny instructions for new *kowtows* of ritual prostrations and offerings. "Go now. Pray. Then maybe gods send wife."

"For months I practice *kowtows*—praying, burning paper money, prostrating myself. The gods do not hear, they send no wife, and I grow disenchanted."

Out of the poverty of loneliness, on Sundays Johnny began to frequent Congo Square, known for its jubilant African music, its calling out and clapping crowds. Once a week, while white men bid at human auction blocks, they allowed their better-behaved Negroes to venture to the square where, freed from their labors, they shuffled in circles in vivid-colored clothes, and stomped their feet and sang out in "shouts" while an answering crowd responded.

Shouts were called out many times as hands clapped in faster and faster rhythms, going counter to their feet, until all of them, young and old, were circling and clapping in unison, shouting and humming to a background rhythm pounded on drums of pigskin and horsehide. One day, Johnny found himself in their circle, swaying, clapping, shouting, shuffling round and round, swept up with the pounding of the drums.

"Music help them remember Africa. Many chants and dances, people calling to family across remembered plains and jungles."

Now he falters at a loss for words, remembering the Negroes at Congo Square, how their memories got mixed up with their grief, so their music had a crying inside it as they called out to their people through the drums of skin. Then a voice, a refrain, a hundred voices joining in, a hundred bodies swaying, shouting, weeping. While in the background, mothers were torn from their children on the auction blocks.

"I go there every week. Congo Square become for me like church. May be I go there just to cry. For me. For them. Nowhere else to go, no one to go to."

He holds up his finger. "But! One day, at Congo Square, I find beautiful part-Creek girl..."

His dozing comrades sit up, suddenly alert, but memories overwhelm him and Johnny abruptly stops talking. He crawls into his tent and pulls a dead man's blanket over his face and closes his eyes, imagining Raindance beside him, her exhalations like slow hoofbeats.

He remembers how they would fall asleep face to face, eye to eye, and when they turned in their dreams how they slept sole to sole, pigtail to pigtail. He remembers the first time he saw her, a deep vibration in his bones, the gods responding to his *kowtows*.

WARREN

Mississippi, Autumn 1862

Dear Mother and Father,

    I again embrace the oportunity to inform you I am tolerably well and mending with my arm. We left Corinth are now encamped near Tupelo though I am hazy to exak location. We got the sutlers here like every camp selling goods for overprice. Boys belly up to their wagons for whisky & tobacco. There are cards and cockfights officers play chess. Rest assured I do not drink or gamble.

    There is still revivaling boys baptizing in the hundreds every week. Still, they like their dancing—fiddles tamborines and such. We have a provos marshal guardhouse stockade and courtmarshaling for there is theft aplenty and desertion. A brave soldier through two major skirmishes was found to be oh hush! a girl following her sweetheart. Month back a hanging for a spy.

    Mother do not be anyways uneasy for my deserting. Boys are running off in thousands on both sides but I rather to die fighting so never bear the name deserter. Two boys in our regiment were shot for cowardice in skirmish causing others to be killed. Two others wear ball and chain.

    Father how is the corn and cotton. Reckon I will miss this years manuring. Remember theres manure aplenty in McGruders stable. Fret not for me. We are ready for whatever comes. Since Shiloh theres been no

clashes of the likes of battles in the eastern states—
Seven Days. Second Bull Run. Antietam.

But as you heard in April New Orleans was took.
In June them Feds overrun Memphis. Now things are
warming up round Vicksburg the South's last major
riverport. Feds are amassing there to take it these are
only rumors. Still who owns that city owns the Mis-
sisippi River. We keep three days rashens cooked prepared to march.

Now days I cannot stomak what is crawling in our
meat. Still we get hardtack and rice aplenty and warm
decoctions of sassafras tea. And oh hush! we had some
of the best soda biscit you ever eat nearly. Forgive my
language here is plenty rough and I am losing my good
ability to speak and write.

Well we are on the march again aiming to push
those Feds back. There is no more talk of peace. Heavy
rains having brung the mud. Plenty boys down with
the ague and flux. When my arm hurts aplenty there
are the bull's eyes more comforting than prayer.

Father you asked what I thought about this war. I
dont know what I think most boys are afraid to think.
General Pierre Beauregard being ill turned over his command to Braxton Bragg. Truth is we don't like Bragg. A
cold sonofabitch who does not give a fig when troops are
sick or hungry. In battle he retreats and loses the advan-
tage so thousands of boys die for naught.

We lost our hero Albert Sidney Johnston at Shiloh. Now our hopes lie with Fightin' Joe Wheeler
new cavalry command, fierce in battle but tender
and loving with his boys. He so inspires us Prattville
troops we up and reenlisted. Now Company H Third
Alabama Cavalry. Wilbur Fisk Mims was voted
Captain.

I reckon the war has reached you. We hear of burning towns in Alabama. Killing and rapine. Keep your guns loaded be prepared to shoot. We are moving on so I will close. Apple trees are starting to put out. A whipperwill hollered so prettily this morning. I cant believe were in a war. Kiss Annabelle for me and rest yourselves contented I am well. I remain your loving son untell death.

W.R. Petticomb

Now driving rains create a shortage of medicine and blankets, and mild infection has set in in his arm. Weak and gaunted, Warren is not yet fit to ride into battle or even skirmishes though he repeatedly volunteers. Once the Army has settled in new campgrounds and his regiment is bivouacked, he sets to regaining his strength by cobbling extra beef from butchers, prodigiously devouring every meal.

He begins to ride again, adjusting to the imbalance of his missing arm. Each day he sits astride a sorrel mare with an easy gait, relishing the clank and jangle of his accoutrements while the horse dances with impatience. He spurs her on, reins held between his teeth, and with his left hand pulls his saber from its saddle skirt, aiming it expertly as the horse gallops toward a melon positioned on a stake.

His thrust is so accurate there is no hesitation in his mount; it is all liquid motion as she gallops forward, the melon now hoisted on his saber. Boys from the Prattville Dragoons cheer him on with a wonderful enjoyment. But in his time of convalescence Warren has given thought to how cumbersome the saber is.

"A weapon that should have been retired with Napoleon. Why, Feds with their advanced rifles are shooting us from twenty yards away! Even clumsy muskets are better than a saber."

Boys glance at his stump, wondering how he will reload a musket with one hand, and Warren grins. "Oh, hell! Just give me a loaded Navy colt."

Drilling with a revolver, his left-handed aim becomes impeccable, never more than an inch off dead center of the target. Slowly, the infection in his arm heals. He begins to regain confidence, to feel again the elixir of fearlessness, the natural superiority of a cavalier.

* * *

He has not seen the nurse for months. With Lincoln's Neutrality Pact between the North and South, nurses and surgeons now move through enemy lines as neutral combatants. Accompanying thousands of wounded soldiers from battlefields to hospital ships on the rivers or to municipal hospitals in Corinth, Memphis, even Nashville, they remain in the cities several months, then rotate back to the battlefields.

Twice now she has gone away. The first time she returned he was aloof, shunning all outward signs of gladness, though he had sorely missed her. The last time she left he rode with a cavalry detail protecting the flank of her ambu-wagon train, though she was not aware of this. Trotting behind hundreds of foul-smelling, fly-ridden wagons—the grievously wounded strapped inside on filthy litters—cavalry escorts had found the stench so overwhelming they rode with their faces covered like bandits. His first long, mounted journey since Shiloh. With each jolt, his stump ached so dreadfully he blacked out in his saddle, a pain he would grow used to, one that would never quite subside.

After long convalescence he sleeps in his own tent again in the vast encampment of the Army. Each night he stares at the moon sliding down wheels of artillery guns, and listens to boys tell of send-offs in their hometowns. Country pavilions, horn and string bands, and waltzing with a sweetheart. Their voices trail off at the memory of holding her, kissing her palm as if drinking her lifeline. A girl most of them will never see again.

He tosses for hours, hearing the wounded in hospital tents, their tongues sliding thick on morphine. Someone walks past his tent with a ticking watch. Someone weeps. He rises and walks out to a field lit with moonlight and sees a horse mounting a horse. He stands in the shadows, watching.

The next day he sits sketching and shading the face of a twelve-year-old bugler. The air shifts, a fragrance. He puts his pencil down and turns. And she comes walking in a crowd of human others. His left hand shakes; he holds it still between his knees. A warm spell has descended, confusing nature, so that there is a cargo of greens and petalled sights that cast a veil over the tents and campgrounds. Seeing her, he no longer sees the world, he hardly knows where he is. Pain falls away, and so does time. She is there, simply and eternally.

"You've come back."

"Why, yes," she answers softly, then gazes at his stump beneath the pinned-up sleeve. "You look fit. You've gained weight…"

They walk off chatting awkwardly, while Warren tries not to sound deranged. "I expect it was hell in the cities, the overcrowded hospitals…"

"A veritable morass, a swamp of dying boys." Era brushes at her eyes, and he fears if she weeps it will unman him.

He stands in a mania of uncertainty, feeling both tenderness and arousal. "I will allow that I have been concerned for you, hoping you were fairing well. That God was looking after you."

"I am obliged. But I don't think God wants any part of this." She gazes up at him and sorrowfully smiles. "Warren, forgive me! I am soiled and unkempt, and have lost all modesty and sensibility."

She sways and he reaches out to steady her. In her exhaustion, she cleaves to him, and he tightens his arm around her waist. In that moment she feels blown clean by the goodness of him, the latent strength of him, and she stares at the upright astonishment of their shadows entwined.

Later, from a distance, he watches as she pours whiskey on a surgeon's infected hand before he operates. When he finishes, she proffers a hairless white limb to an orderly like a gift. Someone cries out; she turns and stares at a groundsheet inside of which is half a man.

At dusk she comes to him in her blood-soaked dress and apron. Even her lashes are stiff with dried blood; it lies compressed beneath her fingernails as she leads him through tall grasses. A kind of fever is upon her as she removes her clothes and slips into a pond and bathes her body clean. He watches, drunk, as she comes to him damp and beautiful, and wordlessly they lie down.

It is not a sly seduction, but rather a carrying him off in a cloud of seriousness, for she is so full of death there is the compulsion to reach for life, for the very act of generation.

"Please hold me," she whispers. "Touch me." She places his hand upon her breast. "I need to know I am still human."

Feeling waves of panic, he gently cups her breast. The softness of it so shocking he cries out.

"I beg of you…Come into me." Her astonishing eyes, the need in them.

In a daze of acceptance of what life is offering, his brain listens and his body follows. When Warren is finally inside her, he moves in ways that confound him, confound them both, drawing them on until they approach exhaustion.

Unexpectedly, her body freezes, goes strict as a rod, then she seems to slowly deflate. His mind reeling, Warren's body yields, he yelps softly and lets go. An exquisite sense of surrender, an openness, a fluency. An interlude in time where God or someone allows them to rest, to at last be tender and human. In this moment they are utterly detached from life. Inviolate.

In that fragile, melancholy twilight, Era strokes his face. "Thank you, thank you! I have felt death crouched up inside me. I have felt like giving in to death. Now I feel alive again, a new and unfamiliar blissfulness, a gladness of the senses."

Warren lies stunned, feeling not just naked but turned inside out. Still, it is thrilling to listen to her talk, for she is truly addressing herself to him, caring what he thinks.

"Oh, Era. You will run rings around me. A girl like you will verily make a man pour his heart out."

She smiles, breathing in sweet gum and broomsage. "I'm not that clever. Nothing I ever learned prepared me for this life."

He turns and pulls her closer. "Oh, you are wrong! In our times together you have asked me questions, not especially to find answers…it was more as if you were tasking me to question *myself*. For the first time in my life I had to struggle to define things, grope to new depths to understand who I am, what I stand for. With you, I have had my finest thoughts."

Finally, he confesses. "I believe I have loved you from the—"

She places her hand across his lips. "When you say a thing, it changes. Words subtract from the feeling."

Yet her face glows, his is transformed, desire stuns them. They lie still, listening to their breathing, and when they move together again he is more confident, holding back until his crying out is like a howling. Afterward, he spreads his arm and holds her, marveling at how she folds to him.

Alone, she will wonder how it happened, how she let loose of her vigilance. Other men's glances alarm her. Perhaps she has turned to him so she can rest from their pursuit. *Or perhaps because he is damaged and vulnerable, and thus cannot hurt me.*

He is lost to her from the beginning. Her body is magic and drives him on. Riding in from scout patrols, he quickly dismounts and looks for her across the grounds. She stands outside a tent and smiles, and the sight of her mouth, her slender throat, brings on a shudder. But, overwhelmed by the wounded and dying, Era rations her strength, holding her body back for days so he lives in a state of constant longing.

Just when he thinks he cannot stand it she comes to him, passionate, even demanding. Later she retreats again. He sees withdrawal in her face, lips tight, unyielding. Some nights when they make love she is not fully there. He feels he can pass his hand right through her.

"I don't know how to be clever with you. You're much quicker than I. I know so little about you..."

Era looks away. "If you knew more, I would lose you."

He finds this puzzling, as puzzling as her name. But when he presses her, her expression confounds him, even pushes him away. He has never been with another woman but suspects she is not like other women, that she is unique and something in her has been hurt. He suspects this because he has begun to study humans, taking their measure while he sketches them when they are least aware, and he has learned to sense when they are calm, and when they are in turmoil.

He tries to tell her this, but his thoughts are a madhouse of insight, delusion, despair, for he is most confused about himself, and understands that though the bones and flesh of his stump are healing, deeper wounds will never heal. He has lost youth, belief in prayer, belief that there will be a tomorrow. All he believes in now is her.

* * *

An overcast and humid day. From a distance he sees Era place her hand on the shoulder of a wounded boy, then bend and whisper to him. The intimacy of the gesture sends a shock through Warren that leaves him breathless. He struggles to inhale and sees how raw and vulnerable he is, how worldly she is. He backs away, imagining the boy with her hand imprinted on his shoulder. *Perhaps she will lie down with him. Perhaps she is collecting innocents.* He stumbles to his tent and steps inside, feeling a mean tug on his stump as if someone had yanked it. Sick at heart, he collapses facedown on his bedding.

In deepest night she comes and crawls in beside him, exhausted, nerves resonant as a tuning fork. Each breath she takes vibrates through him. He prays she will not be clever and vague as she often is. That she will say something familiar and comforting. Instead, she lies quietly panting, trying to clear her head of death, and Warren speaks out in the dark.

"I am verily ashamed," he avows. "I saw you touch that boy, whisper in his ear. I near went blind with jealousy."

"I was persuading him he would be fine."

"Will he?"

"He's already dead."

He turns and pulls her to him. "Forgive me! It's just…I am not always secure in the meaning of your words, your gestures. You're such a mystery to me. Why, I don't even know if you have family."

In an odor of panic she turns away, then turns back to him. "My father's name is Johnny Tom. He's fighting some-where in Virginia."

Warren sits up and lights a candle. "But that is reassur-ing news! We've won about every battle fought back there."

She does not say her father is fighting for the Union. Or that her news of him is derived from unreliable reports.

"So many dead and wounded. So many dying there in prison camps…"

"Era, he's your *father*. Which means he must be mightily courageous. He will be all right, God's truth."

"I've had no word from him. No letters. Most likely they don't trust him."

Feeling utterly hopeless, she speaks out with reckless candor. "My father is…Chinese."

He opens his mouth, then closes it. He stares at her eyes, her skin, with dawning comprehension. "…And your mother? Is she Chinese?"

"Half white, half Alibamo Creek Indian."

"Where is she now?"

Recalling the last sight of her mother, she looks away. "She's somewhere safe. No one can hurt her."

He shakes his head at the wonder of it, then draws her close and holds her.

Johnny Tom

Lying in his moldy, ragged tent, Johnny hears the sorghum-sweet accents of guards as they taunt starving prisoners. He counts his ribs and the sores around his mouth and, with famished senses, slips into a half dream, recalling his first glimpse of Raindance at Congo Square.

…A copper-skinned girl, beside her a woman of a deeper copper. Seeing her he trembled, as if someone had singed his queue. The next Sunday he sought her out again, moved close and caught her eye, then swung his head back and forth to show the length of his pigtail, black and lustrous like hers. Then he winked, an American custom he had learned. She dropped her head and smiled.

On the third Sunday the girl's mother was prepared. She had studied his Oriental eyes, his unlined skin, which meant he was young, but his body strong and manful. She thought of China, a place that sounded far away and safe, and hoped he would return there and take her daughter with him. She saw in his eyes he already loved the girl. She prayed that love would be enough.

The girl, Dinah, was fourteen, child of Jacob as in the Bible. For her mother's white master's name was Jacob. She knew what her daughter's fate would be and had told her that Jacob would one day take her, his own blood, to his bed.

Like many slavers, he dreamed of seeding fields full of mulattos and quadroons, believing that mix-bloods were smarter and more valuable on the auction blocks, that they would not have the rebellious blood of Negro slaves. She had brought the girl here every week, looking for some way to save her. Now she dropped her hand, nodded at Johnny Tom, and whispered, "Run! Make him take you far away."

The girl had hesitated and Johnny moved close, then flipped his queue as if signaling her queue. Perhaps in that moment she saw his pigtail as a ladder with which to climb out of this life that would kill her. The mother reached out her daughter's hand and placed it in that of the Chinese. He saw in her pleading eyes what she was asking. He grabbed the girl's hand, and in terror and elation, they ran.

Folks knew the mother's story: the beautiful Creek woman kidnapped by a slaver, now forever his property. The "white marse" waiting till his half-breed daughter was ready to spawn. Perhaps they started telling it on the drums, spreading the word so folks cleared a path for them, led them out of the city and into the swamp, impenetrable to posses. For days Johnny heard the drums telling their story, and in the deepest bayous humans stepped out of the shadows to guide them. When she grew exhausted, he lifted the girl like a wild bird on his shoulders and they flew.

For weeks they hid, then moved cautiously through rice paddies and cotton fields until they arrived far up the Mississippi River, north of the city of Natchez and south of Vicksburg. There, deep in Nachitochees Parish, was a small backwater town, a community of Chinese thriving in ramshackle farms, growing rice and breeding fowl.

Since the 1820s, when they began fleeing their country, the Chinese had been migrating to such regions as this across America, rural places with rich soil and abundant land for farming. They had jumped trading ships and slave ships docked at New Orleans and other ports along the winding Mississippi and had bonded into groups who spoke similar dialects, small tongs that would one day become benevolent associations like trade unions.

Here in Natchitochees Parish they had named their little
town Shisan, Thirteen, for the original thirteen Chinese who
had settled there. The men labored as menials and in time
pooled their money and leased small plots of land from white
folks. Hardworking, kind, good family men, they attracted
wives among the Indians, Creoles, Negroes, and Spaniards,
even French and Russian immigrants. Some were freed wom-
en, and some the Chinese bought outright from slave masters.
Their children were clever, beautiful little half-breeds who
grew up speaking several tongues.

When Johnny and the girl, Dinah, arrived at Shisan, elders quickly cut off her pigtail and rice-powdered her skin so
she appeared lighter—Spanish or Creole. By then he understood what her father was and what had been done to her
mother, the fate of many Indian women. In one of the white
man's raids on their tribes as they struggled along the Trail of
Tears—robbed of their lands in Alabama, Georgia, the Caro-
linas, and forced to walk a thousand miles to barren, godfor-
saken regions—Dinah's fifty-year-old mother was kidnapped
from her people to be used as a breeder on a Louisiana slave
plantation. So Dinah had been born, half Alibamo Creek, half
white.

When they were married in Shisan, Johnny changed her
name to Raindance, the dance she performed to honor her
lost mother. And when they lay down he held her hips like the
sides of the moon and vowed she would never suffer, never be
near whites again. He would guard her with his life.

A child was born, her skin the color of palomino with a
touch of roan, and they named her Majupi, Chinese for "Pony
Skin." Johnny held her and rejoiced; he had not wished for a
boy, knowing it was unwise in this life to be too fortunate, and
he had already lost one child. Because they would always be
hunted, the girl could never have a Creek name, but proud
Creek blood flowed through her, and she sat a horse like a

warrior. Old Mongol elders brought their ponies just to watch her ride.

At night, when soft dragon mists covered their fields, Majupi told of all she was learning at missionary school. In time, she spoke American English so fluently Johnny began to dream that she might one day become a teacher or nurse, not a lowly farmer's wife, and he gave his daughter a new name appropriate to that dream.

"Era. Because you will bring new era for women of your many bloods."

She helped her father improve his skills in reading and writing of English, but her mother, Raindance, forever refused the language of slavers. And so the years passed, their life one of harmonious labor in the fields, neighbors sharing chores at plowing and sowing and harvest time. Wanting their children to prosper as Americans, their homes grew full of books and thought, each evening composed of query and response in their new adopted tongue. Shisan was so rural and insular they did not notice how parts of the country were splintering, that the North and South were pulling apart.

* * *

As Southern states seceded from the Union war became inevitable, and "secesh" agents rode the land calling for Army volunteers. They began kidnapping immigrants. When they appeared in Shisan, men fled with their families into the swamps, but Johnny stood his ground.

"No wish to fight," he told them.

An agent trotted close, all sour sweat and horse smell. "Listen, Chinee, how many years you been living off our land? It's time, by God, you fight for it!"

Adamant, Johnny shook his head. "So sorry! Not interested in war."

Two men closed in behind him, and when he woke he was trussed up like a pig. The next time he woke he was lined up with other foreign-looking men, all being sworn into the Army. At gunpoint, he pledged allegiance to the Confederacy and swore to abide by the hundred and one articles of war. Outfitted in the gray coat and forage cap of an infantryman, he listened as a sergeant addressed the new recruits.

"We have blown up a Union garrison, Fort Sumter. We are at war! If you run, we'll shoot you dead."

They were dispatched on steamboats down the Mississippi to training camps, where they drilled and formed into companies, regiments, brigades. Johnny learned the fundamentals of saluting, of marching forward to the right, the left, to the flank, and of obliquely shifting arms to various positions. He learned to parry and thrust with bayonet, to load and fire muskets while standing, kneeling, lying down. It all came naturally to him and would have seemed a noble thing to be engaged in if he were not preparing to defend the South and the practice of slavery, which represented all that was vile and base in human nature.

Wondering how to get word to his Raindance, he thought of the life she had escaped, the life her mother was doomed to. He remembered the weight of shackles on his wrists and ankles, the holding cells and human auction blocks, and suddenly he wanted very much to fight, but on the Union side. He began to plan, to bide his time and wait for the most propitious moment.

He wooed his superiors, displaying his expertise at foraging—slipping into barns, stealing chickens, goats, even a cow. He impressed his sergeant and captain by demonstrating how to strangle the enemy from behind, how to leap and sever a neck in one motion. He entertained boys with outlandish stories in his singsong voice. He juggled plates, walked a tightrope strung between two mules, and balanced on his hands on the

back of a galloping horse. He volunteered for the worst assign-
ments—digging garbage pits and sewage pits, always looking
for the opportunity to run.

February 1862, and it seemed the entire Confederate Corps
was moving on troopships back up the Mississippi. Assigned
below decks, Johnny was unaware of when they passed Natchez and Vicksburg, and in between, his little town, Shisan.
He did not see the fires of marauding Rebels. Steaming north,
they passed out of Mississippi and into Tennessee, where they
disembarked and struck an Army camp that sprawled for
miles. Here the infantry, artillery, and cavalry began to prepare for battle.

Almost immediately they were ordered to reinforce two
important Confederate garrisons—Fort Henry on the Tennessee River and Fort Donelson on the Cumberland. These
rivers paralleled each other, crucial commerce waterways that
serviced the city of Nashville, a major Confederate depot and
railroad junction. If the garrisons fell, Nashville would be in
Union hands.

Even miles away, Johnny heard the sound of booming
cannons. Fort Henry was already under siege, bombarded
by Union gunships and twenty thousand ground troops. The
Confederates were holding the fort with only three thousand
men, and by the time his division arrived they had already
evacuated.

Johnny's division regrouped, crossed the Tennessee River
on pontoons, and headed for Fort Donelson. As they quick-
timed closer to the fort, he heard the roar of the battling front,
and began to stumble over dead men. He felt the heat of flying
shells, the brush of grape and canister shot, and quickly understood that strangers were trying to kill him. Midst blinding
smoke and dust, soldiers dodged and whirled as cannonballs
tore them apart. A boy without feet ran by.

Fort Donelson was on high ground, a perfect target for Union gunships, which now commenced to bombard it. Their troops had established a ring around the fort and, with thousands of infantry and cavalry exchanging fire, leaves on the ground and in the woods ignited, boys began to burn to death. They flung their arms out in shock, and many died that way, upright like burning crosses.

Johnny knelt, trying to lift a soldier from the ground. The boy's skeleton slipped away and left him holding smoldering hunks of skin. He held the skin in his two hands and stared at the nightmare surrounding him, burning crosses still eerily upright, their grilled flesh on the wind. He stood and wrapped his queue inside his shirt so it would not ignite, then dropped his musket, threw up his hands, and walked straight through the fire.

* * *

Dead graycoats *and* bluecoats *carpeted the woods and fields. Dead horses rotted. He gazed at a charred landscape of nine thousand captured Rebels, faces powder-blackened, eyes entirely unseeing. Some were corralled in holding pens and many, like him, were made to sit in ditches in their own waste. After two weeks they were shipped to depot prisons in Maryland and Washington, where they were interrogated. As prisoners of the Union Army, they would then be trained in cattle cars to stockades in the North.*

When it was Johnny's turn, the recording officer sat back and stared. As he attempted to tell his story, more officers gathered.

"I am not Confederate," he said. "Want to fight for Union!"

The officers had softly laughed. "How do we know the Rebs didn't plant you here? That you're not a Confederate spy?"

He shook his head emphatically. "Not possible! They kidnap me from hometown of Shisan, near Vicksburg. Force me fight with them. I never aim at Federal soldier, never shoot gun. First chance, I surrender."

A few men reluctantly nodded, having heard of "secesh" scouts kidnapping foreigners at gunpoint, forcing them to fight.

A lieutenant stepped forward. "You're a Chinese. Why do you care who wins this War?"

Johnny looked down, thinking of his wife and child. If the Confederates won, they would be reclaimed as a white man's slaves. He himself was a runaway. But he refused to tell such private things.

He bravely smiled and tossed his queue. "Slavery is wrong. Union right! I want to fight with you."

He was questioned for days, and more officers gathered to stare at him, men of such varying heights and widths and skin tones, Johnny stood open-jawed. They were a new species to him. Unlike soft-spoken Southerners, their Northern accents were clipped and loud. They seemed to bark each time they spoke, and when they finished, the barking echoed. Some men were crude and spoke to him abusively, but he was too fascinated to be insulted.

He was put on a heavily guarded train and sent to a camp outside Washington. Here they continued their interrogation, asking his place of birth, his age—about which he lied, saying he was ten years younger for fear they would not let him fight—where he was kidnapped from, if he had family. He told his story repeatedly until one day a young lieutenant called him to his tent.

"Well, Johnny Tom, it seems your story is true. Now that we control most of the Mississippi, we have agents everywhere. They tell us your town, Shisan, was overrun by Rebs. They burned down most of it, took all the men except the old ones."

He trembled violently, his arms and legs grew cold. When he spoke, his voice sounded like a girl's. "What...happen to... our...families?"

The young man looked down, telling only half the truth of what he knew. "Women and children scattered. Probably taken in by surrounding towns."

"How I can write wife...if no more village?"

"I'm afraid you can't."

Each night he prostrated himself, paid double obeisance to the gods, praying his wife and child were safe.

At first he was allowed to do menial chores—scrubbing laundry, cleaning out latrines. He scraped officers' muddy boots, scoured them with sand and alcohol, then oiled and restored them so they gleamed, and men began to request him. One day, when he returned the boots of a major general, the man's orderly received the boots and handed him a porcelain basin full of phlegm. John bowed and stood confused; except for the phlegm, it was a lovely gift.

In the same way he had wooed the Confederates, he now labored to impress the Federals. His knife-swallowing trick. His "Uncanny Revolving Eye Trick," whereby only the whites of his eyes showed while he disassembled and reassembled a rifle. His "I Begin to Believe Cure," where he rendered boys unconscious by touching certain nerve-points on their necks. He climbed a tree, swift and silent as a cat, and landed noiselessly in the leap of "Butterfly Alighting on Flower." A captain asked how well he shot a rifle.

Johnny grinned. "Like expert. But with knife I slit neck so quick enemy only sigh in dying. Save on bullets. Twice fast as gun."

Disbelieving, they pitted him against an Irish sharpshooter while a crowd encircled them. The man took a marksman's stance, bringing the rifle up to his shoulder. Before he could line him up in his crosshairs, Johnny had rushed him like the wind. Flying feet-first, he kicked the rifle from his hands, spun him round in a stranglehold, and stroked his neck with a gleaming knife that left a thin, red line. The man sat speechless in the dirt.

Within days he stood in Union blues, pledging allegiance to the United States. Vowing to abide by the accepted articles of war, he was sworn in as Private Johnny Tom, assigned a company and regiment. Soon he was on a troop train headed into the Shenandoah Valley of Virginia, into a series of battles that would be known as Jackson's Valley Campaign.

* * *

November now. At Belle Isle, corpses fill the gullies outside barbed wire fences. Rats chew through their canvas covers so the corpses lie naked, staring at the living. Johnny reads the Bible to dying boys, grips their hands as they expire. He lets a boy stroke his pigtail because it reminds him of his mother's. He is obliged to tell more fables in his soft, sing-song voice: how, for instance, his uncle was sentenced to the guillotine for conspiring against the Emperor.

"Night before execution uncle sits in cell, reading *Buddhist Sutras of Angular Severity*. In morning he hears drums roll, execution time. He places bookmark between pages, hands book to guard, commanding him, 'Take care. Do not lose my place!' Then bravely he goes out to be beheaded."

Boys smile at his stories. Johnny smiles too, hoping that if three boys smile, only one of them will die. They compete, trying to tell more outrageous stories, bigger lies than his. This pleases him. If boys argue over what is truth and what is a lie, maybe they will forget they are starving. They will argue themselves into sleep instead of thoughts of suicide.

One day, rumors, an impending prisoner exchange. Boys size each other up, knowing the odds. Two Union privates for one Confederate corporal. Two Union lieutenants for one Confederate captain. A Confederate major general equals thirty enlisted Union boys. Day after day they wait. Finally, they are ordered to line up in ranks and boys drag each other forward, some barely conscious, to stand half-naked in the bitter cold.

A guard advances down the line, examining his list. Johnny stands so straight his buttocks hurt. The boy beside him collapses.

The guard moves closer. "You. Step out."

Johnny hesitates, then points down at the boy. "Please. Take this one first."

The guard looks down and laughs. "You dumb Chinee. Cain't you see he's dead. Step out!"

And so the parting. His comrades left behind, so skeletal and weak they no longer think of food, or even freedom. When he turns and waves, they only stare; many will perish here. And part of him perishes too, because he has come to love them. A private part of him steps into a room that will be forever dark and silent. That part of him now shuts the door.

ERA

Mississippi, Autumn 1862

They thunder down back roads four abreast, like gray flames licking up the dust. Under Fightin' Joe Wheeler, they sortie out, distracting the enemy with incursions and probings. They blow up bridges, cut telegraph wires, attack supply trains. Sometimes their lightning-quick raids escalate into all-out battles with the Federals.

Feeling the heat of minié balls and grapeshot whistling past his head, Warren feels reborn, though he has few illusions now of chivalry. The War has turned them all from idealistic cavaliers into galloping men of death who stalk and slay cold-bloodedly. They are men other men avoid, the ones whose eyes are strangely lit.

Yet when he returns to camp he throws off all thoughts of slaughter, and attempts to look human again. Divesting himself of his accoutrements, he hastily tends his horse, washes his face, and brushes down his hair, then moves across the grounds in search of her where she is in the hospital tents ministering to the wounded.

He stands aside as orderlies bring out the dead. A corpse's face has bleached gray white, yet the ears are blackish-green like spoiled peppers. This has a calming effect on Warren. Still half-crazed from fighting, he stares at the ears in fascination. *Why are they so green?* Then he steps back and tries to pull himself up sane.

The ease with which Era turns and smiles alarms him, her gaze direct, ingenuous. In that moment he feels a fraud, an assassin impersonating a normal man. But when she speaks his name he experiences a rush of feeling, a sense of having moved up in the world for knowing her. She tells him she feels guilty—so busy all day she has forgotten to worry over her father.

Warren takes her hand consolingly. "I reckon to forget now and then is human. Even folks in mourning, distracted by a dog's trick, can momentarily forget their dead."

Era throws back her head and laughs. "You're a wonder! Such homespun wisdom."

"I thought that's what attracted you. My farm-boy sagacity."

"Well, I suppose all attractions are alike; they derive from an inner emptiness. Something missing that we hope to fill." She looks away. "Though nothing ever really lasts, not ever."

When she talks like that, he feels stricken, a fear that she is growing bored. A zest for new things—a new lover?—pouring out of her in his presence.

"Dearest, don't play with me. Have pity on my tender heart."

She takes his arm and leans her head against his chest. "Forgive me. I am so very tired. And I wonder if we survive this War, what will come after? Will life be worth living at all?"

The look on his face is of profound and peaceful desolation. "I know this. If I survive, my life will be worthless without you. I will be unwholesome and unwhole."

"Hush now," she whispers. "We're both exhausted. We need a hill to lie down on."

Dusk. And for a while they seem suspended outside of time, beyond all care. With a joyful surrendering, they lie down on damp mosses and watch their faces fade. He slides his arm round her waist so slender and urgent, and she whispers his name again and again, feeling the deep humanity of him, the intrinsic goodness, a thing she fears she has long ago relinquished. And it is night, a peaceful night that has slipped sideways into the War.

* * *

With the slow encroachment of Union forces intent on taking all of Mississippi and Tennessee, engagements between the armies escalate, sometimes involving a brigade, an entire corps. In the midst of it, litter-bearers feint and dodge, searching through smoke that boils up filthy and gray and rolls along the ground lit with red bursts where muzzles flash. Boys leap and fly apart while canister and cannon chew up their ranks. Others struggle in from the field blank-eyed, lay down their wounded friends, and keep walking into the woods and away, for they are finished with the human race.

She is busy with compresses and syringes when Warren appears, having already struck his tent and packed his haversack.

"I'll be gone a spell. Escorting a battalion of pontooniers and their train."

He nods toward a mule train headed down the road, forty wagons loaded with pontoon boats and lumber for laying bridges.

"The Shawnee River is still swollen with spring rains and the corps has got, by God, to cross it."

Era looks at him confused. "The Shawnee? That's in far west Tennessee. I heard General Bragg is planning to occupy Chattanooga...which is way the *middle* of Tennessee."

Lying just north of the Georgia border, a major railroad center considered the "Gateway to the Deep South," the city of Chattanooga is now a prime objective of the Union Army.

His voice drops to a whisper. "The Shawnee is purely a tactical feint. Joe Wheeler's been ordered to divert the Feds in that region from Bragg's big advance toward Chattanooga, then on to occupy Kentucky before the Union takes it. We'll keep them distracted, raiding and destroying their supplies."

"How in the world will Bragg accomplish such a task?"

"Half of his Army is going by train. A few divisions will stay behind and try to prevent them getting closer to Vicksburg. And some will march, escorting your ambu-wagons part way to Nashville, then press on and meet up with Bragg."

Solemnly, he presses her hand to his lips. "Should we lose each other in this unholy mess, I will write you at the hospital there. I believe you're assigned to Building Number Three."

When they say good-bye, they hardly touch; everything is in their eyes. She watches his regiment ride out, horses snorting and prancing, hooves clattering on stones. The jangle of spurs and sabers. A thousand troopers, four abreast, wheeling their mounts out with the grace and precision of a ballet. A scene romantic and chivalrous. *Southern through and through*, she thinks. Warren fleetingly looks back, his depthless eyes and pinned-up sleeve suggesting the heroic and severe.

That night she engages in conversation with an officer attached to the Quartermaster's Corps. Ignoring the rules against fraternizing, which she has broken a hundred times, she sits visiting outside his tent, petitioning for more quinine and morphine, more linens and supplies. He accepts her soft entreaties as flirtation and offers her a cordial of brandy, which she accepts, knowing the man is a drinker.

The night grows long while he imbibes and chatters amiably. In that way, Era learns that Bragg has already decamped by train with over twenty thousand men, taking a very circuitous route to Chattanooga, and ultimately, Lexington, Kentucky, by heading south to Mobile, Alabama, then

Montgomery, then north to Atlanta, Georgia, then farther
north to Chattanooga and beyond.

"My heavens! Why such a roundabout route?" she asks.

He answers almost lazily. "Because, my deah, Bragg desires the element of *surprise*. The Federals are looking for us
to come at them from the west. Instead, we'll be coming up
theah rear...so to speak. A truly brilliant tactic."

He sips his fifth or sixth cordial, explaining how Bragg
is launching an offensive, which has as its objective the all-
out liberation of Tennessee—half of which, including Nashville, is now in Union hands—and the occupation of "still
neutral" Kentucky. Leaving behind fifteen thousand men
to attack from the west, Bragg's transferring of the twenty
thousand by rail is a maneuver geared to outflank the entire
Federal front in the Western Theater of the war, thus open-
ing the path into Kentucky.

"...Meanwhile unrelenting raids by our cavalry troops
will grievously slow the supporting Federals now advancing
from the west toward Chattanooga."

She leaves him with his brandy and, in the privacy of her
curtained section of the nurses' tent, unfolds a map kept inside her pillowcase and traces Bragg's route while recalling
the officer's words.

"...*Imagine the movement of twenty thousand men over
tracks of five different railroads by such a circuitous route as
down through Mobile, then on to Montgomery, then Atlanta,
and on to Chattanooga. He will accomplish it in two weeks
and shock the bejesus out of the Federals, who will have their
divisions—infantry and artillery—looking to the west!*"

She tries to imagine the consequences: While Union
forces assume that Bragg's Army marching from the west
will take weeks to reach Chattanooga, he will have already
arrived there, successfully taken it, and be heading north to
the bluegrass country of the "stubborn neutral Kentuckians,"

to claim that state for the Confederacy. There he will meet with other Confederate divisions who have come across the Cumberland Mountains to reinforce his Army. This will mean the disruption, over several months, of the entire Federal offensive west of the Appalachians.

The next morning Era meanders into the woods outside the Army campgrounds, scraping her arms on blackjack scrub and scuppernong. Early autumn woods are parched, leaves brittle and dry as locust wings, but there are still roots to be found, healing stems and curing seeds. She walks until she is dangerously close to the picket lines separating Confederates from their enemy. From the distance, a picket sights her and approaches on the run.

"Ma'am! You are surely not safe here. Them Union pickets are so close we can smell 'em across the stream; we can see their *bluecoats*. Why, their sharpshooters in the trees could pick you off in seconds."

She smiles ingenuously. "Oh, you mustn't fret. Why, I'm just looking for yellow root and dandelion, maybe some dried-up mint. They make excellent teas and our wounded boys have precious little home cures…"

While she talks, he stares at the beauty of her, her slenderness, the way her skirt floats, caught on tall grasses.

Era leans forward earnestly. "See this root? Its Latin name is *asafetida*, wild parsley root. Worn in a pouch round the neck, it kills all kinds of disease. Think how it will help our boys! You just go on now and keep watch. Besides, why ever would a Union soldier shoot a nurse? Even they are not that evil."

He hesitates, shifts his rifle, and looks back toward the picket line. "Well, OK, I reckon. But please…Stay low, ma'am. And don't be long!"

She watches him disappear through the trees, cautiously looks around, then moves to a big sycamore, its bark rucked and ruffed as an elephant's hide. Squatting, she slides a mirror from her pocket and flashes it back and forth as it catches the sun's reflections. She does this several times, pausing in between, and waits till she sees the answering reflection from a distant treetop. Then she stands up straight until she imagines she is lined up in the Federal's field glasses, that he is following her moves.

Slowly, with exaggerated gestures, she pulls out a small glass vial inside of which is a rolled-up message in coded cipher. Should it be found by Confederates, it would look like the doodles and sketches a lovesick girl has left here for her sweetheart. Quickly, she digs a hole at the base of the tree, buries the vial, then tamps down the dirt, spreading leaves on top.

Then she leans against the tree, giving him time to determine its exact location, and with a small knife peels off strips of bark. In the dark, their scout can locate the tree by feel. She sits and flashes her mirror again, waits for the responding flash, then moves away and meanders back to the campgrounds.

* * *

The Army finally breaks camp, forming a wagon train that extends for miles. At the front, all is formality and pomp with the generals and their staffs and escorts, and officers of regiments. Behind them are companies, brigades, divisions, endless columns of infantry, even brass men and percussionists, fifers and drummers. Era counts them all, and then counts the massive caissons rolling by, unaccoutred gunners perched atop them, then the endless supply wagons loaded with ammunition.

The white-wagon Army progresses, then slows, then moves again, a great segmented body creeping along, seeming to devour the roads and bridges over which it moves. Behind the ambu-wagons with their wounded men are teams of nurses and surgeons still in their bloody aprons. And behind them, exhausted squads of stretcher-bearers and mess boys. She counts them too, inscribing the numbers in her head.

And still, in the rear of these and extending for miles are the multitude of noncombatants—bakers, cooks, laundresses, camp followers, sutlers, photographers, tailors, barbers, shoemakers, mule skinners, farriers with their portable forges and massive arms—each with a wagon there to supply the Army's needs. As the chain of command dwindles down, order is lost in confusion and attrition. Sutlers gamble in their wagons. Camp whores run alongside farriers, offering their wares. Cavalry details ride alongside their flanks trying to keep order, while boys in the hundreds desert into the woods forever.

At dusk, when they stop and set up camp, there is bedlam, gaming, and drunkenness. Knowing they will soon face another major engagement, boys wander off with their fiddles and play "Aura Lee" or stare silently at their campfires. She sees them clustered in chaplains' tents, lips moving with the Scriptures. They pose for itinerant photographers, making tintype portraits to be sent home in case they die.

Era wanders near a paddock of cavalry mounts and sees a first lieutenant issuing commands. Inexperienced at leading troops, he pores over a manual, then in an odious, stagey voice, lifts an arm and practices shouting orders to the horses. The next evening she sees him lashing his slave boy across the back with a straightened metal barrel hoop.

The lad is small, no more than ten. He has spilled a glass of whiskey on his master. She sees he is already scarred from earlier beatings. Now, with each lashing, old scars are laid open to the bone; even if they heal, they will heal as hideously knotted scars upon scars. A full genealogy of scars. Men watch the beating go on and on until the boy lies unconscious. In the silence, campfires sputter and flicker.

An infantryman speaks softly through the haze. "Guaranteed. One night that sum'bitch will get his own. I plan to *personally* gut him with my Bowie. And I don't mean the little nigra."

She thinks that perhaps such generosity has been awakened in these Southern boys because they are aging and dying fast. It is as if an enchantment has fallen upon them by the force of their sudden affection for life, for the living, for all living things.

She waits until the lieutenant drunkenly staggers off. Then she and an orderly carry the boy to her tent where she gently washes the raw, open wounds, then carefully stitches the flesh together. All night she applies mashed roots and salves, whispering consolingly when he moans. She wants to rage, to tell him things, but no sensible words come. At dawn, when he regains consciousness, she tries to comfort him.

"We're two weeks out of Nashville. The Union owns it now. Soon our Army will branch off, go their separate way, leaving us a few escorts for the wagons. You stay beside me at all times. When we arrive in Nashville…You are *free*."

He stares at her blankly, not understanding what *free* means.

* * *

Each time the Army stops and sets up camp, she tours the hastily thrown-up hospital tents. Now she stares at a fife boy all shot up in his feet, then bends and wipes his feverish brow.

"How old are you, son?"

"Eighteen…"

"You can't lie about your height. Why, you're a baby yet."

"I'm twelve, ma'am. Well…eleven."

They should have taken the feet off. Now there is the gangrene smell. She studies the beauty of his face, sees how it is going over into death. As they are drastically short of morphine, she holds his head and helps him swallow tincture of opium, then two shots of whiskey.

He begins to fade and cries out in his child's voice, "Ma'am! Cain't you help me live?"

She stands in the shadows, staring at her hands, the famished patterns of her lifelines, astonished that she is only eighteen years old. She goes away in her mind, and after a while comes back to the corner of a field tent where certain boys are kept behind partitions. Few nurses venture here except to dispense morphine, and as she moves past a cot, a voice calls out.

"Nurse."

Era turns as a man pulls back his sheet, showing her a pistol.

"Shoot me. Please."

He has no body to speak of below the waist. What is left has been tied together in a huge diaper and tourniquet about his groin. She understands at a glance that if the tourniquet is loosened, all of his insides will fall out. Were they alone, she would shoot him. Instead, she puts her finger to her lips and goes away, then returns with a hypodermic and two stolen vials of morphine.

He lifts the pistol again. "Please."

"Hush now," she says, and carefully administers the morphine.

She slides the pistol into her pocket, watches his face, his heartbeat settle down, then unties his tourniquet and walks into the night.

Exhausted, numb, she leans on a paddock fence, listening to the beasts within. *Mother always said I was part horse.*

She drops her head, soothed by their smell and the sound of their hooves softly stamping. She has seen dead horses scattered across the fields, crushed under massive caissons. She has seen them go insane, gnawing at their trailing intestines. She once saw a dead horse and his dead rider standing poised and still as a statue. No sign of blood, no wound, the trooper's saber raised, the horse's head thrown back as if about to charge. She remembers how she approached and touched them, both horse and rider hard as stone. Their hearts had failed. Together, they had died of shock.

She thinks of that horse and rider, and how for her there is no future, none at all. It is as if her heart had already failed, as if, though outwardly intact, she has already died of shock.

* * *

Ragged couriers from Joe Wheeler's Corps in western Tennessee catch up with their wagon train and relate how Wheeler's cavalry had crossed the Shawnee River, cut their way through Union lines, and burned out their camps. Taking hundreds of prisoners and four hundred mules and horses, they had ransacked Union supply wagons, drinking and eating everything in sight. Their attacks had cost them ninety men, the Federals several hundred. Their plan to divert the enemy seems to have succeeded.

But tending a courier with a broken arm, Era hears otherwise.

"Jesus and Mary, it was queer. We rode down on them, but all we got was skirmishes, no real big engagements. The Feds drove us back, we drove them back, attacks, counterattacks, until the bugle blew the recall…"

He shakes his head, disgusted. "Why, we was fighting a mere scattering of troops. Their larger forces was already heading to cut Bragg off before Chattanooga. There was a *leak*, by God. Them Feds knew our diversion plans."

Patched up and full of whiskey, he stalks out of the hospital tent.

"Sedition is what it is! This whole damn War's about seditious acts. Both sides crawling with traitors."

That night she reads by a candle stub that stutters and trembles. The book is old and familiar, a verse by William Blake that she knows by heart. And so she lets the candle die.

> *Let us agree to give up love/*
> *And root up the Infernal Grove,*
> *Then shall we return and see/*
> *The worlds of happy Eternity/*
> *…And throughout all Eternity/*
> *I forgive you, and you forgive me…*

ERA

Nashville, Autumn 1862

In early spring the government of Tennessee had fled Nashville, leaving it in Union hands and, like most cities under recent siege, crowds still rush to and fro through streets shank-deep in muck and offal. Federals have ransacked stores and slavers' mansions and, drunk on liquor, they dance in the streets, bewigged, in satin ball gowns, cavorting with half-naked prostitutes whose nipples are painted peacock blue.

At Building Number Three to which she is assigned, Era struggles to help orderlies unload the wounded. Part of a sprawling hospital complex, the building resembles the drawing of a huge asylum rendered by a child, a gruesome, gray structure with a large, lopsided door flanked by dozens of obscure windows. Inside, she looks down the length of what seems a gigantic warehouse wherein boys with ghastly faces lie in bloody bedclothes, so neglected their wounds have gone purulent. There are not enough doctors, not enough food or medicine.

She passes through the main ward for abdominal and spine cases, head wounds, double amputations. Then the upper floors. In the right wing, jaw wounds, gas cases, nose, ear, and neck wounds. In the left wing, the blinded, lung and pelvis wounds, and wounds in joints, intestines, testicles. Midst the squalor, volunteers sit murmuring to patients, pressing upon them meager packets of sweets. Since hospitals are open to the public, there are even sightseers strolling the aisles, indulging their morbid curiosity.

An attending doctor coughs into a kerchief. "You have heard the latest madness? The king of Siam has offered Lincoln ten thousand war elephants to put down us 'rebel insurrectionists.' Alas! Lincoln declined. You may depend our starving boys would have tolerably savored elephant meat."

Day after day the wounded arrive. Union soldiers are placed in the best equipped hospitals, while Confederates are housed indiscriminately in grim buildings like No. 3, in churches, stables, even crude outlying tents for the "hopeless." And always in the background, the dull, grinding rasp of the surgeon's saw.

Weeks pass and she falls into the numbing routine—administering bull's eyes, pouring ether into copper face-cones, debriding putrefying skin. When doctors collapse with fatigue, she is disposed to finish surgical procedures—removing bullets with forceps, sterilizing wounds, then like a crafty seamstress, suturing the flesh. She begins to notice how her hands shake as she searches for signs of pyemia, gangrene, and how they shake even when she is still.

Months pass, or is it days? How many miles has she walked in this place? She misses the field hospitals, the scent of pine and cedar, where death seemed more in tune with nature. True, there are no skulls here to rise unbidden from the soil, no pyramid of naked limbs, but there is also a pernicious dearth of fresh air. What she inhales is fetid, a breeding ground for bacteria and microbes. The staff resemble bandits, wearing gauze masks at all times, and though there are not enough masks for patients, most do not care. They no longer have the strength to care.

Some nights Era reads to them and, in the awful humidity, watches glue melt from the spine of her book onto her skirt. Pages drift slowly to the floor, dead sonnets, meditations, and boys call out to her in dying.

"Miss Era, take my hand. I'm going home."

Will I be allowed to forget this? she wonders. *Will there be an afterward?* She feels how death has entered her, become an integral part of her. Only her longing for Warren beats it back. She remembers his hand moving calm across her body, with what soft exaltations he had resurrected her. She wonders how she can ever tell him who she is. What acts she commits.

* * *

She is counting syringes when the superintendent matron summons her. A moment's wavering, then she steps into the office of a stout, motherly figure, a woman who drags a bad foot like an anchor. Blue sacs of fatigue beneath her eyes suggest a further frailty, which prompts Era to envision her on a porch-swing rocking a grandchild, rather than presiding over this infirmary of subterfuge and death.

Matron Phillips greets her, then sits down at her desk, lowering her voice.

"There is much traffic through this office. If you will, Nurse Tom, kindly approach and stand just here where I am pointing to my journal."

Era moves round her desk to stand beside her, and that quick, the woman hands her a heavy packet shaped like a candle stub.

"Well done," she whispers. "And there is a new assignment. Friday, three o'clock. The daguerrean gallery on Myrtle Street. The one owned by the Russian."

A few minutes of conversation, then in parting Era turns back to her. "Forgive me, Matron, but I'm wondering how you came to be in this…business of intelligence gathering. It seems the height of incongruity."

Phillips squares her shoulders, then looks up. "My husband was killed at Bull Run. His death taught me an important thing. War is real. We are not. Good day."

That night in the nurses' dorm she opens the packet. Ten gold-eagle twenty-dollar coins. Remuneration for the dispatch buried beneath the sycamore at Tupelo.

Three days later she steps into the streets where Southern women, gaunt and wretched, wait patiently for handouts of provisions dispensed by Union soldiers. Era keeps her eyes averted as she passes them, then enters a photographer's studio where men beguile the time by lining up for portraits. She hesitates until the owner nods her toward a back room.

A Federal officer is waiting and, though her beauty momentarily disconcerts him, he quickly removes his hat and bows. "Captain Foster Ballard, ma'am."

She frowns as he hands her a dispatch, then steps back while she attends to it. When she looks up, her expression causes him to flinch.

Her voice bespeaks repulsion. "I *cannot* do this. Morphine and opium are for the wounded. I care not if they are North or South."

The captain quietly implores her. "It's a known fact, ma'am, those drugs are helping the Rebs win battles. Nearly half their Army's got the trots…pardon the crudeness. Without opium, they'd be on their hands and knees. It stops the runs, enables them to fight."

"I am aware of that."

"Are you aware that Confederate officers dispense opium pills like sweetmeats when their men are heading into battle? God's truth, some of them just pour it out in powder form; those boys lick it off each other's hands."

"But *morphine* is for grievously wounded patients. What they are asking me to do is a contravention of all human codes."

Ballard sighs and shakes his head. "Forgive me, but I've seen these Rebs in action. They're running out of food, rifles, bullets. They're desperate, jacked up on drugs, whiskey, anything they get their hands on, so numb they don't stop fighting till they're dead."

He leans forward in the posture of beseeching. "We've blocked all ports on major rivers of the South. Most blockade runners from Europe are virtually useless now. But spies keep smuggling drugs across state lines, and poppy fields have virtually sprouted up all over the South."

"So...they are requesting that I help locate the fields."

"They are indulging that hope. Right now Tennessee and Georgia are producing unholy amounts of opium. Grown by women, slaves, even children. They camouflage the poppy blossoms with rows of corn, tobacco. A hundred fields all over this state, virtually invisible from the roads. We mean to track them down and burn them out."

She stalls for time, thinking of her patients. "Are you absolutely sure?"

"We've caught runaway slave girls who confessed they were forced to work a poppy farm. Women harvest the poppy resin, then take it to chemists who process it into opium and morphine powder. They take the powder home and...why, almost every farmhouse in the state has its own little pill mold for making tablets! And a hundred schemes for smuggling it to the Rebs."

"Well, I suppose I can begin to ask around..."

"I'm afraid it must be soon. Last month was the time for sowing. They start scoring poppies and harvesting the gum in thirty, forty days. We got to burn those fields before then. I have been instructed to tell you you will be generously compensated, as usual."

Era turns and faces him full-front. "Captain, by now your General Grenville Dodge or whosoever is in charge of...intelligence gathering...must know I don't give a *damn* about being paid. What I want is word from my father. Why have I not received one letter from him in all this time?"

"I'm sorry, ma'am. I'm just a liaison."

"How do I even know he's *alive*, that he receives the letters I give your couriers?"

"I have been told they reach his regiment."

"I do not believe you! Can it be the Union is withholding them? If he had received them, surely he would answer."

With no sense of it she begins to weep, to clasp her hands before her like a child. "All I know from you people is that he has fought in *this* battle and *that* battle, and that he was captured, then released. How do I know any of it is true? My God, I had to find out from the Confederates who kidnapped him that he had defected to the Union side. Most all the men kidnapped from our town defected to your side. That's why the Rebs came back and burned our village down. They slaughtered women, children."

She looks up with unseeing eyes. "They *murdered* my mother. And now you Federals have taken my father. You won't even tell me where he is, afraid I will make my way to him."

"I'm told he's alive, ma'am. He's well. My word of honor." Moved by her grief, he tries to offer comfort. "Perhaps when the War is going more in our favor you can be transferred closer to your father."

"That is a lie! Up North I would be of no use to you."

She moves so close he feels her breath. "I have not seen my father since the Rebels took him over a year ago. You say he is alive and well. Then bring me a letter from him to prove it."

"That is not my decision. But…I will do my best."

Later, as she passes through the shop, the photographer, Ivan Golgoff, engages her in conversation and asks her to sit for him.

"Such strange, ambiguous beauty," he declares. "A face for the future when all this madness is *kaput*."

Out of loneliness and curiosity, one day Era returns to Golgoff's shop and agrees to sit for photographs. Because he is a foreigner, and because their political sympathies seem to be aligned, she feels somewhat at ease with him and comes again. Bit by bit he recounts his travels in the world, what he has seen and learned of humanity.

"Since history, war has always been the same. Old men talking, young men dying."

In return, Era tells him of her life. How she escaped her burning village, how Federal soldiers found her hiding in the woods, bloody and half-insane. How officers listened to her story, and how she volunteered to serve with them as nurse while searching for her father now fighting with their forces. A major general in charge of intelligence gathering persuaded her to volunteer instead as nurse for the Confederates—where there was such a dearth of nurses—and to gather information on them.

In return, the Federals promised to trace her father, Johnny Tom. Within days, it seemed, she had signed the oath of loyalty to the Union, then learned the grid of Federal Intelligence symbols, a basic coded cipher, and the language of signing with one's hands. Some nights she falls asleep, hands crisscrossed on her breasts, her fingers flicking rapidly. *O father! How did life come to this? Kongpa! Kongpa! I am afraid.*

* * *

After months of rain, the sun. Rivers cease flooding, bridges no longer wash away, and mail wagons reach the city. Warren's tattered letter is smuggled in by a sutler.

Beloved Era,

    I pray this letter finds you in tolerably good health. I know you reached Nashville this displeases me. I hear how vulgor Feds treat womenfolk leastmost coloreds and commoners. You I fear will break yourself down tending soldiers North and South. You will walk backward & forward for them strangers & get nothing in return. I have seen how you don't stop to rest and for that I do not want to hear it.

    Excuse my crabbing am troubled with chronic stomak has reduced me 20 pounds & swept our troops like locusts. Captain passes out bulls eyes when they are aplenty which is less and less. What I eat don't stay put long enuf to do me good. Stomaks like this men no good for walking. God help them infantry.

    My good arm is ailing sore from too much use I reckon. Im still dead fast with that revolver. Boys bullyrag me when I ride out my deck is always full. I rarely waste a bullet. At night I sketch. Cant even sleep for sketching.

    We near routed them Yanks at Perryville but it was costly. Bragg was cocksure we could take them but that Union general Buell struck our 16000 men with heavy forces & just missed a victory. They say we won but then that craven poltroon Bragg retreated stead of finishing off Buells troops. Kentucky was left in Union hands. Yanks burning & destroying with great jollity. Livestock churches homes provisions all they could lay their scurrilous hands on. Pure and out destruction. Nothing to do with soldiering.

    We departed Kentucky in driving rain impassabl fords retreating so slow our Army crept but five miles a day. Yank cavalry harassing us at every mile. As

Braggs rear guard under Joe Wheeler gods truth we fought 26 skirmishes in 24 days. A skirmish is a battle regardless what they call it. You can lose 1000 men a skirmish. I have killed so much I dont know how I stand myself.

Bragg is taking us to Murfreesboro to rest our troops then headed down to Vicksburg they say. With Memphis gone there is only V-burg left to us. Who wins that city owns the Misisippi. God help us all for what is coming. They burned our house down. Poor mama has went to an asylum. Papa wrote he was joining up and little Annabelle of 14 run off following her beau whose regiment is bound for Vicksburg too.

Dearest I try not to think of you but then there is naught to live for. I have drawed your face a hundred times. It looks back & gives me a peaceful astonishment. Though I think when this War is done you will not want a one-armed of little schooling & my talk grows more foul for being in the field.

A lutenant here knows Shakespeere. I lissen when he reads aloud. I don't grasp most things still the sounds of the words pass thru me with a satisfying ravishment. Just as when you read to me. I picture a little ranch someday out in the new West half a dozen horses which you love. You could read. I could sketch. We could just be.

O that I could see you now. My longing is so great I do not sleep. Please take care of your precious self and not run down your health. We are moving out so nothing more. Am mightily tired of this War and want it soon to end. I remain your loveing and devoted untell death.

Warren R. Petticomb

The soiled pages, the plethora of misspelled words. In places, his thoughts are indecipherable, the chaos of a mind wrenched from boyhood innocence into a netherworld, that innocence shattered forever. She suspects the South will be defeated, then what will he be? A galloping man of murder who plunders and moves on until one day he vanishes into the landscape, and she will not be with him. She will have left, with a violent indifference to his life, remembering him only as the enemy.

And yet. She looks up at stars of a porcelain aching, and is momentarily stabbed by the memory of lying in tall grasses, the singing of bare flesh. His ineffable tenderness. His body over hers, crowding out the moon so it spilled round his shoulders. His soft weeping as they held each other, gasping like infants.

She remembers finding him one day outside his tent, bent over in a jeweler's hunch. He was gripping a darning needle, a sock held in place between his knees. She remembers how he squinted, patiently trying with his unpracticed hand to force needle and thread through the sock's worn-out heel. In that moment she saw his stump jerk, the muscle instinctively move as if the missing arm and hand would aid him. When Warren looked up, eyes wide with pain and disbelief, she had felt such love for him she looked away.

Now she is swept by waves of panic as she tries to reconcile her loathing for the Confederates, her abiding need for vengeance, with her profoundly impassioned feelings for this man.

* * *

When Captain Ballard returns, she greets him with impeccable resolve.

"I'm sorry. I have no information on the poppy fields."

He drums his fingers on a desk, then asks her to sit down. "Ma'am, I expect I could be hanged for this. Nonetheless, I am going to confide to you that, in spite of our staggering Union losses in Virginia, your father, Private Johnny Tom, has fought outstandingly in several major engagements. In August he was captured at the Second Battle of Bull Run east of Richmond, and was imprisoned in a Confederate camp named Belle Isle."

Her composure skips a beat as he draws from his pocket a sheet of paper.

"This, of course, is classified, a list of Federal prisoners recently paroled and traded for Confederates."

He hands her the list and points to a name: *Johnny Tom, Private. Army of the Potomac, Third Corps, 70th New York Infantry, Co.D.*

Era hesitates. "It's such a common-sounding name. How do I know it is my father?"

"Well, he was described as Chinese. He gave his hometown as Shisan, Mississippi."

She sobs out and presses the paper to her breast. "When was he released?"

"A few weeks ago. His condition was reported as relative healthy. Many of those prisoners die, but the hearty ones... Mostly, they just need food, rest, time to feel human again. As far as I know, he's back with his regiment, encamped somewhere outside Washington."

"Then I can write him there directly?"

Ballard shakes his head. "I can't say when he'd get your letter. There's a new ordnance to hold all mail till after the next engagement. You see, they're gearing up for a big one near Fredericksburg and men are deserting in the thousands—they've had enough."

"It's happening here too. Wives sending letters full of grief and deprivation. It's breaking down morale incredibly."

"And I guess the higher-ups think your father might desert and come to you. After all, he's not American, no deep sense of allegiance. Then, of course, they'd lose your services."

He is struck by the depth of Era's rage, the way her spine snaps taut. "You are wrong, Captain Ballard! My father would *never* desert from the Union Army. He abhors the institution of slavery. He is a man of enormous integrity."

"Then I suggest you pray, and bide your time till after this Fredericksburg engagement. At least you finally know where he is, that he's alive."

"And I know that he could die at Fredericksburg."

"Ma'am, we could *all* die, at any moment. Johnny Rebs are sneaking in at night, blowing half the buildings in this town."

She thinks on it, finding no solution. "All right. I will wait until after this engagement. Then I mean to hear from him!"

As they prepare to depart, she turns to Ballard, curious. "I do appreciate how you've compromised yourself. As you say, Captain, you could be hanged for treason. Tell me, is it worth the risk?"

Solemnly, he shakes his head. "Maybe I've seen too much killing. I'm sick of how this War is tearing families up. I pray you and your father are reunited."

She briefly shakes his hand. "Thank you again. And I will see about the poppy fields."

* * *

Half-starved women of the farming class and working class gather in changing rooms and tie on freshly laundered smocks. When not working their exhausted fields, they have come to volunteer as nurses' aides, seamstresses, and cooks, in return for which the hospital offers them a modest daily meal, most of which they take home to their children. There is also the opportunity to pilfer. Era sees them pocketing squares of soap, small vials of laudanum.

Even cotton aristocrats have come, some still perversely struggling with rusty hoops beneath their skirts—birdcage chastity belts that now seem an outmoded form of bondage. Having failed to manage their recalcitrant slaves, many of whom have fled, and with their mansions confiscated by Federals, their only concern is staying alive, and keeping their children alive.

They follow alongside her as Era dispenses gauze masks, then instructs them during ward rounds, and she hears them confide how they have begun to fear for their sanity.

"… forced to feed my children sawdust…"

"…every man in my family killed. Beneath this wig I have not one strand of hair left…"

They sit at frugal collations as Era discusses bulletins from the capital of the Confederacy. "Because of the U.S. Naval blockades of our ports, drugs are perilously scarce. The medical purveyor at Richmond is appealing to women of the South to cultivate more poppies so additional opium and morphine might be had for our sick and wounded."

"Why, that is old news!" A redheaded girl speaks out so exultantly her freckles glow. "My name is Cassie, and I vow we have been in the poppy fields two years now, sowing and pruning. Last year Yank patrols near caught us harvesting. Indeed, they arrested several girls for transporting opium packets sewn into their petticoats."

An appallingly thin woman picks up the thread. "Tennessee has the richest soil in the South for growing poppies. We have only an acre or two per farm, but each acre yields about one hundred twenty pounds of opium! It's just…the harvesting is backbreaking and fairly cripples us. Then there is the smuggling. Women have been caught and shot."

Knowing this year's harvest season is fast approaching, Era speaks with quiet urgency. "It appears you need more women in the fields. And in the contrabanding. There are trustworthy women here at Building Number Three who would be willing."

Women drop their heads and moan. "Oh, it seems so useless…"

Yet each day when they gather, she persists, accentuating her soft, Southern tones. "Any disposition to give up will surely defeat us all. Why, ninety percent of our troops, even officers, are suffering from dysentery. Without opium they can barely stand. If they are going to perish…let them die on their feet like *proud* Southern men."

A woman finally takes the floor, hands spread on her generous hips. "I reckon she's right! I'm Lucy Baines, and I tell you there is hope. England and Northern sympathizers have pledged to smuggle in more drugs. Quinine and morphine are entering the city in coffins emptied of their corpses. Why, thousands of children's toys, dolls and such are packed with drugs brought in under the nose of Union patrols. But opium…we need much more of it. If we give up on the home front, our men will surely die."

Rather grudgingly, most of the women agree. Resolving to try harder, to be stronger, they accept Era's offer to help in the poppy fields.

"Then let us proceed. I'll gather sympathetic women from the staff, cooks, and laundry girls, one or two trusted nurses."

Within days, Superintendent Matron Phillips has issued travel passes granting them emergency leave to "tend ailing kinfolk" in the countryside. In creaking wagons, they present their papers to Union sentries and pass out of the city limits.

ERA

The Poppy Fields, Autumn 1862

For hours their wagons roll precipitously along wrecked roads past burnt-out houses and cratered fields. Turning left, then right, down increasingly narrow cowpaths, after six hours they reach a dilapidated farmhouse. A tall, raw-boned woman wearing a holstered pistol greets them.

"I'm Varina Hobbs. This is my home and you are welcome. We got but two rules here. No laggards, each up at dawn. And each empties her own night jar."

Her face is broad and flat as a pie plate with a hint of moustache, a brownish disturbance above her lips. A woman beetling toward thirty, she seems all angles, devoid of curves or indentations, and she moves with a mannish swagger. When they have settled their bags and quilts, she leads them to the fields where other women labor. The woman named Lucy Baines walks alongside Era.

"Don't be put off by the gun. Varina's had to fend off deserters, Home Guard, then the Yanks. She's had her share."

They move through rows of tasseled corn, then tobacco, a violet-blue haze rising off the leaves. Era slowly discerns between them rows of blue-green poppy pods, ovoid and globular in shape. She stands momentarily still, for here is the very genesis of opium.

Lucy reaches out and cups a pod. "*Papaver Somniferum.* Opium poppy.

It's basically a simple plant, a growth cycle of one hundred twenty days."

She guides Era's hand to an egg-shaped husk, and she is struck by its tough resilience. "A veritable light-seeker, it needs eight-hour days of sunlight."

They listen as Varina Hobbs explains the growth process of poppies, how seeds the size of pinheads are sown by the pods when shaken by a breeze. Or when deliberately set they are broadcast or dropped into rows of shallow holes. In moist, temperate soil the seeds germinate quickly.

"Within six weeks, the plants are established and vaguely resemble young cabbages with leaves of a gray-blue tint. Within ten weeks, as the plants mature they reach a height of four inches, the main stem and each shoot ending in a single flower bud..."

Era feels a sudden surge of panic. "I fear it will take me *weeks* to grasp all this."

"Don't fret, dear. Varina loves to digress. I have been at it several years, and all you have to know is when the pod is ready and how to score it for the resin. I will teach you."

As they walk side by side, Era glances at this Lucy Baines, her skin so transparently pale that blue veins swim up to the surface. A faded blonde, midtwenties, her face is lined from hard labor and want, but compared to the others, she seems uncommonly fleshy, with ample breasts and wide childbearing hips. A nurturing sort who smells of lard and underarms, her breath has a musty, familiar odor Era can't quite identify.

Her attentiveness puzzles Era, rouses her suspicions, and she moves to catch up with the others. As dusk moves in, the more established groups of women move toward their quarters in the barn while Varina guides Era's group toward the house, still instructing them in the growth of the poppy plant.

"As the poppy bud matures, the main bud at the head of the peduncle points upward. Within days, the sepals open, the main blossom appears. This usually occurs near the ninetieth day of germination. In the morning, I will instruct you in the incising of the poppy pods. These days are crucial!"

Inside, women gather in small groups, Negroes in rigolettes, former merchant wives and farm wives, then the mix-bloods, their skin colors running the gamut from high yellow to honey and gold. Plantation aristocrats of the now defunct ruling class stand apart, whispering with dread of the poppy fields, women who once considered fieldwork an "abomination." They lay their quilts and blankets side by side, while others labor at a woodstove where skillets sizzle with wild onions and potatoes drizzled with lard.

"You'll learn to forage in the woods," Varina announces. "Even learn to scrape edible fungus off the barks of trees. And you'll set traps for meat. Else you'll be eating the larvae feeding on the fungus."

While she hands out tin plates, offhandedly she tells how her husband marched off to war "verily grinning with anticipation," leaving her alone with two sickly children.

"One at a time, diphtheria took my boys. I ran howling through the woods for weeks. When I was sane again, I decided to live. I sold or bartered most all the furniture for supplies and fuel."

She ladles out food as women gather and eat in circles on the floor. Some have subsisted so close to starvation they bend to the food as if it were a sacrament and gorge themselves on grease. Others turn their heads and gaze into dark, empty rooms, hearing rodents skitter across the floorboards. The moon shines through uncurtained windows, throwing angular shafts of light into the rooms, and the bleak austerity of it moves several women to weep.

"But your husband, surely he is yet alive?"

Varina shrugs. "Two years, not one letter. Not a jot. The South wins or loses, I expect he'll just keep going. The day he left he had his whole life strapped to his back. Evermore I will do my own bidding and care naught for men or vanity."

Yet while she talks she fusses with her hair, brushing at it constantly until the thinner moments in her scalp are covered. Others move off alone, brooding over letters from their husbands, sucking each word to the marrow. Fog engulfs the house. The cold reverberates in their bones and they snuggle close, trying to give each other warmth.

Era lies sleepless, hearing their soft meaningless vocables, their dreamy, overlapping monologues. She thinks of the stories some of them have told of personal tragedies and deprivations. She thinks of her own story, one she will never tell. The details of her history hers alone to fashion, the ellipses hers to select. Wood in the fireplace smolders, its smell reminiscent of her mother's hands when she combed Era's hair. Raindance, who loved eating ashes from the fire. She turns on her side and whispers, "Mother."

* * *

At dawn, the stove fired, Varina bangs pots, waking them. "There's grits, fatback, and stewed apples. Apples aplenty! That orchard won't stop putting out. One bath a week is your limit, so you best be drying out apple rings for wearing under your arms and petticoats for 'freshness.' Specially during your menses."

Out in the fields, she explains about the flowers of the poppy plant. "At first, blossoms appear crumpled like a butterfly emerging from its chrysalis, but the petals quickly expand and smoothen. Some are white, some like pink chiffon, or red, or weakly purple. Inside are a ring of anthers on top of what will become the pod."

"But where are the flowers?" someone asks.

Varina grins. "Oh, the blossoms are short-lived. Within a few days, the petals drop, exposing a pod resembling a large pea. This matures to the size of a small hen's egg, bluish-green with a waxy appearance, as you see now. The top is surrounded by a small crown from which the stigmas rise."

She beckons women closer. "Imagine, inside each pod are maybe a thousand seeds. When mature, they lie loose in the pod, then are dispersed through these small holes just under the crown."

"And when are they matured?" Era asks.

"Now! Why, just think of what a seed is capable of producing. A drug that brings the end of pain, that might could help our boys win the War."

Varina's hands are busy touching pods, pressing at petals, stroking a stem. Everything she has to say runs through her fingers. It's as if her life depends on the sowing and harvesting of this crop, or perhaps it is because she is passionate by nature and must have a focus for that passion, or because the rest of her life has abandoned her.

In its raw state, opium is the dried juice of the seed pod, an opaque, milky sap produced during a ten- to twelve-day period when the pod is ripening.

"Once the pod has reached maturity, the sap is no longer potent."

Era quickly grasps why harvesting is done by women.

"Oh, yes, it takes delicate hands and requires patience and dexterity."

Now, two weeks after the petals have dropped, the harvesting begins. They gather in groups to watch experienced women bend to examine each pod and crown of the poppy. The sap is obtained by tapping each individual pod, a process unchanged for centuries, perhaps not since the Bible.

"The points of this crown are standing straight out, which means the pod is ready."

Since pods mature variously, they must keep a close watch on them over a period of weeks. In late afternoon, the incising of unripened pods begins and will continue until dusk. Lucy Baines moves close to Era, patiently instructing her. Using a small scoring knife made of four sharp, parallel blades mounted on a handle, she runs it vertically over three sides of each pod.

"Careful, careful," she whispers. "If the blades cut too deeply into the pod, the opium will flow too quickly, drip to the earth, and be wasted. But too-shallow cuts will cause the flow to run too slow. It will harden on the pod wall and—scab-like—seal the cut."

She takes Era's hand in hers and leans closer. "The ideal depth is about one-sixteenth of an inch. This is achieved by slanting the knife blades."

Era turns her head, overwhelmed again by the odor of underarms and the woman's moldy breath, so bafflingly familiar. At the same time, she experiences a felicitous sense of excitement, of anticipation.

"My father taught me an old Chinese belief: 'Each time we learn a new, important thing, it means we are born again.'"

Lucy smiles, intrigued, for this is Era's first reference to a family, to her life at all. She has been drawn to her because she is a nurse and part-Chinese, people said to be uncommonly wise. And because she seems solitary, a woman Lucy might take into her confidence, one she might confess to. As they move along, she explains how incisions are cut in the poppies in late afternoon so that the sap will ooze out overnight and coagulate slowly on the pod's surface.

"By morning the hardened sap, now gum, will have darkened, ready to be scraped off. Each pod will continue secreting for days,

and will be incised half a dozen times in twenty-four-hour periods. The gum can then be stored and retain its potency for years."
Era commences slowly, making careful incisions with her scoring knife. Thus she begins to understand why poppy-harvesting is considered crippling work. At first it fascinates her: how resin from these simple pods is transformed into opium and morphine that grant humans deliverance from appalling pain, and with what euphoria it transports them into death. But after long hours she feels near-paralyzed from bending down. When she tries to straighten up, flames consume her spine, her shoulders rack with pain.

She turns to see Cassie, the redheaded girl, weeping silently. After scoring pods all day, her fingers are a mass of weeping blisters.

Touched by the girl's stoic silence, Era gently takes her arm. "We must tend to this before your hands become infected."

At the house, she gently washes Cassie's hands, applies poultices made of healing roots—mullein, burdock, yarrow—then tends to others. Women groan, their backs bent like hoops, wondering how they can face another day. Midst the rumbling litany of their agonies, Varina swings through the door carrying big clay jugs.

"This home brew has got a whang! Sure to set you right."

She pours hard cider into cups, its smell haphazard and rusty. At first, women frown at the bite of it, then begin to relax as the liquor takes hold. Others roll crushed tobacco leaves into crude cigarettes, then strike Lucifer matches and pass the smokes around. They drink and smoke, then lean back sighing, liquor and the general camaraderie bringing a sundown blush to their faces. They are so weary no one thinks of food.

Outside, blue air congeals with mist and they talk again of the War, of their children sick or perished, husbands vanished. A young wife tells of begging for food along the roads, carrying her swaddled infant for a week before admitting the child was dead. She slept atop the grave for days because of prowling wolves. Another woman hints at having bartered her body for food and cloth from Yankees.

Several Negroes and mix-bloods speak softly of rape, their faces expressionless. At night, they will sleep with their hands still clenching their scoring knives. As she listens to their stories, it is as if everything Era had learned, or surmised, about Southern women is being told again so she can reinterpret it. The whisper of ambivalence takes her unaware, the smallest suggestion of compassion as she learns how they are marked by lives as desperate as hers.

That night the girl Cassie crawls in beside her, nestling deep inside her quilt. She is a strange girl, dreamy in the extreme. Her words come out slowly, each sentence the end of a journey. Whispering softly, she confides how her mother died and her father was conscripted, so she ran off to see what this world was about. She has lived mostly on the handouts of widows who taught her to smuggle drugs past the Federals and who first brought her to the poppy fields. When she confides that she is fourteen, Era gasps.

"Only four years between us! You are but a *child*. While I am ancient."

The girl falls silent, then rolls over in the dark, and Era smells the richness of her flame-red hair, a curious scent of chestnuts, sweat, and dog. She lies there envying her—young, innocent, and dauntless. All of life before her. Across the room, women lie face-to-face, murmuring softly about married love, lost or wasted love, love betrayed or unexpressed. She thinks longingly of Warren, wondering, *Is he safe? Is he well?* Wondering how she can ever confront him with her sordid truth. As she falls into sleep, thoughts of her father dominate, her drummer in the background keeping cadence.

* * *

As days pass, Era grows to anticipate the mild hypnosis induced by the rhythm of scoring, and the *smell* of the scoring as poppy resin flows, and even the pain, the harvest pain, a part of the ritual. Some days there is no talk; men and their battles seem to evaporate in myth, and there is only the dronelike quietude in which they labor. And in the evenings, there will be the balm of hard cider, the fireflies of their homemade smokes accentuating their gestures, and even the protean relief of laughter.

Opium sap first appears as cloudy white. On contact with the air, it oxidizes, turning a brown viscous substance sticky to the touch, but with a delicate perfume. Each morning the congealed dark mass, now a resinous gum, waits to be carefully scraped from its pod with a blunt iron blade.

To prevent the blades from growing tacky with gum, between each scraping women learn to dip their blades in water. The more experienced simply lick their blades clean, and these are the women who complain least about backaches and fatigue, who through the hours move like dreamers. Women who have inadvertently become addicted.

One day, Era touches her tongue to her scraping knife. The taste is bitter but not repellent. She does this several times within an hour and begins to feel a sense of ease and consummate well-being. Her back pains disappear, the sun hums on her shoulders, tuning her spine in yellow octaves. Its heat drips through her marrow. Images soften as light assumes an aquarium quality, and women drift in private reverie.

She watches crows swoop down and lift off with poppy pods, pecking at the wet, white seeds inside. She sees them nodding in the crooks of trees and in clusters on the grass. One crow swoops back and forth, executing lazy 8's, romancing his shadow sailing along beneath him. Era sinks slowly onto her back, swooning into the curvature of the earth. Lucy comes to lie beside her.

Infused with the mellowness of the poppy and in the grip of affectionate curiosity, she eventually asks if Era still has family. Rather dreamily, Era replies that her mother died, and her father is fighting in Virginia.

"And do you have a sweetheart?"

"Yes, in the cavalry. His name is Warren Rowan Petticomb." How predictably Southern and romantic it sounds. How personally shocking to her.

Lucy leans back and sighs. "My husband, Horatio, is in the infantry, a man direly afraid of guns! One of piety and Sabbath hush. In truth, I found him...boring."

She weeps softly. "I've been alone two years now, and Horatio was the last time I felt *safe*. If God will allow him to come home, I vow I'll never again contradict or goad him, never mishandle his devotion."

Era turns and comforts her. "You're a lovely, generous woman. You keep praying. I'm sure God will bring your husband home."

The woman hesitates. "Well, there is this habit I've acquired. My little supplies of opium gum. My bull's eyes hidden in tins. Precious vials of laudanum. I suppose I've become rather...dependent."

Era finally recognizes the moldy smell on Lucy's breath, so prevalent among her patients.

"In truth, I am verily *addicted*. I am seeking your advice."

"You are asking me how to find a cure?"

"Oh, no!" Lucy cries. "I don't want to be cured. I believe we are going to lose this War. The future is going to be dreadful, unimaginable. I don't think I can possibly survive without my...medications."

She moves closer, her head cocked sideways in a child-like attitude of listening. "Era, you're a nurse. You deal in life and death, questions of morality. I expect you have heard thousands of confessions. What I wonder is: Must I confess this addiction to my husband when he returns? Am I dishonoring him if I do not?"

Era thinks of legions of men sent home from the battlefields, each man crippled and ravaged one way or the other. Most of them addicted to drugs or liquor, or just trying to find an end to it.

"I suspect you are right about the outcome of the War, and women will bear the brunt of the South's defeat. If he survives, it may be your husband will not even notice your dependence. More likely he himself will be addicted. I don't believe your telling, or not telling him, will be a moral issue. Morality is a luxury when people are struggling to survive. But meantime try to be moderate, else you will end up asylum'ed like so many women lost to drugs."

She wonders if her advice is morally sound, then watches long lines of women licking at their knives and wonders what morality means in this day and age. Small groups move to a slow, fluvial pace cadenced by their bending to the pods as they work their way backward, tapping lower pods before the taller ones, so as not to spill the precious gum. In varying études, they dreamily pause before lowering their arms and depositing the gum into containers round their waists.

Then a new corps of women drifts into view, trailing long, bright-colored ribbons. In a slow contrapuntal dance, they tie the fluttering streamers to larger, more potent pods to mark them for the future when they will be gathered in whole and opened, the seeds dried in the sun and collected for next season's harvesting. For days the brilliant streamers will flutter and float, staining the air.

At dusk, they hear shots. Varina staggers in with a full-grown turkey and, with fabulating zeal, tells how she stalked and killed it with one shot.

"Them other shots you heard was for the wolves. They tried to ambush me and take my bird." She glances at Cassie. "You'd best keep an eye on your hound; they'll be claiming him for supper."

The girl travels with a dog named Atticus, a handsome mixed-breed with the head of a German shepherd and the coat of a golden retriever. He runs loose in the woods all day and sleeps on the porch at night, and some mornings they find Cassie curled up with him in her blankets. Now, emboldened by the threat of wolves, she bounds to the door and drags him in, and he settles down before the fireplace, head between his paws, looking devotedly at Cassie.

Perhaps she is let loose by hard cider, or the ingestions of poppy gum, or just a need to tell. Without preamble, she describes how one day when Atticus was off hunting rabbits, five Yankee scouts ambushed her in the woods. They tied her down, hands above her head, and stuffed wet moss into her mouth, and each had his way with her. Within months, her stomach showed.

"When my time came, I went into a town, but folks threw me out. I crawled into deep woods, no one to care for me but Atticus. He stood guard over me, whimpering when I cried out."

A day and a night passed while she howled, then the child dropped out of her.

"I could see it wasn't right, its head all big and soft. It didn't cry. I guess it was dead, but I held it while I slept."

When she woke, there was no evidence of a baby or an afterbirth. Her legs and thighs were clean. At first, she thought she had dreamt the child, but there was a lot of blood on the ragged quilt beneath her, and she vaguely remembered Atticus licking her arms and legs.

"And now he sat quietly licking his paws. Then he came and licked my face and whimpered, and lay down across my stomach, keeping me warm."

In profoundest silence the women stare at her, then at Atticus, her child/dog. She stands in the middle of the room, defiant, her slender body upright as an obelisk. As if seeing her for the first time, they are struck by the jaw-slackening beauty of her, the long graceful doe legs, the flaming hair, and tiny amber freckles, giving her face a luminous, otherworldly quality.

"That's my story," she says. "Maybe I shouldna' told it. But I once heard a preacher say when you speak out about a thing, you come to know it in a different way than when it just sits on your mind. He said spoken words give events real flesh and blood, real sounds and smells, and help you grasp the certainty of wrongs done."

Moments pass, then Varina Hobbs rushes forward, clasping the girl to her chest protectively.

That night Cassie shifts in her blankets and whispers, "I reckon you hate me now."

Era takes her in her arms and holds her, and talks through the night until dawn.

* * *

In gum form, raw opium contains a high percentage of water. Reduced by evaporation, it will achieve a sticky, brown substance with a strong odor. Thus, one day at the end of their harvesting in the hours of late afternoon, the women gather in a barn to stir what they have collected in long rows of large, heated cooking trays. They will cook the gum until it is dark and shiny like icing. With a mineral slowness, the walls of the barn begin to drip with condensed vapor. The cooking opium enters their pores.

Minutes fade, then hours. Time ceases to exist. And there is the warmth of animate heat as women dreamily disrobe. Perspiring profusely, they tie each other's hair back from their necks, then languidly remove their dresses, petticoats, threadbare camisoles, leaving their arms and torsos bared. In foglike vapors, white skin flushes to shimmering pink, brown skin turns luminous as women swoon and sink into each other's arms.

Their faces shine, their voices ride the long and lovely arias of ease. And there is light, a choral light, that seems to lift them as each woman lays a quieting hand on her neighbor's heart. Past war's deprivations, past rage at men who have abandoned them, they surrender to an exaltation, a sense of transcending life and death, grief and joy, of knowing if only briefly a quiet and ecstatic fire midst their catastrophic lives.

Era's arms fall softly like the movements of a marionette whose strings are worked by loving hands. She gazes round her, accepting that these women now have a claim on her. She has witnessed the tragedy of them. War will end and the South will be their burden. They will be the guardians, entrusted with the dead. Their only joy may be the memory of these innocent, unmodulated hours.

With spectacular delicacy, Lucy draws Era into her arms, her breasts like mammoth totems. Era rests her head there while the woman rocks her, singing songs she will forget and then remember. A pulse at the side of her forehead, a humming cadence in a small blue vein, tells her she is safe. She will never be this safe again.

In the morning, when they wake, they form the opium into small loaves and wrap them in cloth, wherein they will harden even further. The loaves will be broken down to packets small enough for them to carry beneath their skirts, tied to the waists of their petticoats. Or packed in coffins, or carpetbags, and smuggled to Confederate troops. These will be shaped into little balls and swallowed as bull's eyes. Or chemists will mix the opium with lime and chloride, cook, then crush it to powder which will be smuggled into Army camps in dried-out lemons, shoes, even ladies' bonnets. Or it will be molded into pills, or processed into morphine.

Week by week, Era will move with the small army of women from farm to farm, wherever there are crops to be harvested and cooked. Each night she will sleep on cold, bare floors while in her head she draws a grid that gives the location of each poppy field. When she prepares to depart from Varina Hobbs, the woman hugs her almost passionately, her holster digging into Era's hipbone.

"You're a quiet one, keeping to yourself. But you're a damned good harvester! You come back next fall."

Then Cassie comes running, hair wild and aflame. The one who has touched her most deeply. The parting that most cuts her.

"Era! Write me, don't forget! I'm staying on here. Varina can read me your letters."

"Of course I will..."

"And when the War's over, we'll meet up! You promise?"

"I promise!" She embraces the girl, forcing herself to let go. "Meanwhile, I want you to learn to read and write."

As her wagon pulls away, Cassie waves and calls after her, "I remember everything you told me. I never will forget!"

She watches them diminish, the big, raw-boned woman, the long-legged girl, and her child/dog.

A last few weeks of harvesting, one last farm, then women will disperse to their starving families. On their last night together Lucy pinches off a wad of poppy gum, which she prepares to swallow, anticipating the long, lovely dive into euphoria and sleep. Era sits up and stays her hand.

"Lucy, I ask you to wait and listen. I did not give you good counsel before. I have thought on it, and my advice was not *sound*. When he comes home, you must tell your husband of your dependence."

Alarmed, the woman stares at her. "But why? He may be wounded; I will wound him further. He's deeply Christian."

"If he's badly wounded he will need your attention and care. He himself may be addicted, then he will need your forbearance and…sobriety. If he is *not* wounded, you must tell him. He will understand and try to help you."

She begins to weep. "Oh, I am too proud to confide such a thing! He will see me as weak and damaged."

Era looks off into the night and thinks of Warren. "My dear, we are *all* damaged, don't you see? Cassie was right; things become real only when they are *spoken*. How else can we address the wrongs done? How else make them right? You cannot deceive your husband who loves you. How then can he truly *know* you? Tell him. Honor him."

* * *

In Nashville, she stares at herself in the mirror, wondering again what the truth is. She has never before felt sympathy for whites. The dying boys she tends are colorless and gen-derless, innocents that death is claiming for itself. But there is a nobility to these women she has labored with and slept beside for months. The nobility of those irrefutably doomed. Theirs is now a losing battle of endurance, slow starvation, and a dawning realization that the color of their skin will not save them.

She hangs her head, remembering what acts their husbands and fathers and brothers committed upon her, upon her mother, and her mother's mother. She presses a fist against her mouth. Still, something moves within her, a desire to help these women prevail, to overcome this wretched mess that men had made. She grows calm and smooths her hair, and looks into the mirror again.

She has missed several meetings with Captain Ballard. Now she sits and draws crude maps showing the location of seven thriving poppy fields within a sixty-mile radius of Nashville. In two days, she will deliver the maps to him. She pictures his consternation, his pursed lips. By then the poppies will have been harvested. Her information will be too late.

Johnny Tom

Battle of Fredericksburg, December 1862

During the months of Johnny's imprisonment, the battle of Antietam proved another disastrous defeat for the Union's Army of the Potomac. General George McClellan demonstrated once again that he was too cautious, perhaps too cowardly, to lead his troops with valor.

Lincoln has replaced him with an equally feckless general, Ambrose Burnside, who is now amassing divisions to invade Richmond, the capital of the Confederacy, by way of the town called Fredericksburg. The Army of the Potomac is now encamped north of there, with only the Rappahannock River between them and Robert E. Lee's Confederate Army of North Virginia.

Having returned to his regimental comrades, who welcome him back with clamorous shouts and embraces, Johnny sits for long periods remembering friends left behind in prison camp. For weeks he withdraws into himself, recalling their faces, their voices, a weight he will carry with him always. Eventually, he begins to feel his senses reawaken to the urgency of life, of being alive. The camaraderie of friends, and even the prospect of battle, lifts his spirits.

"I am OK," he tells the regimental physician.

"No, you're not," the man argues. "Your eyes are jaundiced; you're coughing phlegm. You parolees are carrying diseases you never even heard of."

He hands Johnny half a dozen chits. "Tell the butcher you want extra hunks of beef, and get yourself more sleep."

Still, he is exhilarated by the familiar bugle call for reveille, the splendid regiments in rows. It is only when the bugle sounds for "drill" and he marches in formation that Johnny begins to sense his frailty. After twenty minutes he can barely lift his feet; his limbs cry out from months of deprivation. Excused from drilling, he assists at the quartermaster's tent, polishing buckles and buttons and weapons of the dead. He presses his nose to their jackets, smelling gunpowder and sweat. And he wonders, *Who were you, brave boy? Was your courage twice your height? Did you die with a mouth full of pearls and coins?*

He thinks of the fathers of these boys, whose grief will be imperishable. He imagines Era and his beloved Raindance dying before he can find them. The thought is so shocking tears suddenly spill forth, which he has tried manfully to resist, having kept them so bottled up that now they pour out in rivulets between his fingers. It is of course the terrible longing for his wife and daughter, but it is also a letting go of rage and sorrow for friends who have battered at his mind since his parole from prison camp, and now demand his acknowledgment of guilt for the ignobility of having survived while others died. His sobs make such a racket Johnny stumbles into the woods until grief runs down to exhaustion.

He chides himself, knowing it is best to keep a wintering heart, detached and self-composed. But it is difficult, especially at mustering for mail call when whooping boys receive letters from home, which they handle delicately with their fingertips. He continues writing long, heartfelt letters to Raindance with nowhere to send them, during which he strokes his queue, hearing the comb he dipped in birch oil dragging through her wild black hair.

One day, he notices a boy who stands apart during the rush for mail call, a slender Irish lad named Casey O'Shea. At first his face seems hard, all angles, but when he smiles it turns angelic, his blue eyes dance with childlike exuberance. Johnny initiates an easy conversation and eventually Casey tells how he arrived in Boston on an orphan ship from Ireland, and on his sixteenth birthday enlisted.

"It's a tolerable life....except for mail call."

Johnny is more than twice his age. He has often seen him sitting alone, watching boys lark off together to share smokes and delicacies from home. He looks at the shock of wiry reddish-golden hair and crooked teeth, the boy's gangly wrists hanging out of his jacket, and something moves within him.

"You are too much thinking," Johnny says. "Always *Moong cha cha!* In a fog. You need learn better instincts for survival. *Ho Ts'ai Techniques of Camaraderie.* How to make friends, so in battle you watch friend's back, he watch yours. I will teach you."

The boy gamely agrees, and it is not coincidental that Johnny arranges his *Ho Ts'ai Techniques of Camaraderie* away from the weekly, rowdy mustering for mail call.

"First lesson, if nothing to share with others, no need for shame. You sit quiet; make clever things to catch the eye." He shows him how to carve brooches and thimbles from acorns and little animal skulls, how to dry leaves and roots for homemade smokes to share round the campfire.

"If no education, not important. Knowledge not permanent; every day facts change. If not good English, speak slow. Make you seem wise, a thinker."

Casey begins to appreciate how Johnny compresses large thoughts into smaller words like gifts.

"When wrong, apologize. When not wrong, not right, be still! Old Chinese proverb: 'Nothing more accurate than silence.' Most important: avoid cowardice in battle. Show courage at all times, even when scared! Courage contagious like fire."

While Johnny lectures, Casey's body seems to dance in visible glints and tremors. His eager attentiveness, the quirky way he squints when he listens, the endearing way he bends at the waist when he laughs, recalls for Johnny memories of his younger brother, Ah Fat, lost in the passage of decades.

At night by their campfire, he recalls the desperate years of the two brothers running from starvation, the euphoria of finding a rice ball, a rotting duck foot. In turn, Casey tells of the unrelenting sweep of Ireland's potato famines, wiping out whole villages, entire genealogies, and how on the ship to America each night the newly dead were tossed overboard. They fall silent, lost in their reveries, the boy slowly grasping how Johnny's kindness has had a calamitous effect upon his heart.

He turns and claps his hand on Johnny's shoulder and, in a soft Irish brogue, declares, "You're my first real mate in this Army."

That night he falls asleep contemplating his feelings for the boy, his concern for his welfare. With his youth, his innocence, his longing for adventure, he seems the embodiment of what a son would be. The son he suspects he will never have.

* * *

Johnny gains weight and grows stronger, anticipating the major events of Sundays when regiments are formed by companies, after which brigade commanders proceed up and down the ranks, inspecting personnel and equipment as men stack arms, unsling and open knapsacks. Then it is the soldiers' day—sporting, playing cards, worshipping with chaplains.

But now rumors fly of an impending major engagement. Throughout the camp men grow restless with a morbid, desperate gaiety. Round every campfire music is heard—sweet, haunting violins, guitars, and flutes. Irish balladeers wring the hearts of their messmates, and officers step from their tents to listen. Battle-scarred veterans off by themselves playing euchre, turn their heads to the singing, stand up from their games and move closer.

Corn liquor begins to flow. Soon ballads and violins give way to banjoes and fiddles twining out "Billy in the Low Grounds," "The Goose Hangs High." Men swig at jugs of "Oh Be Joyful," then slap their knees and grab partners, spinning and yipping in womanless dances. It spreads from campfire to campfire as bogus sweethearts whirl and stomp and pass their jugs.

Soon the fiddling and dancing spread across the entire Army encampment and even beyond the horizon so that the landscape is aglow with fires, howling figures stomping in and out of shadows. From miles away, Confederate soldiers see the glow, hear the shouting, and calculate it is a religious revival. Up closer, their cavalry scouts sit in the shadows and watch.

"Some pagan thing, I reckon."

"Naw. They just celebratin' they ain't dead."

A big, brawny redhead holds out his cup for another splash of "Joyful," then grabs Johnny round the waist, and soon he is whooping and whirling. They pass him from man to man, loving how his long pigtail flies out like a girl's, how he dips and twirls like a feather. A liquored-up man grows enamored and grasps at Johnny's buttocks. He steps back, takes the man's measure, then flying feet-first, knocks him unconscious with a blow to the chest. He lies spread-eagled as Johnny moves on to a new partner, yipping and whirling, and his comrades fall to their knees with laughter.

Here is acceptance, the friendships he has longed for, earned with each battle fought, each brave and selfless act. Here is a sign of loyalties built between him and these men through memories of bloody trenches, of prison camps.

They might die in the coming battle, but they have survived the last one, so there is immense exhilaration. Men seem to glow with the sudden awareness that they are alive, that their campfires are alive, and the trees, and the land, and it makes them want to be honorable and decent, desiring only justice and victory and human concord.

And so there is a grandeur to them as they shout and dance, a momentary godliness, as if they have just discovered what's best in themselves and in the world, and exactly why they are fighting. Johnny dances to exhaustion, intermittently pulling on a jug and a cigar, and when he passes out they gently lay him down. At dawn, he wakes, the rank stub cold between his lips, his comrades snoring around him.

* * *

After weeks of driving rain and snow, the weather breaks and General Ambrose Burnside moves to cross the Rappahannock River, occupy Fredericksburg, and drive on to Richmond, but the War Department lets him down. Engineers sent to build pontoon bridges to cross the river are weeks late, leaving over one hundred thousand soldiers stranded. Burnside broods in his tent, a fat-shouldered man with a mournful physiognomy and flamboyant sideburns.

Troops sit in camp and wait while, across the Rappahannock, Robert E. Lee's Confederate Army gather their forces behind Fredericksburg along a ridge called Marye's Heights.

Johnny's commanding officer huffs past him. "Sixty thousand of them sons a bitches stretched over six miles along that ridge. That whole town's evacuating."

Their troops silently watch the long, pitiful procession out of Fredericksburg, six thousand humans dragging their children and infants and meager possessions through deep snows. Johnny hangs his head in sorrow, for the scene conjures up his boyhood—whole towns fleeing floods, starvation, war.

It begins to snow again, and to the right of him Casey O'Shea is shouting and pointing. In a nearby snow-covered field, a horse stands abandoned, so purely white he is barely discernable. He snorts through pink nostrils that send falling snow into tiny whirlwinds, then magisterially lifts his head as Casey runs toward him, flinging off his hat. The horse whinnies and nods his head repeatedly, and in one graceful bound the boy mounts him, and they gallop off into the landscape, the horse's mane floating up and down. A haunting image, only the flame-like flicker of the boy's red-gold hair interrupting the whiteness of the horse and the falling snow.

Thinking he is deserting, boys run after him. "G'wan, you coward! Hope you get shot! You crummy Mick!"

Johnny rises to his feet, silent and astonished. Ten minutes pass, then twenty. In the background, officers shout orders at their massing troops, eyes trained on the river they must cross. His shoulders feel weighted. His heartbeats seem to slow as sadness presses down. The boy he had chosen would not be brave; he would be a "turntail." Another ten minutes pass and Johnny turns to go, but then hears boys shouting again.

He turns back to see Casey trotting out of the landscape, the horse snorting with exhaustion, the boy's grinning face aglow. Still euphoric, he trots the horse in easy circles, cooling him down. Boys run forward, calling to him now in a rush of awe and admiration.

"Say, where'd you learn to ride like that?"

He grins. "Didn't you know, boys? Irishmen are all half horse!"

They fall back as their sergeant approaches and stands with his hands squarely on his hips. "You'll get the stockade for that, O'Shea. What the *hell* did you think you were doing?"

He looks down, embarrassed. "I couldn't help it, Sarge. He was just so... beautiful..."

The man steps up to him and shouts, "*Beautiful?* That word is not part of combat discipline! Fall into line! Get ready for battle! I'll deal with you later!"

Johnny moves up and walks beside him. The boy is suddenly jittery; his skin looks tight. Perhaps it is the anticipation of battle, the looming possibility that he might die. He looks back longingly at the horse, and Johnny sees the aching in his young Irish heart.

He takes him gently by the arm. "It is *important* that you rode the horse."

"Why, Johnny?"

He cannot say that, so close to death, one needs to acknowledge beauty. He says it in a plainer way. "The horse expected it."

In time, he will forget the day, the month, the details of the coming battle, but he will carry the image of the flame-haired boy galloping on a white horse through whirling snow. It will give him moments of deliverance.

* * *

Engineers finally arrive and commence building pontoon bridges so Federal troops can cross the river and take Fredericksburg. A crackling of rifle fire from Rebel snipers in the town, the answering crack of Union snipers. Before the bridges are completed, Burnside impetuously sends men over in assault boats to "purge" the town, and they methodically begin to burn it down. Johnny's company arrives with

fresh troops to see the awful conflagration. Stately historical buildings aflame, homes entirely consumed. As the day
winds down, a strange golden haze lies on the land and on a
town reduced to ash.

He looks up to where the Confederates continue strength-
ening their entrenchment of sixty thousand men on Marye's
Heights, their artillery now massed to cover all approaches
to the ridge. A four-foot stone wall runs along the base of a
hill approaching the ridge, a virtually impenetrable trench
behind which four lines of Rebel infantry are poised.

Word is slowly passed down through the ranks that, unable to grasp the impossibility of taking Marye's Heights,
Burnside is issuing orders to prepare for attack, envisioning
the taking of the ridge as the breakthrough to Richmond.

Corps commanders argue that he is asking them to sacrifice their boys up those slopes to deliberate death. "There
is nothing but open fields and the Rebs will be firing *down*
on them."

Seasoned generals warn that to attack Marye's Heights
is outright murder, not warfare. Oblivious, Burnside repeats
his orders. The signal is given and over fifty thousand Federals pour out in columns until the meadows are black with
them. Johnny is there in the thick of it, keeping time with his
heartbeat. The route-step tramp of thousands drumming in
his head, he glances left, then right, at endless blue columns
bright with flags, the sun reflecting on waves of glittering
bayonets.

His arms are numb with hardly the strength to hold and
load his musket, a sensation stemming not from fear but an
abiding lack of strength—his body still in recovery, his muscles and ligaments still reluctantly adjoining. He feels for the
knife in his belt, hoping he will get that close to a Rebel. As
morning fog lifts, the Army of the Potomac is spread across
the plain south of Fredericksburg, rank upon rank, banners

snapping smartly. All magnificent and doomed. Behind their fortifications, Confederate gunners and cannoneers stare at the limitless target before them.

Artillery guns barrage the Rebels and, finally, Johnny's regiment goes in. And there is the high unearthly keen of the Rebel yell as they come storming down the hills onto the plains. The Federals push them back with superior guns and the Confederates—too easily—retreat, a ploy to make the enemy rush Marye's Heights, now bristling with cannons.

At the foot of the Heights is the wide, sunken road with its four-foot stone wall, behind it four lines of waiting Rebel infantry, above them on the hill more infantry. Higher and extending to the left and right—prepared to lay down devastating crossfire—are Confederate cannon guns. Burnside's men stand on open plains, a perfect target at shotgun range, and as they halt to deliver their fire, the stone wall ahead blazes from end to end with a crackling sheet of flame. The guns on Marye's Heights commence crashing and thundering.

Now Union brigades approach and fall apart. Up comes a third brigade, a double line of blue a quarter mile from end to end. They are instantly mowed down. A fourth brigade is leveled, the wounded falling upon the already dead. Johnny bites off a cartridge, pours powder, stokes, and aims his musket and shoots blindly. Knocked down by reverberations from a cannon, he crouches in the blown-out pelvis of a dead boy, his eyes a startling porcelain blue.

He struggles to bite off another cap, then stops to watch his troops advance. How beautiful they are! How young. Faces determined and aglow. Shells suddenly burst their ranks, creating huge gaps, then canister that staggers them. Johnny struggles to rise but is engulfed in slippery flesh. The boy's bloody gore has plugged the barrel of his gun.

Half turning now, he sees Confederates rise up below Marye's Heights and, sighting along their rifle barrels, let loose a storm of lead into advancing troops. They fall like paper dolls. A rifle lands aside his head and he hoists himself up, shooting two Rebels before flying metal tucks him down against the corpse. Around him men lie in layers in the thousands. The land is carpeted with flesh.

"Hang on, hang on!" a sergeant shouts. "Fresh troops are forming and advancing."

Johnny wonders where Casey is, if he is still alive. He wonders if he himself will die. Will it be fast or slow, and will he be able to stand it? Will he scream and cry aloud like some do? He has never thought this way before. He blames it on the prison camps. They have robbed him of his physical strength, his soldierly discipline, his pride. Now all he can think is: *Is this my time? And how will I behave?*

He tries to imagine new boys assembling, staring at ambu-wagons filled with limbless men, and at the pandemonium of smoke and flame and charging troops, each succeeding brigade hindered by the fallen. A last brigade forges up, and with a startling crash—a blinding sheet of fire and flame—the Confederates hurl upon them the full force of their infantry and artillery. The field is lit as if by sunlight. Afterward, no Federal banners fly. In every regiment, all color-bearers gone.

A dying boy cries out. "Our flag…Who will carry the flag!"

Eventually fourteen assaults will have been beaten back from Marye's Heights. Twelve thousand Federal soldiers will fall. Across the field appalling sights, a weird, unearthly writhing of the half-dead crying out for help, for pity, for someone to finish them off. Johnny lies still and thinks of the endless succession of doomed assaults, the shimmering rows of steel borne by boys facing certain death but never faltering, always moving bravely at the quick time. He calls out to Casey, to others of his comrades; a hundred voices answer.

* * *

Dusk now. Temperatures fall; the wounded begin to freeze to death. He squeezes himself between two corpses and draws another crosswise for a pillow, pulling the boy's coat over his face for warmth. In deepening dusk, enemy shells explode knapsacks, sending scattered clouds of letters high into the air, even photos of sweethearts. Bits of their faces float down like confetti.

Stretcher-bearers move cautiously about the field, for no truce yet exists. There is only the dark, and piteous appeals. Something smacks his shoulder; he whirls and stops it with a knife. The man goes down, and by the smell of him Johnny knows he is a Rebel busy stripping the dead and near-dead. They are out there in droves; by morning most of the corpses will be naked.

In the growing dark, he hears whispering, men crawling back to the Union lines. He thinks to join them, but something holds him back. He looks up toward Marye's Heights where the enemy's bivouac fires are flickering amongst the stars, the beauty of it astonishing. He thinks of the beauty of advancing brigades and porcelain-blue eyes, and cannot find the logic.

Midst his musing, someone tugs his arm. "Water...please..."

Johnny gropes in the dark and presses a canteen to near-frozen lips. Others cry out, and he begins to understand why he has remained: for these, the near-dead, abandoned by stretcher-bearers as hopeless. Boys so shattered when they try to move their bodies come apart. He passes the night crawling back and forth across blown-open skulls, across blue intestines shining like snakes, as he doles out water, a semblance of prayer, a moment of magic for them to hold: a white horse running through falling snow. Boys listen, grasp his hand, and die.

Someone shouts and he looks up. From end to end of the horizon, the sky comes alive with waves of light. Dazzling reds and greens and whites in shimmering undulations. It seems to go on forever, and boys lift their arms as if the light will take them home.

A man steeped in blood speaks out in a fading baritone. "God gave the Israelites...fire by night...to keep them... from despair."

It sounds like a quote from the Bible. Greatly fatigued now, his boots filled with blood and gore, Johnny crawls close to the deep-voiced man, wedging himself between him and a dead boy. If he should perish, he would like to die beside someone who knows the Good Book.

Dawn brings the full horror. Naked and swollen corpses riddled with minié balls and metal blanket the valley. Many lie entangled in layers of twos and threes. Vultures perch amongst them, like grumbling old women. When a body unexpectedly moves, they cackle and hop about and turn their heads sharply, lengths of organs dangling from their beaks.

During the night the defeated Army of the Potomac has pulled up stakes and retreated across the Rappahannock. Lee's victorious Army now moves to reoccupy Fredericksburg. Carefully stretching half-frozen limbs, Johnny endeavors to crawl out from the dead and make his way back to Federal lines. From Marye's Heights, snipers suddenly come alive, picking off anything that moves. It will take him all day and most of the night to reach the river. Moving mere inches at a time, he drags the corpse of the deep-voiced man on top of him, using him as a shield while he crawls over several acres of dead bodies.

When he finally reaches the Rappahannock, troops out searching for survivors shine their torches his way. Seeing the face of the man he has dragged, they grow uncommonly quiet. With great care, the body is lifted into an empty wagon, then Johnny—filthy, half-conscious—is helped into another wagon full of wounded boys.

Two days later he wakes, bathed and lying in clean sheets. He reaches frantically for his queue. It lies beside him like a good pet, freshly washed and braided. He feels for his privates. There, intact. A matron leans over him and smiles.

"Well, Private Tom, its seems you're a hero. You saved the life of a brigadier general."

Johnny Tom

Army Encampment, December 1862

They come to visit, his first sergeant, his captain, others wearing bars and clustered stars. Even the major general whose orderly once handed him a bowl of phlegm. He means nothing to them, only a curio to be examined: his yellow skin, his shaved foreskull and queue. But, good military men, they do not wish to gainsay his act of heroism.

In terse, chiseled English, they speak of selflessness and valor, of a promotion. They do not speak of the dismal defeat at Fredericksburg, the appalling casualties of twelve thousand men, or of President Lincoln's rumored depression. Johnny smiles, inordinately relieved when they depart. Then warmth flows through him; he hears the voices of his comrades as they lean over him.

Casey and Rudi, the Italian boy, Andy with the long, pointed nose like a hunting dog, half a dozen more. He buries his face in their words.

"Say, Johnny, you're a dang hero!"

"Rumor is, they're gonna make you full general...You'll ride up there with Grant!"

They joke and cut capers, making him smile, yet deep in their eyes he sees a new indifference, to life, the War. Mostly rough farm boys, conscripts of ill grace and no fervor for the Cause, combat has manifestly changed them; even their posture has changed. In Casey's expression, he sees that an inner ease is gone, replaced by a strange, incomprehensible bitterness. Like the rest of them, the boy seems jolly and morbid, profane and lost. They seem to believe in nothing now but each other. Still, they play cards and gamble, drill and prepare for another siege, and they visit him daily, affectionately joking and tugging at his queue, assuring him there is no gangrene in his toes, that he still has all his body parts.

"My general," he asks. "How is my general?"

"Oh, half a leg gone. One lung. But hell, he's already demanding his saber and his regiments."

"I am not hero," Johnny whispers. "I thought he was corpse. I used his body for cover."

They laugh, and Casey slaps his thigh. "Oh, hell, pard, we're all corpses…We just don't know it yet!"

He looks at each of them, feeling fatherly. Not one of them over twenty. He wonders what life will expect of them when this is over. All the Army has given them is instinct, a hard edge so they don't go to pieces when they kill. *I have traveled*, he thinks. *I have family somewhere. Have seen much life before this. These boys, mere children. Went from innocence to death.* He worries especially for Casey, and feels such love for him just now he would give his life for him. He turns his head, and they drift off to let him rest.

In a half doze, he composes a letter to Raindance. Still scratching with his fingernail on his palm, he memorizes every word. When he is fully awake, he will put them down on paper, then read them softly to the wind and hope the wind will find her. How many letters now, his twentieth, or thirtieth? How many prayers offered to Kuan Yin, goddess of mercy, beseeching her to find his wife and child.

My honorable and cherished Raindance,

To continue with my story…I am true soldier now, many battles fought. But at night still this boy carving your face against my face in sleep. Oh wife, a long time since they tell me Rebels overrun our village. How many times I ask what happen to our daughter and to you? No one can give such answers. I miss smell of ashes in your hair. Smell of deerskin mocassins you dance in. My longing like a bear's paw.

We are now in Tung-Chih, time of winter when Yang forces rule. Days white and thick. Much snow. No good for fighting so we go to winter rest. Our horses graze and fatten. I see running mare and think of Era. Our part-horse girl!

Oh where she is now? Without father's guidance such headstrong girl can be cut down. Own pride cut her down. She was born in Year of Monkey. Quick learners, selfish, vain. Like empty bowl, always searching for fillment. You need be firm with her.

I have freeze bite in toes, weight lost from battle. Nurse brings many nourish-ments. She is old and warty tai tai, not beautiful like you. With deep humility, never kowtowing to vanity, I inform you I am soon greeted with high honor. New title, Corporal Johnny Tom. Who leads men in battle.

There is young soldier, not of my platoon, but we grow close in other ways. His name Casey, like the nighthawk's cry. His ways much like my long-lost brother, Ah Fat, childlike mischief in his eyes, how he dips at waist in laughter. His hair hung hsiao, red radiance, his laughter cools my eyelids. But many shadows run beneath his surface. His heart a ragged tent that I must mend. May be he is also mending me.

Most honored wife, I say goodnight with cherishment and longing, wondering where you are, beseeching our gods to protect you. My prayers are constant, flowing east to west like ancient scrolls. I ask again you write me to War Department, Washington, D.C.

> Your dutiful husband,
> Corporal Johnny Tom

* * *

The Army settles into its new encampment below the town of Falmouth. Across the Rappahannock, Lee's Confederate Army once more occupies Fredericksburg and the hills outside which they so well defended. Between the two armies the river slows, begins to freeze, signaling a truce. Now the quiet months of winter, a time to rest from battle. Christmas passes quietly, the nights moonlit catastrophes of longing. Boys crawl into mildewed tents and think of home.

Squads are formed to forage in the woods for logs with which to build crude winter cabins. Other squads raid farmers' barns of cured tobacco leaves; the Army riots in cigars. Boys gather to sew pine-needle mattresses to cover bunks. They fashion stools to set before crude tables and pack wet clay in chinks between log walls. Their commanding officers keep them busy, hoping they will forget the shame of having lost at Fredericksburg, of fighting under egregiously inept leaders, and of the Union Army's mounting defeats.

Then, against the advice of his commanders, General Ambrose Burnside attempts another charge on Lee in Fredericksburg. The disaster that ensues will become known as Burnside's "Mud Campaign," an army of eighty thousand exhausted men slogging through weeks of lashing, freezing rains, their artillery and supply wagons so deeply mired in seas of mud they fail to engage the enemy. Thoroughly detested by his officers and men, Burnside is rapidly replaced as commander of the Army by General Joseph Hooker.

As Johnny convalesces, his boys tell how they are preparing their winter cabin for him, and they debate Joe Hooker. Here is a man of dubious character, a reputed drinker with a penchant for prostitutes for which his name will become synonymous. Yet he is a proven fighter, a hero of the Mexican War, and always unequivocal about the welfare of his troops. Hearing the news of his command, across the campgrounds soldiers cheer, hailing him as their deliverer.

Finally released from the hospital, Johnny grins and bows upon entering the cabin he will share with friends.

"*Zhuhe nin*! Congratulations! For building such fine house. *Xiexie. Feichang ganxie*! Thank you very much for allowing me."

The boys gather round, slapping his back, affectionately mimicking his Chinese as he carefully unfolds his kit, displaying all he owns.

"*Qita*! My miscellaneous. For you to share."

Struck silent, they gaze at his possessions. No commonplace book. No Bible. No pocket watch or sewing kit, or playing cards or mirror. No letters, no tintype of a loved one. Only an Army-issue coffee tin, a spoon, random acorn carvings, a packet of papers upon which sentences are scribbled. His boys surround him and gently press upon him warm pairs of socks, rolled-up thread, eight buttons. Extra laces for his shoes. They tug his queue affectionately, remembering his ministrations in the prison camps: dying boys he had held and sang to, wild tales he had told starving others that made them laugh and want to live.

* * *

In driving snow, his regiment lines up across the campgrounds while men singled out for promotions step out to their commander.

Finally, his named is called. "Corporal Johnny Tom!"

He steps forward smartly and is presented with his stripes. His commander shakes his hand and salutes him. The brigadier general whose life he saved has been hoisted into his saddle for the viewing and ceremoniously nods to Johnny. Ever the prodigious noticer, Johnny looks around with mild disappointment. No blazing trumpets, no marching bands to honor him. That quick the drill is over and company dismissed as men dissemble for their cabins.

Then someone shouts his name. Johnny turns, is hit hard in the chest. His eyes seize the culprit, Casey, who has broken from his own platoon. Johnny bends and packs a good, tight snowball, then shouts and lets it fly. Snowballs commence sailing back and forth until a dozen men, then two, three dozen, are engaged in battle. It grows to companies, then regiments, massing and bearing down on each other. Soon it appears as if the sky and all the elements and even the men are made of snow as several thousand join in the fray.

Hour upon hour a pulsing tapestry of *bluecoats* exhaust themselves, shouting and cursing and letting fly. Some men are knocked out cold; two will lose an eye. Fresh troops join the battle, skidding in on sled boards, yipping across frozen ponds like banshees. Johnny full-heartedly engages in the shouting and laughing until his hands are numb, his queue frozen stiff against his neck.

He sinks down in the snow and Casey exhaustedly falls beside him, lips half-frozen, his cheeks deeply flushed. Dusk now, as lanterns are lit in hospital tents and cooking tents surrounding the army of battling men whose teeth and eyes and cheeks dart out of the snow like sparkling jewels. Snow swirls so thickly their blue coats rise to a pulsing white as their voices still ring out in merry aggression. The two men stare, trying to hold the moment, and it is as though they are watching a winter carnival ringed in lights, in the foreground boys shouting and laughing, forever young and innocent.

"How can it be so pretty?" Casey asks. "How can we frolic and forget? I've killed boys younger than me. I wake up asking their forgiveness."

Johnny looks down. "We are soldiers. Better not to dwell."

The boy persists in his soft Irish brogue. "When I think of going into battle now, my nose bleeds. Next, I'll be fainting like a girl. I'm bloody brave, I'm not afraid of dying! But, Johnny...I don't want to kill no more."

Johnny reaches out and grips his arm. "You need talk, come talk to me. Meanwhile, find something beautiful to look at, beautiful to hold. Make you turn away from ugliness, regret."

Casey looks at him, intrigued. "Do you have a beautiful something? What do you look at and hold?"

"Faces of my Raindance, and my girl."

Because he is young and callow, he asks the question before he thinks. "The Rebs burned down your village. How do you know they're still alive?"

Johnny smiles. "In sleep, Raindance combs my hair. I feel her heartbeats. I wake with my queue freshly braided. And in sleep, my daughter reads to me. I wake with new words on my tongue. Hope is also a thing beautiful to hold."

Winter grows deeper. Men retreat, turning thoughtful in their cabins. A boy dying of wounds gives Johnny his Bible, and he spends hours poring over the Scriptures. Salvation. Revelation. Retribution. Wondering again how he will ever master such words without swallowing his tongue. The stories themselves he will never fully fathom. They seem to be about slaughter and vengeance, dictated by a God with no logic, no foresight or hindsight.

"This man, Cain, very good man. Tiller of earth. God refuse his gift of fruit. Prefer sheep from brother, Abel. Why?"

He is reading to a Cherokee scout who smiles. "Maybe this god is one smart Indian. Knows meat more valuable than grapes."

Two officers pass their campfire. "Now, don't that beat all? A heathen Chinee reading the Christian Bible to a Redskin!"

Inspection. Drill. The days agonizingly repetitive. Boys write letters home on wallpaper stripped from burnt-out houses. They have spent their pay on gambling and liquor and have no money for stationery. Johnny gives them what he has purchased from a sutler, and in return they share letters from their families. But while they read aloud, they glance at him self-consciously.

For over a year they have watched him scribble letters, then tuck them away in his knapsack. Every week when the mail wagon arrives he steps forward, hopeful. Names are called, a cheer goes up, boys rush to grab their letters. After a while, crowds dwindle, boys disperse. Johnny smiles and walks away. But now he listens dreamily, eyes half-closed, to news from a family in Maine.

"...*a new litter of healthy coon pups...Papa's lobster traps stolen...Jenny, oldest sister, ran off with a dandyman, Mama took her portrait down...Grandpa has the winter gout...Reverend Thompson's wife won't give up wearing hoopskirts... Scandalous, with metal so scarce in this time of sacrifice... Did you receive the woolen socks? And cornstarch for the rash?...*"

And he knows momentary peace, lost in the intimate surround of a family and a home. He carries that precious world to his cabin and lies down, clinging to those images—the healthy squealing of newborn pups, the runaway sister in thrall, the reverend's wife's scandalous love for her metal hoops—until the bugle sounds the last tattoo, signaling silence and sleep.

ERA

Beloved Era,

Imagine my joy receiving your letter. Your packet a godsend are mightily low on supplies here. Camp so filthy slops thrown every which way no one cares. You cant hear revelle for thousands spitting up their lungs. My stomak once more tolerable with the bulls eye thank you from my heart it strengthens me I am in your thoughts.

After disaster of Kentucky we fled south passing close to Nashville. Was sorely tempted to sneak into city & find you. Our corps of 40,000 ready to settle in for winter when like number of Federals broke off from their hold on Nashville came after us at Murfreesobro. We went at them Feds like demons near slaughtered them to pieces.

Battle of Murfreesboro don't compare in size & butchery to Shiloh but Lord so much blood men verily drowned. Ten hours fighting with no letup. We sank down to rest so weak & starved could hardly slice off meat from dead horses. Don't remember Christmas but O Mankind! All New Years day we slept.

Then Bragg ordered another full out charge. We kept going rain & sleet cutting down them Yanks. Dearest we almost had them. Their lines broke but their artillery tore our ranks to pieces. Bragg chickenheartedly gave up. 10,000 dead & wounded & what for we gained nothing. Some claim Murfreesboro a draw the Feds call it a victory.

I was hit by shrapnel in the thigh Doc cleaned it good then sprinkled morphine. Am healing tolerably. So many wounded we commandeered town of Tullahoma just below Murfreesboro bout 40 miles south of Nashville. Rumor is medics & supply wagons are speedily making their way here to set up hundreds of hospital-tents. I pray you will be among those angels that you will recognize me & not be put off.

In this everlasting carnage I give thanks how you have laid claim to my existence. You are beautiful & good & such qualities is the only thing that beats off death. I have growed mean and testy with my pards, bursting forth in outraged sallies & insults. But thoughts of seeing you again has turned me sane. I am more careful riding out to skirmish with the enemy, for I don't want to die. Though I now declare that I would surely die without you.

Oh dearest, even with all my thoughts half-jelled & tumbled you stand bright & clear in my mind. All the pettifoggery & evils of war melt away. The vagaries and ailments of my body fade. You are a cleansing. I hear your voice felicitious & soft as when you read to me. The shape & shadow of your form, the remembered scent & softness of your arms reduces me.

I am then but a poor thing in a rapture of desire who in this perdurable nightmare longs mightily for you & vows to stay alive for you. I pray my words do not put you to the blush. Please forgive my fervor & intemperate notions. I will never discomfort you but will always show control & not this liquefaction in my heart as I feel now from thoughts of you.

I desire only to hold you again & know you are real. Hearing from you gives me hope that you still

*care & that you will take pity on the harsh thing I
have become. I confess I don't know how to sleep no
more. At night I calm myself sketching I have drawed
so many likenesses of you think I am verily gone in
the head.*

*We will rest here through winter & prepare for
what is coming. The Yanks equally tired will leave us
be for now. Still I am not sanguine as to a final Confederate victory. Thus ends our first year of fighting in
the West.*

*Will stop my foolishness for now. Dearest I pray
if ever you do come it will be soon & with hearten-
ing news of your father. Tell then please rest yourself
contented I am well. I remain your loving & devoted
untell death.*

Warren R. Petticomb

Makeshift words, disjointed thoughts, the stained and
pungent pages. He has begun to embody for her the dying South, a thing barely holding on—valiant, touching,
doomed. Much of his letter moves her to weeping—scenes
of death and deprivation—but much of it fills her with joy.
A plaintive, childlike voice inside her calls his name as she
remembers the tannic scent of him, his handsome face bi-
sected by haggard planes. The way his eyes softened as he
beheld her.

She pores over his letter again, the humble phrases, the
brave, resolute declarations that laid his soul bare. She covers her face with her hands, weighed down with a past and a
place and a heritage no one else can understand. How could
he, the enemy, understand? Yet she is battered with longing,
nearly paralyzed with love for him.

She thinks of the women in the poppy fields, spectral
and over-boned, their children starving. Their war is lost,

they know it, yet press on. *How can I betray them?* she wonders. *How can I betray this man?*

The Federals will surely send her to Tullahoma. Ulysses S. Grant has entered upon full invasion of Vicksburg, Mississippi, last Confederate stronghold. Bragg's Army will endeavor to defeat him, ambushing and skirmishing, blowing up railroads and communications lines. U.S. Army Intelligence will want to know his plans, his strategies, his every strength and weakness.

Should she and Warren meet again, no matter how innocent his questions, she will have to be devious and lie. She will begin to confound him and he will think the matter is with him. Finally, because such truths cannot be hidden—that she is not with him, but against him—there will be nothing left to recommend her.

* * *

Summoned again by Superintendent Matron Phillips, Era is struck anew by blue sacs of fatigue beneath her eyes. Though clearly exhausted, she exudes a disquieting air of authority.

"Miss Tom, I assume you're prepared to leave for Tullahoma soon. Thousands of wounded Confederates there, a great need for surgeons, nurses, and the like…"

Deferentially, she nods. Longing for Warren, but dreading the transferral and ensuing deceit, Era is half-prepared to argue against it.

Matron Phillips shocks her. "But I have lately been informed that you are…somewhat attached to a soldier now encamped down there with Bragg. My dear, this is folly! I would be remiss in my duties if I did not reprove you. You are jeopardizing your credibility, your very *life*."

Era vehemently shakes her head. "He means nothing to me. In fact, on several occasions he has unwittingly given me valuable information."

The woman gathers her broad shoulders round her neck. "He is a Rebel and a *cavalryman*. They're sly as jackals, remorseless. If he discovered you 'scout' for the Federals, he would kill you in an instant."

"He would *not*. He knows they have lost. He wants it to end."

"Nevertheless, my instructions are to keep you in Nashville. Your work here is excellent. You can be valuable in other ways."

She keeps her face expressionless. "Why should I follow their instructions? They have not kept their word. I've had no news of my father. He could be dead."

Phillips stands and takes Era's hand in a mothering way and leads her to the door. "Be patient, dear. Things take time. You will remain here for the present."

That night she pulls from her pocket the shiny knob of bone. She rubs it thoughtfully, thinking how part of her had not wanted to go to Tullahoma, had not wanted to face Warren and again deceive him. But things begin to stir within. She is suddenly weary of instructions, of doing their bidding, weary of betraying and being betrayed. Thus far her loyalties to the Union have never swayed.

But what about love? she wonders. *Is one allowed to compromise one's loyalties for love? What is really loyalty, and what in war is steadfast?* She ponders this because definitions keep changing; her sympathies keep changing. With no physical proof that her father is alive, Warren is all she is sure of in this world.

She goes to Ivan Golgoff's studio and tells him they want to keep her in Nashville, but sick of the chaos, the fetid air, she is determined to leave.

"Of course, I need a traveling pass." She opens her pouch of gold coins. "I will pay anything."

He pulls forms from a drawer and waves his hand, dismissing the gold. "So...you are running. And whose signature shall it be?"

She shows him Superintendent Phillips' signature. He practices a few times, then forges the name with a flourish.

"And can you find a sutler for my transportation? Many are headed in that direction."

"What direction would that be?"

"A town called Tullahoma."

"Ah, yes! To your one-armed cavalier. You see, even the spies are spied upon. So. I will arrange the sutler."

As she leaves, Golgoff bows and takes her hand. "I will not forget you. Such a face."

* * *

Just before dawn she departs with only a carpetbag, the hood of her cloak pulled low on her face. Pushing through filthy streets, she approaches a checkpoint, shows her credentials to sentries, and passes out of the gates of the city. A sutler waits in his wagon, wearing a rakishly slanted crimson hat. Seeing her, he whips off the hat and bows with great flourish like a musketeer.

They move down potholed roads bordered on either side by miles of Union Army tents forming a ghostly city outside the city. On the parade grounds ragged regiments drill in formation. Even their horses look exhausted.

"Wait till you see the Rebs," he says. "You will not believe your eyes."

They move slowly, his mules braying and backing up at mud holes. Era grips her seat as the wagon lists and threatens to topple, spilling his wares—liquor, tobacco, magazines—luxuries the Army does not provide, which soldiers purchase from these itinerant merchants who follow the armies, some following the same units through the war.

They are famously a seedy lot, men who deal in stolen goods, some gathering information for the Other Side. This one seems more presentable than most: cleaner, more cautious and respectful with his words. As they move along, he flicks his whip, intermittently looks at her, then briefly tips his attitudinal red hat.

"The name is Wickett, ma'am. I know you're leaving against instructions. I don't shoulder trouble, but I'll take you the forty miles to Murfreesboro—the Feds occupy it now. Their scouts will ride you close as they can to Tullahoma where Bragg's Army is dug in. They'll drop you near Rebel picket lines…Then I guess you're on your own."

Era looks at him, alarmed. "You go back and forth. Yank camps to Rebels. Why can't you take me all the way?"

He answers in soft Southern tones. "Beg pardon, but as I see it, to escort you into Bragg's encampment would be imprudent. I 'scout' independently. In case you're ever identified, well…no double executions."

She studies him, taking his measure. "You're a clever man, Mr. Wickett. Quite frankly…I feel I might be wearing down. I don't know what more information I can gather."

He glances at her face, imagines her slender beauty beneath those grim black clothes. "You'll find plenty. Women have a way. You get weary, just think of three hundred more years of slavery."

Era studies him again. "If I may ask, where are you from, exactly?"

"East Tennessee, ma'am. But not all us Southerners support the Cause. We're poor folks, don't own slaves, and don't believe in dying for the rich."

Late afternoon as they near Murfreesboro. He helps her from the wagon and half bows. "I recommend you be extra cautious at all times. Those Rebs catch you spying, they will not be frolicsome."

At a stand of frozen willows, six weathered Federals await her with an extra horse. She greets them perfunctorily, then, gathering her skirts, slips a foot in the stirrup, swings her leg over the horse, and digs her heels in like a man. Riding two abreast, they trot off, leaving the sutler behind.

Ice melts. The road becomes muddier, and in places disappears. They cautiously pick their way round blown-out bridges. Where the road is halfway clear they gallop for a while, and sometimes they can only walk their mounts. The landscape is a void, no trees, no wildlife, only cratered earth, blown-up breastworks and artillery.

A trooper speaks out solemnly. "The Battle of Murfreesboro."

Rags of uniforms, gray and blue, skirr and flutter in the wind. Skulls grin, surfacing from hastily dug graves. She passes them slowly and forever.

A few miles outside Tullahoma, they meet up with sentries picketing their border. Era shows her pass and they wave her through, warning her she is leaving Federal territory. Her escorts take her another mile, then rein in.

"You're now in Reb turf. Godspeed!" They ride off with the extra horse.

Daylight begins to fail as she picks her way through blown-open graves. Lest she recline in the lap of a corpse, by meager starlight she finds high ground between boulders, wraps up in her cloak, and fitfully dozes. At dawn, she chews a piece of hardtack, makes her way to a stream and splashes her face. When she looks up, she sees what had been a farmhouse, nothing left but half a roof, a wall, and something else.

Struggling through brush and vine, Era finds beneath the roof a wooden bathtub. Inside, the corpses of two women, Indians or half-bloods. Moving closer, she sees their bloody thighs, blank-eyed stares. The bullet holes. She starts to tremble and sits down. *How she screamed and fought, how she clawed until her fingernails were packed with Rebel skin.* She drops her head, remembering.

Finally, she moves closer, and examines their fingernails. Under one woman's nails she finds not skin but bits of cloth. The dark blue wool of Federal uniforms. It could have been the same troopers who escorted her here. Then she sees the eerie absence, the thing missing from between their legs. Their private parts are gone. What is left looks like raw meat from which something has been crazily sliced off. As if the women had been scalped down there. She turns away and vomits.

Later, she sits beside a crude, hastily dug grave, having buried them facing each other with their arms crossed. She had even prayed for them. Now she broods on what was visible under the nails of one of them. Minute rags of dark-blue cloth. She has heard that Confederate soldiers are taking enemy scalps, hanging them from their belts like trophies. She wonders what Federals are wearing on *their* belts.

Exhausted, she sits scraping mud from her hem and shoes, and that is how they come upon her. Four of them bearing down at a gallop with their guns drawn. One of them trots forward, spits a long stream of tobacco juice, and speaks in a soft, menacing voice.

"Whar ya from, miss? State ya business quick."

She tells her story, a nurse fleeing Nashville, trying to get to her sweetheart in the troops with Bragg. Weathered and grizzled, while they listen their stench comes off them.

"How do we know ya story's true? Ya might could be a spy sent by them rabbity Yanks. We shoot women too. It's nothing."

Wearily, Era stands and hands up Warren's letter. One of them takes it and stares with a certain fixity, and by his expression she knows he cannot read. Two of them dismount, passing her letter back and forth with elbowing jocularity. In greasy nutmegs and ragged boots, they could be beggars except for their hard, wolflike expressions.

They hand the letter back. "This don't prove nothin.' We know ya type. Sashay into our camps as 'fancy gals,' then gob up military information."

She folds her arms and stares at each of them in turn. "I am not a *whore,* neither am I a *spy.* I'm a trained nurse. I worked with your wounded at Shiloh and went with your ambu-wagons to Nashville. Now I'm here, and I'm *not* going back."

The man who had pretended to read scratches at his beard. "Wal, now...What then's the name of ya so-called sweetheart?"

"Warren Rowan Petticomb. He's with the cavalry. Third Alabama, under General Joseph Wheeler."

Hearing Wheeler's name, they grin. "Wal...guess there's nothin' for it but to take ya in. See if this Petticomb will claim ya."

He reaches down and recklessly lifts her up into the saddle in front of him, his breath on her face like a judgment.

WARREN

Tullahoma, January 1863

Ambu-wagons clog the roads for miles. Across the land, every factory, barn, and church has been commandeered as operating theaters, every house filled with wounded men. The sprawling encampment of Bragg's Army—renamed the Army of Tennessee—resembles a hastily thrown-up city of crude log cabins and sod huts, all arranged in a haphazard fashion along company and regimental roads.

At a security blockade, the Rebel scouts deliver her to sentries. Era smooths her hair, brushes her dress and cloak, then enters a cabin where Confederate officers stand around in frock coats. They turn and silently inspect her, then straighten the skirts of their coats and begin their interrogation. She answers each question thoughtfully, anticipating the next question so that she is always a step ahead of them.

The commanding officer studies her, discerning in her one of those hard-eyed mixed-bloods, women difficult to read. One generally steps around them and moves on. But he is inclined to believe her story because he remembers her enigmatic eyes, her cheekbones like closed knives under skin the color of fresh lumber. A field nurse at the Battle of Shiloh, efficient, kind to the wounded, otherwise distant and aloof.

What would a soldier want with her? he wonders. *She carries more than one race in her, more than one history.* He discerns very little white blood there and assumes that in her history is the usual hatred of whites. Then he recalls Petticomb, one of those cold-eyed cavalrymen from Wheeler's corps. He glances again at Era, thinking how like calls to like. He knows there are goings-on between nurses and the men but sees no sense in addressing it. *They would not grasp the concept of propriety.*

After an hour of questioning her, they call in a hospital matron who recognizes Era and highly praises her services. An adjutant is finally dispatched to fetch the trooper, Petticomb, and she is detained in a room alone. Through a window, she watches the raising of hundreds of hospital tents, orderlies carrying operating tables and surgical instruments. Era leans her weary head against the wall, then finally sits and drifts into a half sleep. Hours pass.

In the outer room a chair is scraped back, voices murmuring in conversation. Silence, then a knock. Her door is opened, and without turning, she smells tired flesh, the aged and tannic scent of leather.

"Era…" Even his voice is old.

With reflexive wariness, she turns and it is like a scratch on her cornea, his face marked almost beyond belief—deeply lined and haggard. A man now familiar with death to the point of grace. He removes his hat, and from its soft, ragged lining she inhales someone else's former life. He holds out his hand and it shakes.

His lips tremble as she moves to him, his silence telling her what it is to wait, what it is to have looked into a thousand faces when none of them were hers. It tells her how, night after night, through slaughter and hunger, he has asked the dark with a certain poise, "Let her come. O, let her come."

He takes her in the circle of his arm, feels the pounding of his heart, or is it hers? He presses his lips to her head, breathes in the scent of her hair, and moans. He feels her shuddering, clutching the folds of his shirt, as if to keep herself steady.

"Warren." In quiet incantation, she whispers his name over and over. That is all she can do, whisper his name.

Finally, with the lassitude and helplessness of a child, she weeps. She leans her head against his chest and weeps with aching and fathomless relief. And when he lifts her face to his, she weeps again in exaltations of pure joy. They seem paralyzed in the moment, incapable of words, only of pulling back, staring at each other, then flooding into each other's arms again.

After a while, a tapping at the door. Reluctantly, they pull apart. She is aware of being dismissed by the officers, then led by the adjutant across icy roads to the hospital superintendent's quarters while, in a highly agitated state, Warren follows behind. The superintendent is so desperate for nurses he clasps her hand repeatedly, then consults with her over a schedule.

A matron then escorts her to the nurses' compound while Era repeatedly looks over her shoulder, afraid Warren will disappear. In a large tent fashioned like a barracks with curtains separating each cot, she settles her belongings, then steps outside where he is waiting.

Warren takes her arm and carefully walks her down "corduroy roads," made of logs laid across frozen mud. There is a tension now, she can feel the trembling in his arm as he nervously chatters, directing her gaze toward thousands of makeshift cabins outfitted for winter.

"Some are hewn from logs, sawed and notched and put in place, others made from scavenged parts and ingenuity…"

There is a humming in her head; she can't absorb his words. All she is aware of is his arm trembling against her side, and the heaving of her chest. Finally approaching his cabin, she smells pine and cedar. Inside, the wondrously clean scent of green wood and freshly split logs.

Warren turns suddenly shy and rather formal, as if learning to be human again. "As you see, I have been in preparation. With some assistance from my boys."

Wood is laid in a fireplace with a chimney built of logs
and chinked and lined with clay. He lights the kindling, and
in the warmth of the sudden blaze, again she sees how badly
he is trembling, trying to hold back, not lose control and
overwhelm her. He points to pots hanging jauntily from
hooks. He has even built a cooking stove, and a table from a
barrel upon which are set out dishes and utensils. A bayonet
is thrust into the floor, a candle inserted in the socket for
illumination. Even a crude mantel over the fireplace holds
sketches of her face, full front and in profile.

He lights the candle in the bayonet, and stares into the
flame. In trying to express his love, his voice comes close
to breaking. "I tried to build generously. I have even set up
a bedstead and overlaid it with pine boughs for a mattress,
and covered the boughs with sheets and quilts for a counter-
pane. And everything is freshly washed."

At last, he moves closer. "How hopefully I have gazed
upon this place, praying you would come."

Light seems to flow from her incandescent eyes, from
the exultant glow on her lips, her cheeks. She sobs out and
sinks against his chest.

"Oh, my beloved. Hold me! Don't ever let me go…"

She feels euphoria spiraling out from her being, radiant, unignorable. The brittle aloofness with which she has
armored herself against the world now melts away. With
convulsive urgency, she kisses his face, his neck, feeling a
welling up from deep inside her after having felt nothing for
so long.

"Era…Era…"

He tries with a certain amount of propriety to unpin her
hair and is struck almost helpless with the scent of it, the

wealth of it cascading down her back. She thinks to help remove his jacket and his shirt but turns clumsy, a fire cours-
ing along the edges of her extremities. They are both so
chaotically desirous of each other it is like dementia. Warren can only stand there holding her, so much bottled up
inside him he bows his head and weeps.

Finally, she steps back and slowly unbuttons her dress
and then her petticoat, slipping out of everything until she
stands before him naked, candlelight burnishing her pale
skin. He cries out softly and sits down, and with trembling
hand pulls her to him, and leans his head against her stomach for the longest time. When they finally lie down together, she feels rescued, and when he touches her she feels
cleansed, absolved of all the ugliness and violence in the
world.

He enters her silently except for the sound of his breathing, and they move together wordlessly, profoundly, and
forever. His hand slides over her breasts, her stomach, the
smoothness of her skin. Her hands lightly pause at the
shrapnel scars across his back, a scar below his ear, then
glide over the soft blond hair, the tender eyelids. Because
words fail her, she tries with each touch to express what he
means to her. How she has never felt this way before.

After all this time apart they seem inexhaustible, crying
out in ecstasy, then finally lying still, whispering and resting,
then coming together again. Later, they lie side by side like
children, watching light from the candle, a dancing moth.
She tries to explain to him this brilliant, this extraordinary,
thing that has happened to her, how she feels alive and innocent again, a side of her nature that lay dormant so long
she had thought it was dead.

She tells him how she loves him for what he has suffered, what he has lost, and she loves him for his fine intelligence and sensitivities, and because she understands she

can never doubt his love. Mostly, she loves him because she
has seen his soul.

"There is a bond that unites certain people," she whispers. "What that bond is God alone knows. I think of it as
timeless and placeless, without logic. I was bound to you the
first time I saw you. We have been united since that day."

He spreads her hair across the pillow and draws her
close. "Although, I believe that at first you resisted me."

"Oh, yes. I was wary and unsure. Things happened that
one day I will tell you of in detail. My father went to war. My
mother died. I was lost and bitter."

"I pray you will tell me everything. I want to share your
burden. I want ever to protect and worship you."

As they grow calm and more relaxed, she senses his need
to talk about the War, to explain to her how it has been. How
he has learned to stand far enough back so that each battle
takes the shape of a celebration.

"Before it starts it's already happening in my head. I feel
it creeping up like the background of a drawing that slowly
becomes the foreground."

While he talks, he scratches repeatedly at his neck and
chest. She is not sure it is body lice; she has seen these ner-
vous tics before. She listens calmly, feeling his urgent need
to give voice to his deep guilt and shock.

"Some of the boys have gone insane. They're scalping
Yanks. I came upon one while he twitched. The nerves to
his brain were severed with the top of his scalp, but his
eyes still moved, his lips. He was asking me to shoot him
and I did."

When he finally sleeps, she strokes his chest and runs
her hands along his ribs, his bones barely covered by flesh
that unconsciously shrivels away from her.

During the night he wakes and talks again, describing
New York Zouaves coming out of their trenches in pantaloons

and fezes. "...Like raving harem dancers. I thought I was shooting women. I did not care."

Era tells him how she, too, has changed. Until today, she has felt very old. "I thought if I could find my father, I could be a girl again. But it was too late; I had seen too much. I felt even my soul had flown from me in horror. Now, here with you..." She smoothes blond spirals of hair on his chest. "I feel I've been given a second chance to live."

Somewhere out on the picket line a man plays his coronet; across the miles a Union picket answers with his horn. It goes on for hours, the playing and responding, a sound that will haunt them all their lives when they recall these winter months. Each night Era gathers Warren to her, acknowledging with soft murmurations her love for him, expressing with her body how that love is not feigned or imagined.

But one night he sits up and stares into the dark. "Dearest, I believe we will lose this War. It may be I will die fighting. I have thought deeply on these things. I want to tell you that after they cut off my arm—the months you tended me, the nights you read and talked to me, the scent of you sitting close, showing me how to sharpen pencils with one hand— well, they were enough to fill a life. I am prepared to die."

Era cries out, "Hush! Oh, hush!" She looks down, struggling for words. "In truth, I no longer fear death either. There have been times when I *wished* for it. Yet I think we are dying to know life in every breath, waiting to see our destiny revealed. I have come to understand that *you* are part of my destiny."

She weeps a little, then reaches up and presses her palms against his face. "I know now if you should die, I will die too. It makes life very simple."

Years later, she will remember this winter as a time both infinite and evanescent. A time when their powers were so acute they could see what was ahead, but could not say it. It would be their best time, magical and fleeting. Each dawn paints itself on makeshift cabins that a thin veil of snow has rendered blue, a tender, luminescent blue. They walk out, feeling for a moment absolute fulfillment. On sudden clear days, the slaughter of bright sun on snow is blinding; in the glare, they drunkenly laugh and run like hares zigzagging through a hail of shot.

At dusk, when thousands of cabins and huts stand out against the snow, here and there open doorways fill with that bluish light when, for a while, homesick boys pause before lighting their candles. At such moments, Era stands still, her cheekbones hoarding the going light, and she wonders, *When shall I tell him? How shall I tell him? What then will we do?* Then night and the huge encampment closes its doors, each boy left with his candle and his thoughts.

She and Warren lie down again in softest murmurations, hands reaching out beneath the quilts, the slapping flesh so meager their bones rub against each other. All is tinted blue, even their faces, from the snow's reflections shining through chinks in mudded walls. They doze and wake to the convulsions of their bodies in expressions of love, until they fall asleep exhausted.

Some nights in a half sleep he turns and sketches on her naked back with an imaginary pencil. Era wakes and lies still, imagining the landscape growing between her shoulder blades—a riderless mount, an orchard beneath whose drifting petals dead boys lie. Then his finger rubs her back as if smudging the sketch, creating depth or shadows, so that her back becomes a narrative of his fingerprints, a mosaic of his hands.

* * *

A stillness across the encampment. A Union "scout" has been caught at the picket line with detailed sketches and assessments of Bragg's artilleries. Divisions of infantry and cavalry stand at attention to witness his hanging. Era moves close to the gallows and sees the rope snap tight, his neck bone wrenched sideways. The tongue protrudes slowly as it fills with blood. The face goes black. His mouth opens like the maw of hell, and as he dangles, his bowels are loosed in his trousers, a filthy death.

A man beside her grins. "I seen a woman hanged. It's war."

His words reverberate, branch and fork in her brain. They abide with her on rare, warm days when she and Warren walk through fields outside the camp to a sunstruck boulder. They remain with her even when Warren lies back and tries to imagine a future.

"Should I survive, I would want to live quietly. Do quiet things. Not rouse the old instincts."

His voice has a hoarseness suggesting age, yet he is still a handsome man, more fleshed out now that she is looking after him. He talks again of his dream to have a ranch out West with horses. There would be a bedroom for her father, a reading room for her, and a room where he can draw and maybe learn to paint with oils.

"I have come to fancy the names of colors. Porcelain... crimson...vermilion..." He draws the words out like a prayer. "Though I reckon they do not sound manly."

Era looks at his pinned-up sleeve, thinks of the shrapnel in his back and thighs that will work its way out for the rest of his life.

"You've been manly enough. I doubt that a love of colors will impugn your masculinity."

Some days, while stretched out on the rock, he draws crude maps, answering her casual inquiries about the Army's recent campaigns.

"There's Perryville, Kentucky, where we almost took a victory, but for Bragg's dastardly retreat."

Wetting his sketching pencil with his tongue, he draws the route down which they came from Kentucky into Tennessee, engaging in daily skirmishes while blowing up bridges along the Cumberland River.

"Bragg thought to reclaim Nashville from the Feds, but our troops were near starving and exhausted. We passed east of the city and came on down to Murfreesboro, where we captured the Union garrison that commands major rail lines and river valleys."

There they had planned to rest and regroup while their generals worked out strategies. Meanwhile, Wheeler's cavalry had run nightly raids, ambushing Federal units, snipping away at their telegraph wires.

Warren smiles and shakes his head. "Sure enough, they come after us. Forty-five thousand troops and artillery. You know the rest. History might call the Battle of Murfreesboro a 'minor campaign,' but it suffered some of the bloodiest assaults I ever heard of. And there weren't no victory. Just all-out slaughter."

He broods in silence, then draws almost a direct line south of Murfreesboro to Tullahoma. Then a farther line south to the broad Tennessee River, which he sketches in long lines.

"A mighty body of water. It cuts through the South like a slithering snake from Paducah, Kentucky, all the way to Knoxville, Tennessee."

Era leans in, paying close attention.

"Why, after the Mississippi, the Tennessee is our most vital river. The course of the War here in the West is following its meanderings because of all the traffic it bears—supply ships and such—connecting cities with major rail connections. That's why we've set up bastions all along its banks, why every week we ride out to reinforce them."

She follows his pencil as he sketches, absorbing each thing he says. He draws a circle, denoting Chattanooga, maybe forty miles southeast of them.

"See the direction we're heading in? I think, come spring, Bragg is going to hit that city again, make up for his earlier defeat by taking it back from the Feds. You see, major railroads connect in Chattanooga."

He points again to the Tennessee, showing how it flows past Chattanooga, and how, in a roundabout western route, then turning in a northern route, it connects with the great Mississippi, which flows from Missouri all the way down to the Gulf of Mexico.

"Every town along ole Miss is now Union-occupied except for Vicksburg, our last major port. And the Feds are moving to take it. That will be a battle to behold…"

She tracks the distance from one city to another. Chattanooga to Vicksburg appears to be about four hundred miles apart.

"But, how will Bragg's forces help defend Vicksburg if he's reclaiming Chattanooga?"

Warren shakes his head. "That's the sad part. We're now conscripting ten-year-olds and grandfathers. Some don't even shave yet; some are halfway blind. But, by God! They can shoot. Come spring, we'll have near a hundred thousand new troopers. Probably break them in by taking Chattanooga first."

"What about weaponry, artillery?"

He smiles, warmed by her interest. "Well, now…smugglers and blockade runners are still delivering us arms from Europe and Northern sympathizers. And as you know, we're natural foragers—stealing everything we can from Feds.

Guns, bullets, cannons. And every household in the South is donating pots and pans to melt down for bullets. Even their blessed church bells."

Era shakes her head in wonder.

"I know," he whispers. "I reckon it's hopeless. But Southern men…we're born to fight. We don't know how to stop."

She hesitates, then takes his hand. "Dearest, I think you have fought enough. And suffered enough. Is there some way you could just…walk away?"

"You mean desert? I've thought of it. I'm sick to death of war. I thought how we could both head out. I could get us across the Mississippi, down to Texas and beyond. But, could I live with it? Anymore, I don't know if we're right or wrong. All's I know is the North invaded us. And I know you take a side. And you stay true."

As he speaks, he sees how her eyes look strange against the light, implacable and cold. He feels that an important moment has passed, that he has let her down. He turns his hand now lying in her palm, and studies his lifeline.

"It may be that what we do each day—me killing, you saving lives—is our destiny. That thing you said we've been waiting for."

* * *

In spite of her love for him, she begins to feel a slight disdain toward Warren for how wholly he trusts her, how easily he confides in her—broad bits of information not exactly vital but enough to help confirm rumors flying between the North and South. As talk of the next battle accelerates, she starts to panic, feeling a resurgence of fear that she will never find her father, never flee this endless butchery. She begins to relish her panic when passing on bits of information while "foraging" for roots and herbs, burying the dispatches in coded cipher, afraid if she stops informing she will lose all possible connections to her father. On days when she feels no panic she is irritable and jumpy, like a woman long deprived of sleep.

Sometimes she comes off twelve-hour shifts, then bathes, and quietly approaches where, on warm days, Warren sits outside their cabin sketching. He pauses and broods, his long, gaunt hand wearily raking his hair in a way that makes her ache. She stands still, admiring the focus of him, the calmness as he captures the sinuous veins in the muscular arm of a farrier, or the faultless pitch of grapeshot stacked in pyramids. A man alone in the heart of his world, trying to grasp the meaning of the short time in which he has been given to be a man.

At such times she is wracked with the need to confess to him her deception, her sordid *duality* of roles. But she is paralyzed with fear, her lips unable to form that simple but obdurately unspeakable word. *Spy.* She imagines his reaction: In his eyes, she will become a thing completely vile, not only a traitor, but one who has enlisted his help in her duplicity.

She walks away with a corrosive sense of guilt welling up like a scream. *Time*, she thinks, *I need more time.* She broods on how she will slowly lead up to it, telling him what happened to her village, her mother, to her. She will arouse his sympathy, working on him such tricks of alchemy he will be transformed. A man sympathetic to both sides, or neither.

But there are days when Warren rides in from skirmishes full of blood, his eyes cold, expressionless. He rinses off the dust, steps outside the cabin, and stands pensive in moonlight.

"I'm so full of killing I scarcely have a sense of myself as human. Maybe I have truly come to love it."

At such times, Era remembers who he is, what he represents, and her guilt momentarily recedes.

One afternoon, she is startled to see Wickett, the sutler who had brought her out of Nashville. He tips his red hat and smiles.

"Good day, ma'am. Have a gander at my magazines… Here is *Harper's Weekly*, and even rose water for the hands."

She stands at a distance from soldiers bellying up to the bar for whiskey, and leafs through old copies of *Harper's* as he approaches, offering a book. Thackeray's *Vanity Fair.*

She shakes her head politely. "I believe I have this book."

Wickett's eyes bore into hers. "Why, ma'am…I don't believe you have this *new* edition."

She pays and walks away, meandering back to the nurse's tent. That night, within the book, she finds lightly marked pages, and begins to decipher the coded message achieved through certain groupings of letters.

WHEELER…VITAL…MORE…INFO…WHAT…
RAIL…LINES…BRIDGES…HE…TARGETS…
NEXT.   BRAGG…MORE…INFO…ON…SPRING…
PLANS…MAJOR…THRUST…VICKSBURG FIRST…
OR…CHATTANOOGA?…

"Fightin' Joe Wheeler, now general of Braxton Bragg's cavalry troops, is reputedly a brilliant and fearless strategist, though standing just over five feet tall. Deeply loved by his men, he has been wounded three times, had sixteen horses shot from under him, and is known to walk through the camps before each battle, rallying his cavaliers, "Up, men, up! The war child rides tonight!"

When she asks about Wheeler, Warren fairly glows. "Greatest cavalry leader in this War. Mightily superior to that overly theatrical and self-serving Nathan Bedford Forrest. Joe is brave, tender, loving, and daring. We would follow him through hell."

Now the Federals are asking her to spy on Wheeler, even set him up for an ambush. She knows there are other "scouts" here gathering like information, and thus does not feel compelled to help them. *What has the Union done for me? There is still no word from my father.* Ignoring their request, she throws herself into tending her patients.

For over a year Era has watched how nonwhite soldiers are ignored and mistreated by surgeons, even by nurses and orderlies. Indians, mixed-bloods, Creoles, occasional Orientals, and of course, Negroes, now that they are allowed to serve as soldiers. All volunteers, they are the last to be brought in from battles, raids, or skirmishes. Some are left wounded in the field for days and bleed or freeze to death, while white boys are gathered in and tended.

She thinks of her father captured by Confederates, the Army he deserted from. *Did they torture him?* she wonders. *Was he beaten? Starved?* She ponders the state of his health after months in prison camp, and worse, his desolation at having no word of his family. The Federals would tell her nothing more than that he was now encamped at a place called Falmouth, in Virginia.

She studies maps, the distances unfathomable. In order to reach him, she would have to cross the Great Smoky Mountains, then the Blue Ridge Mountains in ice and snow. Or travel along the Atlantic Coast, be caught without a pass by one side or the other, and imprisoned as a runaway or spy. She thinks how in spring, when winter snows are melted, she could go to him, work her way slowly, state by state. Other women are doing it, wives following their husbands from camp to camp.

The thought of seeing her father sets off antiphonal chords deep within her. Her only blood, her genesis. She hears him calling out her name in singsong, hears his laughter like a boy's. She remembers how he cherished her, his great pride in her. She knows what the odds are each time a man goes into battle. Her need to find him grows more urgent.

And what about Warren? she wonders. *Must I sacrifice one love for the other?*

When she is with him now, she feels helpless with desperation, wanting to confess to him, yet terrified. She expresses that terror when they make love, giving herself over mindlessly to the flesh, allowing sensations to plunge her to such depths it is like dying again and again, the two of them whirling downward in an indivisibility of flesh. At such times, her passion seems inexhaustible, almost gluttonous, and Warren momentarily pulls back, as if watching her devour herself, devour both of them.

She goes back to the sutler, Wickett. "Tell them I want news of my father, Johnny Tom. He's with the Army of the Potomac in Falmouth, Virginia. They *promised* me a letter, but I've heard nothing since before the Battle of Fredericksburg."

Wickett frowns. "Why, that's a force of a hundred twenty thousand soldiers. Near impossible to track one man..."

Era steps closer. "How many Chinese are fighting in this War! How many Federal soldiers are 'pigtails'?"

He looks at her skin, the shape of her eyes, and finally understands.

"You get me news from my father. Something written in his own hand. Do that, and I will bring them Wheeler's plans. I will verily bring them Wheeler's *head*."

Only with her patients is she calm. The presence of so much dying and death does not allow her the luxury of spinning off and losing her composure. One night, when she enters the cabin exhausted, Warren is laying precious wood and coal, with which he has lit a fire that warms the room and jumps out in little bat wings. He has seen how she is tense and agitated, how each day seems a torment. Sometimes she is in such bad tempers she seems almost savage, and because he loves her so, he suffers. Later, when they are settled and lying close, he confides a thing that shocks her.

"Dearest, I know you are distraught about your father. I see how it is robbing you of composure, perhaps even of your sanity. I have tried to think how I can help. Today I asked my commanding officer if our Intelligence people could help locate your father..."

Era sits up and looks at him in shock.

"The man near went convulsive, shouting indecorously on how our troops are starving, ammo nearly gone, how we are verily losing the War, and I stroll in asking to find somebody's father. He suggested I look alive, comport myself as a cavalryman, not a lovelorn boy!"

Before she can respond, he draws her close. "We will think of another way. I want so badly to help you, to take away your torment."

When she finally speaks, her voice is low and urgent. "Warren, you must not do this...You *cannot* do this. You don't understand..."

"I understand you are bewildered and uncertain. Some days you look afraid. Frightened for your life! I want to help you find your father, reclaim your peace of mind."

She inhales deeply, then exhales, feeling her chest heave. "There are things I want to tell you. Things I *must* tell you. I've been struggling to find the words..."

He is so full of thoughts, again he interrupts her. "You *will* find the words when you are ready. And *only* when you are ready, for you are strong-willed and wayward like a child, which I find mightily endearing. Plus, on a good day, I believe I make you laugh. Though something in you does not want to laugh..."

His words grow soft as he falls into slumber. "Era, you must give in to me...for I would not know how to stop loving you."

In the flickering light, she whispers, "Can you vow that you will love me always? No matter what I have to tell you?"

Half-asleep, he murmurs, "We will find your father...We will find a way..."

The moment to tell him has passed. She lies back, shaking. Through the night she listens to his snores and feels his warmth, and thinks of starving families dragging their church bells to foundries, melting down pots and pans for bullets. She thinks of the women in the poppy fields. The gallantry and desperation of it all. And she thinks of what she is doing for the Other Side. In that moment, she wants to climb over the barricades of rage and hate, and beg his forgiveness. She wants to gather him and run.

Johnny Tom

Chancellorsville, January 1863

Now there are skirmishes every day. Federal cavalry encounter Rebel troops, who suspect they will try to take Richmond by once more attempting to overrun Fredericksburg. Or that they will attack the Rebels first in a town named Chancellorsville.

Eager for combat after months of convalescence, Johnny begins to practice his leaps. "Tiger Clawing at a Sheep." "Phoenix Spreading Wings." His "Butterfly Kick." Various strangleholds and knife thrusts. Having learned how onerous muskets are in close combat, his boys beg him for like instructions.

As corporal, he is now ranking man of his squad, and beardless lads appeal to him, "Our very lives are in your hands!"

He begins to train them methodically until they achieve a certain buoyancy in motion, the focus of men ecstatically charged when they attack. One day, a Negro approaches and watches him, a freed slave who has foraged his way up from North Carolina to fight with the Union. He is accompanied by his own slave, a fact that confuses Johnny.

The man's name is Zebedee. "After Fort Sumter, marse say I'm free, he selling out and going North. He give this slave to me. 'What I do with a slave?' I ask. 'He your property, work him or free him,' he say. Well, I free him. But he won't stay free."

"Got no where to go," the boy, Virgil, explains. "I stayin' with my daddy."

"Stop that!" the older man shouts. "I ain't your daddy. I'm your liberator."

"You're my daddy," Virgil insists. "If I ain't your slave, then I'm your son."

"Oh, give me peace!" Zebedee turns back to Johnny. "Well, Corporal, I come to show you how they use to break our thumbs. You break both a man's thumbs, he no good for holding muskets, bayonets, can't hardly hold his head up for the pain. You might could disable a whole Rebel company that way."

Johnny strokes his queue and frowns. "What good is broken thumbs for slaves? Then master have no workers."

"Oh, this only done to old slaves worked to uselessness. First thumbs, then all ten fingers. Pain kills appetite. They jest sit drooling till they starve to death."

He holds up his big dark hand, then shows Johnny a certain way to jerk the thumb back, a motion almost quicker than the eye.

"Jest this swift, cracking sound. Works every time."

Two soldiers follow his instructions, a trick so easy and swiftly executed one boy accidentally breaks his friend's thumb and faints dead away.

"Ah, so!" Johnny smiles. "In my country, this called 'Snapping Drake's Foot.' I forget, because so simple…"

"Spectacle," Zebedee says. "It lacks of spectacle, flamboyance."

Johnny studies him. "You know big American words. I like learn such."

"Well, marse taught me reading and writing. I also dabble in such foolishness as verse." He points to Virgil at his side. "This boy here afraid of guns. You teach him tricks of survival, I teach you a whole prodigality of words."

Through the ensuing days and weeks, they become a kind of trio, Johnny coaching them at dusk when camp duties are finished. The "Tiger Leap," the "Butterfly." In return, Zebedee endeavors to improve his English with nightly readings from the Good Book. In that way, a friendship takes root that will become like a protective cape thrown over their lives. Feeling a growing kinship with the big, dark man, in his hesitant English Johnny talks a bit about his life—China, the cane fields of the Hawaiian Isles, the girl named Laughter.

Zebedee regards him while he talks: a small, yellow, pigtailed man with a shaven foreskull shiny as a child's, fighting a war that will profit him nothing. He feels a sorrow for him then, so far from his people and his homeland. At least Negroes have each other, their language, and their drums. And they have a country now, which they have earned.

Softly, as if relating a fairy tale, he tells Johnny how, for three hundred years and more, his people have been brought in chains on gigantic slave ships out of Africa to cities like Charleston, Savannah, New Orleans. How they were packed together like wet moss, laid side by side in endless rows. How, as they starved and suffocated and began to die, tens of thousands were tossed overboard so that the migration of sharks changed drastically as they followed the death ships across the Atlantic.

Johnny listens in shock and finally wipes his cheeks dry. Then he tells about Raindance, how her Creek mother had been kidnapped, used as a breeding slave. In time, he pours his heart out, telling everything—his kidnapping, the slave ship, the human auction blocks, and white men who stabbed at his private parts with sticks. Then being taken by the Rebels and defecting to the North.

"For this I lose Raindance and our child. Second family lost. So I am man of double shame. Not knowing how to find them, how to make amends."

Zebedee taps his finger on the Bible. "You keep on with the Good Book. Sometimes answers come in jest the turning of a page."

* * *

At the end of March, General Joseph Hooker prepares to launch an attack on Lee and his Confederates. Once they have captured the town of Chancellorsville ten miles up the Rappahannock, they will then press on, attack Lee's flanks, and finally take Fredericksburg.

Midst preparations for the siege, Johnny is summoned before a major general who addresses him with almost effusive geniality.

"Corporal Tom, I have good news. We have located your daughter, and have a letter for you. Fortunately, it has not been censored much."

He bows deeply, attempting to respond, but words recede beyond his grasp. An adjutant passes him the letter and stares at how prodigiously his hand shakes. He escorts Johnny back to his cabin, which is deserted, his mates having been instructed to give him privacy.

"I'm sorry, Corporal Tom, but you have only twenty-four hours to answer this letter. Hooker has sent down orders. You break camp in two days."

My dearest father,

I have written many letters but no word from you. For months we thought you were fighting with the Rebels. They raided Shisan again, and thus we learned that most of you deserted for the Union side. They burned down our village, took the rest of our men for soldiering.

We women and children were marched to a Confederate camp near Natchez, a long, hard march of many weeks. Mother took sick and I am grieved to tell you that she died. Your name was the last word she spoke. I buried her in a stand of birches and carry part of her with me always. Forgive me, Father, for bringing you this news. My grieving will never end. Until they told me you were alive I no longer wished to live, but now I do.

Please know I am in tolerably good health and presently nursing in Nashville, Tennessee. I tend all wounded, Union and Confederate. I pray the North will soon win this terrible war, our country is running out of boys. I know you have been captured and released, I know that you are brave.

If I could come to you, I would. They tell me it is not possible because ####################### ### ###################### and to keep this letter short. I will write again when I know you have received this, which I will know by your reply.

Please answer as soon as possible. They will allow you only one page. Father, I have nothing left but you. My poor heart has been shattered, only the thought of one day seeing you keeps me alive. I am trying to persuade them to ######## ################## ### #########

May God have mercy on us both and keep you safe till I am at your side. You have all my devotion and my love. Your daughter, Era Tom

He weeps. He curls up on his bunk, pressing her letter to his nose, trying to retrieve her scent. *Cherished daughter!*

Whose hands have held this paper. But there is only the dank smell of leather and tobacco from couriers. He holds the page up to candlelight, searching for her fingerprints. He reads the letter through the night, then hunches over, struggling to compose his reply.

In late afternoon, the adjutant returns and walks away with his letter. When Johnny looks up at dusk, Zebedee is there. He takes the Negro's large, black hand and strokes it with his own, then turns it over, awed by the length and beauty of the fingers, the petal pinkness of his palm. Not knowing where to look, he stares at the palm as if at a consoling face.

"My beautiful Raindance…is dead."

* * *

Hooker issues hourly bulletins, ready to launch his attack, his "perfect plan." Once they take Chancellorsville, a small virtually unguarded town, several Army divisions will demonstrate against Lee's front at Fredericksburg, while the main body, commanded by Hooker himself, will march up the Rappahannock River on a flanking maneuver that will ingeniously bring it down *behind* Lee's forces and take him by surprise. Finally claiming Fredericksburg, the Union Army will then press on to Richmond.

At dawn divisions break camp and march up the northern banks of the river, making wide detours behind the hills to conceal their movement from the Rebels. After agonizing hours, thousands of men, wagons, and pack mules reach the Rapidan, a fork of the Rappahannock. They strip and wade shoulder-deep across swift-running currents, bearing equipment aloft on their heads and on their bayonets. The crossings take all night and they sit shivering till dawn, then press on toward the point of concentration,

Chancellorsville. In late afternoon they bivouac a mile outside the town.

A boy in Johnny's platoon drops his equipment near a
fallen tree and collapses, leaning back against the log. In
the chaos of setting up camp—men shouting and joking—
no one hears his cries for help. Finally, they turn and run
forward, viewing a sight they will not forget. The boy has
reclined in a nest of pit vipers. They writhe all over him.
One slides from beneath his arm and raises up, its mouth
hideously wide, showing a glistening, white interior.

"Jesus wept," someone cries. "Them's cottonmouths!
He's done for."

They count as many as seven snakes whipping around in
a frenzy, sinking their fangs into the boy. Men curse aloud,
helplessly waving their pistols, afraid they will accidentally
shoot him. One of the vipers rears up and sinks his fangs
into an eye and hangs there while the helpless boy screams.

Men of sounder mind run forward, flipping vipers into
the air with branches, shooting them before they hit the
ground. But one is still gruesomely attached to the boy's eye,
its big head covering half his face as if it will swallow the face
entirely. A soldier, whispering oaths, lies down paralleling
the boy, takes careful aim, and fires, and most of the snake is
blown away. The head remains; the fangs cling passionately.

His body relaxes and they know the boy is dead, yet his
jacket moves in undulations. With a sickening sensation,
they see there is another snake inside it. From the distance,
Johnny runs up, rips open the jacket, slaps the snake from
the boy's chest, and plunges his knife into its belly, pointing
it in the air like a trophy. The thing flips and writhes in its
death throes.

In that moment, the shot-apart cottonmouth lets go its
fangs and falls away from the dead boy's face. Men stare in
horror, for his eye is the size of an egg, still expanding, ready

to pop. Even Johnny stops and stares, and that quick, the snake hanging from his knife sinks its fangs into his wrist.

He falls slowly to his knees, staring at the brown-and-black cross-banded markings of the reptile's head, its hideous, vindictive eyes. He feels venom shoot through his veins, mad palpitations of his heart, a sense of suffocation. Around him, men are engaged in an orgy of shooting until each snake is scattered into rags and bits. They turn to see Johnny unconscious, the snake clinging to him in its death throes, and they stand momentarily paralyzed.

Zebedee comes running, shouting profanities, then picks up a stone and smashes the serpent's head until it is pulverized. He digs the fangs from Johnny's wrist and places his mouth there, then turns and spits, and turns back again, sucking out more venom. Men run for help while others go into another frenzy, obliterating the snake while Zebedee kneels, his mouth working vigorously at Johnny's wrist.

Medics arrive and quickly wrap his arm in poultices of Klamath weed, ironweed, and warm manure, then carry him off while Zebedee bends over spitting and rinsing out his mouth repeatedly. Then, very slowly, he stands and turns to the crowd of men still waving their pistols. When he speaks, his voice is deep and dignified, his words carefully enunciated.

"I know you soldiers is trained in how to suck a snakebite. Every...single...one of you! Instead, you frolicked, waved guns, and played cowboys...while Corporal Tom near died. Think now. What was you most afraid of? Tasting snake venom? Or tasting Chinese?"

* * *

Visions of Era nursing the soldier with the popping eye. His beautiful Raindance girdled in vipers, her body shot to rags and dust. He comes out of his nightmares feverish and screaming. Nurses administer laudanum, apply fresh herbs and poultices of warm manure. Eventually come nights of deepest sleep, fevers abated, his body purged of venom. He awakens to the sound of whip-poor-wills, the scent of things sweet and clean. His boys come bearing scuppernong jelly, beaten biscuits from home. They weep with relief that he is alive—purged and cured, not paralyzed.

Weeks pass before he is steady on his feet again. By then the debacle of Chancellorsville is over, seventeen thousand Union casualties. Another hugely crushing defeat for the Union Army, one they say that has left Lincoln in deep despair. Joseph Hooker, with more than one hundred and twenty thousand battle-ready men had—in three instances of cowardice—refused to issue the command to charge, thereby yielding the initiative and leaving his troops floundering. With half that number of troops, Robert E. Lee had, through brilliant strategizing and a blatant refusal to believe he could be whipped, emerged victorious.

When Johnny is strong enough, he sits with his boys asking how they had been so terribly crushed under Hooker, who had held their greatest hope.

"A coward," someone volunteers. "Kept pullin' us back, and pullin' us back."

"God's truth, he left us stranded! Whole divisions out there with no leader. Soon's he got a little wounded, he departed the battlefield all shook up like a baby."

Casey, the Irish boy, sums it up dispassionately. "Fact is, Hooker was out-generaled. It's time we face that we are *losing* this damned War."

ERA

Tullahoma, April 1863

The days have become an agony. She tries to approach him, to confess she has been scouting for the Federals, but Warren's preoccupation with the War, his brooding insularity, makes him seem suddenly forbidding and aloof. She turns away, imagining she gives off emanations, an odious, traitor's smell.

The War now seems a distraction, receding into the background, while the full significance of her deception leaps into the foreground. She grows less attentive to the numbers of new conscripts arriving, new supplies of guns, to the gossip of nurses and camp whores. Tending wounded officers who have grown homesick and loose-tongued, she neglects to ask about the numbers of deserters among the ranks, and if the next big campaign will be Vicksburg or Chattanooga.

Alone, Era prays for a final, decisive battle that will end this War, end her subterfuge and lies, but then she thinks of the odds for Warren, and for her father. *Each battle increases their chances of being killed.* Some days she is so wretched and fearful she thinks of taking her own life. *But what about my father?* She has collaborated in hopes of finding him; it has all been for him. Her death would nullify everything. Yet so would her confession. She would be hanged without ever seeing him again.

She resolves once more to go to Warren and confess. She imagines how he will be appalled, how he will regard her as instantly repulsive. He will look upon their lovemaking as having been grotesque. And worse, he will be presented with the sordid humiliation of having been her accomplice. Nonetheless, one evening she hurries to their cabin. He is all she is sure of in this world, and she will fall upon his mercy, his essential goodness, imploring him to help her, to rescue her.

She finds him sitting on the porch with one of his pards, Wilbur Mims, a cavalry captain. They stand and greet her, and she passes into the cabin while they continue their conversation. Era sits waiting for Mims to depart, but they are engrossed in reports lately sent down from Confederate scouts. Five massive Union gunships, eight transports, and a like number of mortar vessels have been sighted heading up the Tennessee River for Chattanooga to strengthen Federal troops there.

Era begins to pace, anxious for their talk to end, but at the margin of her consciousness, she hears the soft drawl of Wilbur Mims. "Just now that river's mighty cold and sluggish; those Feds will be moving slow. There's a deep bend twelve miles past Decatur. Word is, our engineers are setting up to blow them there."

"And you may depend," Warren says, "we will be there full force with Fightin' Joe!"

Dark now, and she has lit a fire. When Warren finally comes inside, she sees he is distracted by the talk with Mims. He leans at the fireplace, his handsome features cast in flickering blue flames. He speaks of "those godless, motherless invaders" with such unregenerate hate her heart races, then slows as she acknowledges her loss of nerve, her inability to confront him.

During their meal the conversation is cleft by silences, prolonged moments of ruminant nonspeech. When his gaze lingers on her too long, she imagines his suspicions and inwardly shudders. A ponderous drowsiness and lassitude overcome her, yet later, she lies sleepless, thinking how once again she has allowed the crucial moment to pass.

In her paranoia, Era begins to imagine a change in him, as if the euphoria of their first weeks together has been despoiled by the consciousness of something troubling in the air between them, a sense of things held back. And perhaps subconsciously roused to a sense of danger, Warren *does* become alert and tense, especially when she loses her composure.

"I want it to end," she cries. "All of it! I am so weary."

He thinks her strain is from fatigue. "Era, you must slow down. You are wearing yourself ragged in servitude to those doctors."

Yet her exhausting schedule is what keeps her sane. It keeps her from thinking. For days, a Chinese mess boy has been feverish with typhoid. Hour after hour, Era places damp cloths on his face and holds him while he shudders. One night, she holds him until dawn; then he grows still. She shakes his shoulders almost violently. "Live! Live!"

A surgeon pats her shoulder. "Nurse. He's gone."

Era weeps. She weeps convulsively and cannot stop. A matron walks her up and down the road for hours.

That night she tells Warren about the boy. "He looked like my *father*." She grips him almost fiercely. "My father could be dead by now, and I will never know. Oh, dearest, never leave me. You're all I am sure of in this world…"

"Don't you know I'm bound to you?" he tells her. "I begrudge each hour we're apart…"

Her voice begins to fade as exhaustion overcomes her. "You must promise to *always* love me. Even when you know the truth…"

He lies beside her, puzzled, then falls into sleep.

* * *

She has not seen the sutler, Wickett, for weeks, but one day he is back in camp, his wagon replenished with "luxuries and varieties." He tips his crimson hat as she casually approaches, then spreads out a handsome shawl sewn from swatches of fine velvet and silk.

Era moves close to him, fingers a spool of yellow thread and whispers, "I want you to relay this message. Tell them I am *finished* with this sordid business. They have *used* me, made false promises. I will find my father on my own."

He smooths the shawl and speaks loudly as if he has not heard her, as if they are engaged in a transaction. "Fetching, isn't it? From the ball gown of a Nashville lady." Then he leans closer. "Your papa is well. He came out of Fredericksburg a hero. Promoted to corporal."

Era steps back as if struck, then struggles for composure. "How do I know you're not lying? Trying to gob information from me."

"Ma'am, his letter is sewn inside this shawl. I assume you know your papa's handwriting…?"

Her eyes grow so wide she looks momentarily degenerate. After a moment, she steadies herself, slides her hand beneath the shawl, and grabs his wrist.

"If you're lying, I vow I will track you down and *shoot* you. I have nothing to lose."

"The letter's real. Been through the hands of seven couriers." He has not yet let loose of the shawl. "Things are quickening. Feds need information bad. Now, do you have anything for me?"

Era tries to pull the shawl from him; Wickett holds on to it firmly. Half-crazed, she hesitates, then, with lips barely moving, tells him of the Confederate plans to blow up the Union naval fleet on the Tennessee River twelve miles past Decatur. "Wheeler will be there in full force with his cavalry."

He smiles, finally releases the shawl, and takes her money. "I may be gone a spell. I recommend you take extra caution when—"

Era shakes her head. "I told you, I'm finished. I *will not* do this anymore."

Wickett looks off in the distance and smiles and keeps his voice low. "After all this searching, you finally found your papa. You want to lose him again, just like that?"

She whispers frantically, "In my heart and soul, I'm sick of it! I've got nothing left to give them."

"Then *find* something. Or I guarantee you won't hear from him again. Nor he from you. You might could say the Feds are holding him hostage. They want *information*. Look, this War is near over. Give them what they want. Then you can have your papa."

She clutches the shawl against her chest, feeling his letter in its folds. "How should I…proceed?"

He casually glances around, then looks back at her. "Best you stick to 'foraging.' Our signalmen are in the trees, waiting for a sign. Use the mirror. They sight you in their glasses, you sign in deaf man's code. Don't be putting nothing down on paper anymore."

Most cherished daughter,

I write you with glad and bursting heart for your survival. With profound bewilderment and deepest grief for Raindance, most honorable wife and mother. Such news causes me to weep. I did not protect my family. But grief gives me courage for coming battles. Auspicious winds blow through me full of Union victory. Daughter, you are all I live for now, my flesh and destiny.

I am promoted Corporal Johnny Tom. One day will be American citizen. Without you all would be for nothing. What would happen to my pigtail, my Chinese tongue, my manifolds? Without you would be no honor, no pride of valor to look back on. You are now holder of my dreams so must stay safe for me. In nursing wounded must be kind to tend yourself as well.

We will soon gaze upon each other, will sit with Raindance near birch trees, honor her with fruit and sweets so fou dogs of Afterlife give her entrance. She will call down and blow ashes from her lips. We will build a house in blues and reds of fiery raindance colors.

Forgive me, precious daughter, aide now comes for this letter which travels many miles to you. May all our ancients keep you safe. Please send more words when can. Soon we embrace in more auspicious times.

I am not worthy,
Your father, Johnny Tom

Small, discreet, and so familiar, his handwriting takes her breath, leaves her weeping like a child. His letter tells her little, yet the remembered sound of his voice, the scent of his skin, provides a balm that soothes her heart. Here is her blood, her genesis. Each word rescues her from chaos.

She lies back, remembering summer nights when he pointed out the stars. Venus. Casseopeia. *Nights of your long, black hair undone while you and Mother raindanced. Mother singing out in Creek, you chanting martial dialects. Oh, the laughter! The good earth.* She thinks how one day the battles will be over. *Then let me run on swift legs to find you. Oh, Father! Only your voice can convince me I am not beyond repair…*

* * *

The months of wintering are over. As preparation for major spring campaigns begins, she listens to Warren's daily harangues against the enemy, his impatience to gallop back into the carnage. When she reaches out with a nervously placating hand, he ignores her and she begins to back away, feeling once more the imperative to move toward her father, to aid the Union side. There is no hesitation now. Each lie she tells, each act she commits, is a gift to herself because it will bring her father closer.

Between nursing shifts, she makes notes on artillery reinforcements arriving in the camp. Thirty-two pounders, forty-four pounders, eight-inch Columbiads, nine-inch Dahlgrens. Mortars, howitzers. She draws quick sketches and slides them into her shoes to memorize at night. What she cannot memorize, she rolls into tiny paper cylinders the width of toothpicks and folds them into her hair beneath her hairnet, or slides them between the seams of her waistband.

When Warren and his troops ride out for that crucial bend in the Tennessee River past Decatur, she carefully packs him thick socks and bull's eyes, and packets of white powder that troopers will pour into their palms and lick off in the tonguefuls. But while he is gone, she is once more riven with guilt, imagining him wounded or dead. Imagining her life without him.

Weeks later, when Warren returns he is subdued. The attack on the Union ships heading up the Tennessee had been adjudged a dismal failure.

"The ambush our engineers set up was pretty near useless. Bridges ready to be blown, artillery with cannons at the ready. A whole division poised on their stomachs with rifles trained on the river. Then those scurrilous bastards surprised us, came up *behind* us, two whole brigades. Drew us out before their ships ever reached that bend. We only sank two of them."

He shakes his head. "There was a major leak, that's sure. They were after Fightin' Joe. Their troops kept shouting, 'Get that *sum'bitch* Wheeler!' A miracle he escaped."

* * *

An overcast morning. Men shouting and galloping by on horseback. They have caught a Union spy. Soldiers fix bayonets and hack him to pieces before officers can intervene. Later, a private broadcasts the news.

"Damned Yankee sutler! Decoding our dispatches right there in his wagon."

She does not ask the name of the sutler; she cannot afford to ask. But days later, she sees a soldier prancing round a campfire, wearing a rakishly tilted bright-red hat.

New reinforcements drill in the mud and sleet of early spring. A Council of War is held, and she watches General Braxton Bragg as he rides across the campgrounds, looking thin and gray, worn down by infighting amongst his officers, half of whom are calling for his resignation. Joe Wheeler, with his sweet, boyish face, rides beside him. Barely twenty-six, sitting small in his saddle, his proud posture makes him seem a taller man.

Rumors fly that in the interest of boosting morale for the coming spring campaigns—and to brighten his own tarnished image—Bragg will tour the regiments of his vast Army corps, speaking personally to his infantry troops. Perhaps to prove his mettle, he promises to visit even the outermost campsites near the picket lines, mere shouting distance from Union pickets and their deadly sharpshooters.

Incredulous, Warren paces outside their cabin. "Bragg has lost his damned mind! He thinks his officers can shield him. Why, his men despise him so, one of his *own pickets* might shoot him. Hell, *I* myself would like to shoot him."

Era stands riveted. In her mind she sees the still-snowy fields run down to scattered woods, then deeper woods, then Rebel picket lines. Beyond it, a neutral stretch of woods, then the Union Army pickets, and in the treetops, their signalmen with sophisticated field glasses crouched beside sharpshooters whose rifles are far advanced of the Confederates. Weapons capable of debraining a man from half a mile away.

At night she tosses, thinking how Bragg is hated, how many battles he has forfeited out of cowardice, how many boys he has sacrificed. She would be doing his troops a favor. She thinks how easy it might be to deliver to those sharp-shooters the prime—the most sought after—target. One day, she tells Warren she must soon go "foraging" again, that medical supplies are grievously low.

He gazes at her thoughtfully. "Whatever do you find out there in half-frozen ground?"

Era feels her cheeks flush. "Why, so much thrives under snow. Rotten apples make vinegar, which takes the mold off teeth. There's yellow root for scurvy and pellagra. We even gather spiderwebs from inside logs. They're cold, and that stops bleeding."

He broods as she rushes on, describing this and that. "And leaves…so good for teas and balms. And violet for clearing lungs. Then there's wolfsbane…"

"That's poison. It can kill a man."

"But ground with oils, it makes the best rub for aching joints. And rotten pokeberries! Boys swear its juice kills lice."

He lights his pipe and exhaustedly exhales. "Best thing for lice is sulfur and hog fat. Now all we have to do is find a hog."

At night she feels his breath on her, his soft declarations of love throwing her again into a miasma of guilt. She vows that this will be her last time; she will send no more messages. She can no longer betray his trust. *Now I know where my father is, I will seek him out on my own.*

In his sleep Warren loosens his hold on her, his damp hand leaving fingerprints of condensation on her hips. She lies very still, feeling the prints dry.

* * *

The day is crystal clear and cold. She moves slowly, hugging herself inside her cloak while thoughtfully kicking snow aside. Occasionally, she plucks up frozen roots and wizened berries and drops them in a bucket, then straightens up, shades her eyes, and looks into the distance, listening to pickets, North and South, shouting taunts back and forth.

Panic rises in her throat. Her mouth goes dry. She bends and pulls more roots, then casually moves to the shadow of a tree so as not to stand out against the landscape. She breathes in deeply, sets the bucket down, and squats, spreading her hands before her, preparing to send the message by signing with her fingers.

It is a form of ciphered code similar to sign language used by the deaf, except that each sign signifies an entire word or phrase and each Confederate general has his particular sign. That of Braxton Bragg is signified by two tight fists with forefingers extended and crossed, suggesting the dead center of a bull's-eye. She has practiced the code signs repeatedly, timing herself with a pocket watch.

URGENT...URGENT...GENERAL BRAGG...INSPECTING...NEAR...PICKET...LINES...TOMOR-

ROW...TIME...NOT...KNOWN...BE PREPARED...BE PREPARED...

She looks around, then pulls a mirror from her pocket and flashes it, letting it catch the sun's reflection. She waits, then flashes it again, praying a Union signalman in distant trees will see her, that no Rebel picket will turn back and look her way. She stops, inhales deeply, flashes the mirror again, turning it this way and that.

There is a returning flash, repeated several times; they have lined her up in their glasses. Stepping from the shadow of the tree, Era begins signing her message, arranging her fingers into the shape of code words. She takes her time, straining for accuracy. The mirror flashes rapidly from the other side, signifying that they have not grasped the full message. They want her to REPEAT... REPEAT...

Slowly, meticulously, she begins again. GENERAL... BRAGG...INSPECTING...NEAR...PICKET...LINES...

"Era."

She snaps her head around, then looks back at the rapidly flashing mirror. It is clear they have not yet picked out Warren in their glasses. Then they do, and there is a moment of silence before the crack of a rifle shot, then a bullet hitting rock. They are trying to avoid hitting her.

He rushes forward and pulls her to the ground, his frightened horse dancing behind them. She wonders at how silently he rode up, how silently he must have followed her. She struggles, but his arm surrounds her, holding her elbows tight against her ribs.

"What are you doing? Tell me! What are you doing?"

She shakes her head and, again, there is the crack of a rifle. The earth spits up beside them. Warren drags her behind the tree, and they lie panting like dogs.

"Era, are you a...scout? Have you been *spying* all this time?"

In the distance, shouts, the returning fire of Rebel pickets.

He is confused and still unsure; he does not want to be sure. Almost serenely, he asks her again. "Are you...working for the Federals?"

Her silence tells him everything. Moments pass swiftly, yet she has a sense that it is happening in slow motion. The Federals retreat, under attack from a squad of Confederate cavalry. The back-and-forth of rifle fire eventually wears down. She can still hear Rebel pickets swearing, not comprehending what has taken place behind them.

He drags her to her feet, forcing her hands from her pocket, and finds the mirror there. He hangs his head at the wealth of information he has given her, time after time.

"My God. What have I done?"

Her voice comes out devoid of all emotion. "You said one had to take a side. Be true to that."

"But why? *Why?* Your own father is fighting for the Confederacy."

"My father is a corporal in the *Union* Army."

"You lied. Everything was lies..."

Something is finally let loose in her. She steps closer. "Yes! I lied. Rebel soldiers kidnapped my father and all men from our village, forced them to fight for slavery. Many defected to the Union side."

Her eyes have a depthless quality now. "The Rebels came back for retribution. Shall I tell you what they did to our women? To my *mother* and to young girls...like me? So many soldiers I could not count. When my mother fought back with a knife, they strung her up. Hanged her from a tree, then set her on fire while they kept on, on top of me. I watched my mother burn to death while they kept on...on me."

She is shaking so badly her teeth chatter. "My Creek grandmother was a white man's slave. And so my mother was born his slave. He was planning to breed more slaves with her, his *daughter*. If the South wins this War, I, too, am his slave. His property."

Warren shakes his head in disbelief.

"Do you think I would ever fight for them? That my father would fight for them? He was brought to New Orleans in chains, on a slave ship of kidnapped Chinese. They auctioned them off on the blocks because they were cheaper than Negroes. My father got away. But I have seen Chinese with their feet cut off who did not get away."

"Be still," he whispers. "Be still!"

"How can you fight for such filth? The South should not *exist*."

His arm flinches as if he would strike her. He steps back. "I will not raise a hand to you. But I mean to take you in."

"You will *not*."

How she has betrayed him. How she has lied to him. He has been laid open, filleted of any information she could use. He feels he has meant nothing more to her.

"God help me, woman. I will take you in! They will stand you before a firing squad."

She steps forward, reaches out her hand. "Give me the horse. Just give me the horse."

His mount has approached, and now it stands pawing the snow where patches of grass show through. Warren hangs his head, shaking it, trying to comprehend what has happened. In that moment, Era lunges, grabs the reins, and mounts the horse in one motion, then kicks it so it rears. She lashes the reins against its flanks and its great muscles gather, then it surges forward, urged by the high, yipping sounds issuing from her throat.

Disbelieving, Warren shouts, then pulls his gun from its holster, calls out her name and fires. He sees her back arch, sees her fall forward, her body half-sliding from the saddle, hands still clutching at the reins. Down on the picket line, Rebels shout out in confusion. More gunshots, the sound of galloping hoofbeats, the woman falling. Era, woman of lightning, forever falling.

For days he sits in shock. Then a soldier from the picket line walks into camp, leading his horse.

"We hollered over to the Feds. They don't know nothin' bout a woman goin' through their lines. But we found blood trails, lot of blood. We think the woman's dead, sir."

He presents himself to his commanding officer and tells him half the truth. "I believe she was suffering from terrible fatigue. She wanted us to run off together. I could not do that. In a moment's madness, she stole my horse, tried to break through the picket lines, and was shot. We don't rightly know which side. I believe she's dead, sir. Out in those woods somewhere."

The major shakes his head. "A tragic thing, Petticomb. These nurses are grievously overworked, laboring without letup in these filthy hospital tents. Even dying of our diseases. Well, I pray she is at peace."

He clears his throat and tactfully looks down. "In future, I would heartily recommend that you troopers refrain from…alliances with these frail, lonely women."

For weeks Warren will ride out on raids he will not clearly remember. A Federal train is blown; two of his friends are killed. He will not recall their deaths. He is not fully conscious of eating, or sleeping, or even evacuating in the saddle during skirmishes. He simply rides on, his waste frozen in his trousers.

It is late afternoon when a Negro from a burial squad appears in front of his cabin. "They'se sent me to tell you, sir...we'un's found that woman and...we'se buried her."

He stands up and struggles to steady his voice. "Where? Where did you bury her?"

The man hesitates. "Tha' empty stretch jest aside our picket line. We'se bringin' in a mess of frozen bodies and they'se buryin' them togetha."

"Show me!"

He follows the man for a mile beyond the campgrounds, a stretch running just inside the perimeter of the picket line. As he approaches, several Negroes step back from a mass grave they have tamped down with shovels.

He dismounts from his horse. "I would like to see the woman."

A detail of limers stand off to the side, looking not unlike the dead themselves. White with lime and nearly phosphorescent in the dusk, they stand in a faint miasma of carbolic and look at him, confused.

"Sir, they'se already limed."

"I mean to see her corpse!"

Two of them begin to shovel dirt, slowly uncovering the grave. A shovel hits something solid, and they moan and shake their heads. He sees the beginning of a leg gone black, already eaten to the bone. He sees long, dark hair, a hollowed-out eye socket, the remains of a face.

"Stop, for the love of God." He rides away.

* * *

Now Federal forces are gathering at Vicksburg. Sitting high on a bluff over the Mississippi, the city is central to a total Union victory.

Lincoln has announced that Vicksburg is the key. "And we must put that key in our pocket."

For over a year, their Naval forces have tried to take the city, but Mississippians are proud and do not know how to surrender. The Federals try to take it by land and are stopped at Chickasaw Bluffs. Ulysses S. Grant has recently tried again, leading forty-five thousand men through tangled bayous on the river to seize the bluffs north and south of Vicksburg. Though he surrounded the city and entrapped thirty thousand Confederate soldiers, he was still beaten back.

Now he has settled in for a siege, attacking the city with guns and cannons while gunships pound it from the river so that Vicksburg is now surrounded by a ring of fire. Still refusing to surrender, families burrow under the city into caves of yellow clay, turning the caves into crude homes with makeshift stoves and beds.

Rumors abound that, attempting to distract Grant and draw his troops away from Vicksburg, Robert E. Lee, fighting in the East, plans to invade the North, striking somewhere in Pennsylvania. Warren's troops receive the news in a kind of wonder, for across the land Confederate armies are starving and weakening, eating their dead horses and marching barefoot. And here there is unholy fire surrounding the city of the last Confederate hope.

We will die for nothing, Warren thinks. *We will lose. And you were an instrument of our defeat. I am glad you are dead. Glad I delivered you to death.*

When he thinks of her, his heart seizes up with hate. He studies an ambrotype in its metal frame, the two of them standing side by side, looking stern so as not to show passion or affection. It had been taken by one of the itinerant photographers who followed the armies camp to camp, advertising *Ambrotypes and Tintypes* on their wagons and carrying their portable darkrooms inside.

He remembers posing self-consciously before the camera, wanting to take Era's hand behind her skirt. Remembers how she blushed and pulled away, how the camera stood on three legs, aiming its knowing eye at them. He does not destroy the ambrotype. Studying her face, recalling the immense deception of her, helps him nurse his hate.

Now he trusts no one, neither fellow troopers nor his superiors. Men are deserting every day. Whole squads of infantry and cavalry talk of surrendering. He ignores them, wanting to be left alone, wanting their desires to leave him alone. He no longer cares who lives or dies, who wins this War. The world is now an empty space he merely fills.

His stump aches constantly. Some days he feels a near-paralysis that keeps him from sitting up, even as it prevents him from lying down. Standing seems equally impossible. He watches schoolboys parade in serried ranks, new conscripts ready to sacrifice their lives, and feels no compassion. With equal apathy, he regards his wounded pards of the Prattville Dragoons. Yet in his darkest moments, something in him weeps, a small voice telling him it wants to start over, discover what he might have been, what he did not have time to experience.

And sometimes, in a half doze, he remembers how he held her until all her hair fell down. The golden globes of her shoulders, the modest and uplifted breasts. How, in sleep, she pressed her cheek against his naked stump and woke with the scars imprinted on her face. He remembers her last words, telling what was done to her. All the men she could not count. He remembers how those words came out of her, as if her insides were in flames.

He thinks of the damaged core of her, and how he might have healed it. There were so many silences, so many warn-

ings he had missed, so many things that escaped him because he was not attentive enough, or smart enough. And
because he did not know how to encompass the sorrow of
her, and the richness of her, that had entered him and overwhelmed him.

Johnny Tom

Gettysburg, July 1863

His rice barrel seems to overflow. He has saved the life of a brigadier general and survived the venom of a cottonmouth. He has never been shot, nor does he suffer from dysentery, which altogether bestows upon him double-hero status. Johnny's boys follow him about, emulating his gestures, even heeding his exhortations to eat soil, which abounds in minerals that redress their baneful diet of rancid meat and hardtack.

He has come to love the taste of American soil. In his daily jottings to Era, which have become like his journal, he describes this taste, this gritty flavor of freedom. *But freedom what for?* he wonders. *Raindance is gone. My Yuanfen.* That apportionment of love that is allotted to each man in his life. *She whose bones fit my bones perfectly, whose sighs of pleasure like temple bells at night.* Sometimes his grief is so deep he slaps his face to make his heart feel lighter. This gives his face a radiance that inspires his boys as they drill and prepare for the next engagement.

Rumors fly that, in the Western Theater of War, Ulysses S. Grant has surrounded Vicksburg, Mississippi. Believing that his invasion of the North will force Grant to rush back to defend Washington, capital of the Union, Lee is now marching his forces through the Shenandoah Valley, crossing the Potomac and headed into Maryland. His troops are said to be one hundred thousand strong with which he is planning to invade Pennsylvania, then take control of Washington. The War now seems to hinge on Vicksburg in the West, Pennsylvania in the East.

As Confederates move ever north, Union troops—still under Joseph Hooker—begin a similar course to the east, keeping between Lee and their capital. With the ghastly defeats of Fredericksburg and Chancellorsville fresh in their minds, boys are disposed to kneel and pray. They line up at streams, waiting to be baptized, as the Rebels cross into Pennsylvania, threatening to destroy their families and their homelands.

Even as they prepare to face the enemy, Johnny thinks how the fickle gods might turn on him, reverse his fortunes after such good luck. He thinks how he might die and never see his daughter. And he ponders how the South tried to enslave him, then tried to kill him, and now the North has turned him into an assassin. He wonders if fighting and killing is an honorable way to make his progress in America. *Is there not a better, more noble way?* Yet he fears this is the only way for him; he has seen how Yankees treat foreigners and nonwhites much like the Rebels do. Because of his yellow skin, his slanted eyes—even when he becomes an American citizen—he suspects he will always be thought of as a "pigtail."

Encamped once again north of the Rappahannock, his Third Corps waits for orders while they drill in heat and choking dust. Exhausted, he sits outside his tent, wondering if Era received his letter, if he will hear from her again. In the distance, a Confederate sharpshooter with a telescopic rifle aims at Johnny's head, but sighting someone else, he shifts his aim. An adjutant approaching with a letter half holds it out to Johnny.

When the first bullet hits him, he stands there disbelieving. The second bullet knocks him down. It pierces the letter before entering his head, and the enormous force of it sets the envelope aflame. Johnny shouts and kneels, ministering to him, and watches the letter from his daughter turn to ash. Nearly inconsolable, he sits with Zebedee and Virgil and tells how the War had killed Raindance and now it will take Era from him too.

"Listen, now," Zebedee tells him. "This burned-up letter means she got *yours*. So you know she alive, and soon you going find her."

"But...now letter man is dead. I have much to tell. No one to tell to."

"Oh, hell, they'll get other couriers. Meanwhile, John Tom, write to me. Yeah, me and Virgil. Jest put it all down in your Bible, and now and then you might let me read of it. When I get bored with Job and Proverbs, I going read the Book of Tom!"

Profoundly touched, Johnny begins to write his memories of his youth in tertiary hatchback across whole pages of Scripture. In that way, his Bible becomes a compendium of his thoughts, his life. Should he never find his daughter, at least Zebedee will know his personal history; someone will have been his witness. At night he scribbles feverishly with the *yang* concentration of a scholar.

* * *

All through June's heat and rain, cherries have been ripening. Along the roads, boys reel, half-drunk with the musty, winey fragrance. Squads break ranks and gulp them in the handfuls, gasping at their sweetness, so that thousands of them will die with their intestines bursting bright-red cherry pulp. Its nostalgic fruity smell will permeate the battlefields.

As Lee's troops spread over southern Pennsylvania, the Federals keep vigilantly between them and Washington, and suddenly, there is a new commander of their Army. Lincoln replaces Joe Hooker with General George Meade, a man the rank and file are not familiar with. Disheartened, confused, the boys feel they have no steady leader now, no one to look up to. In the past ten months they have fought four major battles—Second Bull Run, Antietam, Fredericksburg, Chancellorsville—each with a different commander who led them to appalling defeat. An unspoken pact is seeded and spreads like wildfire through brigades and divisions. They will depend only on each other now. They will be their *own* heroes.

They are marching thirty miles a day. At night, they progress by the light of candles stuck in the muzzle of their rifles, a flickering locomotion that stretches twenty miles. The Confederates are now rumored to be somewhere between the towns of York on the east and Chambersburg on the west, and they are moving fast.

One night, during bivouac, Casey O'Shea, his lips bright red from gorging on cherries, sits at Johnny's campfire. "Those Rebs are dumping their equipment along the roads. Throwing off *everything*, even their shelter tents. What can it mean?"

Johnny answers softly, "Are moving fast to infiltrate. When have gone deep enough…will turn and face us."

"Mother Mary. It's going be a big one, ain't it?"

Johnny sees the hesitation in his eyes, the resolute, luminous flame inside him flickering. "Yes. Will be big. You remember what I taught you? Be still, no panic. When waiting for enemy, only eyes move, watching out for comrades. So they watch out for you."

"Yes, I remember everything!" His brogue seems more pronounced, yet his voice turns laconic, measured, almost elderly. "But I don't want to be killing no more, and I don't want to die. I ain't afraid to die. Thing is, Johnny…I ain't *ready* to die. I ain't hardly lived! I don't have no memories yet…"

"You are wrong, brave boy. Being orphan, starving, sailing ship to America—this is already memory. Every day is memory, like precious grain of rice. At end of each day you must think, I am one grain stronger! One grain richer!"

Casey squints his eyes the way he does when he's listening while Johnny gestures theatrically, knowing how gestures add meat and bones to words and captivate the listener.

"Like me, you come from nothing, so must invent yourself. Every minute pure invention. So even *minutes* become memory. Also, you must learn to *listen,* so other boys' stories become your memories too."

Trying to distract him, he reads aloud from his notes in the Bible, reminiscences of his boyhood, poignant thoughts written in his broken English that still convey sly humor so that while he reads Casey laughs, bending a little from the waist. Johnny reads to exhaustion and finally closes the Good Book.

"Now, how rich you are in memory! When you are old, will tell your children of Johnny Tom from China, his brother Ah Fat, and how they ventured out into the world. You see? In listening, you have inhaled my life. My memories now possess your bones. You will not forget me."

He looks at him, concerned. "But, Johnny…we'll stay close pards, won't we? When the War is over?"

His smile is gentle, almost shy. "Oh, yes! Do you not see how I think of you as… son? Your memories now possess *my* bones."

The boy looks down in quiet exultation.

* * *

Seven corps of the Union Army approach the environs of a town called Gettysburg. Tidy Dutch barns, fastidious orchards and cemeteries. A soft, green country of rolling hills, except that there are no cattle in the fields, no horses. Rebels have already scoured the land. Meade's troops slow down, sensing that enemy troops are somewhere up ahead and imagine them springing phantomlike from the soil—barefoot, sunburned, screaming that eerie Rebel scream.

Marching aside Johnny, Zebedee calls out, "You ever seen a picture of Lee? White hair, white beard, soft blue eyes. Look like an angel, not a killer."

"Angel of death," Virgil whispers.

With Lincoln's Emancipation Proclamation, they have been officially sworn in as Union soldiers, issued uniforms and rifles, and assigned to Corporal Tom as his "tagalongs" until they can join an official Colored Infantry Regiment. It has all happened so fast Virgil continues to gaze at his musket in horror, holding it out in two hands as if forced to hold a snake.

Troops begin to falter as they pass fields of dead Rebels and Yanks gone down in skirmishes. Rags flicker in the wind, so corpses seem alive as buzzards gather, the *haw! haw!* of crows snatching up human offal. Feral hogs come out of the bush to snuffle, and boys turn aside to retch. Day fades to dusk as, once again, they go into bivouac. They have marched over one hundred miles in four days. No longer boys of harum-scarum jocularity, they write letters home and pray.

It is a small town of two thousand people in open, hilly country where many roads converge. West of it, the land rolls to the mountains in long, easy ground swells. A gentle land, rich and bountiful, with shallow valleys between broad ridges running north and south. On the first day of July, a Federal cavalry troop commandeers one of the ridges outside the town. Their pickets look west, and dawn comes up behind them, lighting the blue crest of a mountain before them.

As light dawns, a column of Confederate troops comes heaving eastward. The general of this division has heard that stores have been lately stocked with shipments of shoes. Thousands of his men are barefoot, walking in tied-up rags. It is assumed that there are only a few Yankee militia in the town, and so the Confederate division—four thousand men and scouts—comes booming over the western ridge, headlong into the rising sun, too blinded to see the enemy. The Federals spot them and begin an exchange of heavy fire. And in this way, over the simple need for shoes, the Battle of Gettysburg begins.

The Confederates are stronger and push back the Union troops who retreat and form defensive positions south of Gettysburg on a saddle of high ground called Cemetery Hill and, just beyond it to a higher point, Culp's Hill. Rebels quickly take up position facing them on Seminary Ridge, a scant mile away and, by early afternoon, have formed a long semicircle from the southwest around to the northeast outside the town. As more divisions gather, the fields surrounding Gettysburg explode. Confederates bombard the enemy with volley after volley, and Union cannons come alive. As dusk falls, Union couriers are frantically dispatched in search of still-approaching divisions comprising over fifty thousand men.

All day, Johnny's Third Corps has marched while rumors of the fighting ahead are carried back by couriers. Now outlying battlefields come into view, the dead and dying thickly entwined. Through charred, broken trees, wounded soldiers crawl forward, reaching out to passing troops.

"Look away! Look away!" A sergeant cries as boys offer their canteens.

A captain trotting alongside Johnny's company shouts imprecations, "Keep it tight! Keep it close! Eyes front!"

Ahead, in the smoke-stained evening, the day's fighting has ended. Advance corps of Federals have sustained appalling losses—nine to ten thousand dead or wounded. At Cemetery Hill, there are barely two thousand soldiers left, and commanders pace, desperate for the sound of approaching reinforcements. Facing them one mile away, the enemy's campfires glow.

Johnny's corps bivouacs off Taneytown Road, which will lead them to the rear of Cemetery Hill, and all night, from across the fields, comes a long, thick sigh he knows so well: the exhalation of dying men. Already he feels tired, a weariness of soul, and he thinks again of Era, most precious daughter. Now that he has found her, he must be prudent in his actions. *Must stay alive, for she is all alone in the world.* Yet, in the next instant he thinks how, as corporal, he must now be fearless in leading his boys, in taking care of them. He hears them in their tents talking quietly to God. By noon, many will have lost their minds.

* * *

July 2. In the early hours of dawn, they fall into line, tugging at crotches, groaning with the labor of drawing on accoutrements. It has rained all night and mist drapes the valleys, but soon it will vanish; meadows will stand green and stark. Through the night, divisions of both armies have gathered south of Gettysburg so that over sixty-five thousand Confederates will now confront almost eighty-five thousand Federals.

The morning grows hot, the air heavy. Johnny's division joins others as they grimly assemble in the rear of Cemetery Hill. Ranked beside divisions of infantry and cavalry are thousands of caissons, artillery batteries, and ambu-wagons with stretchers hanging from their sides. At the head of their regiment, a colonel announces that scouts have spotted Robert E. Lee astride his horse a mere mile away on Seminary Ridge. He is pointing at the heights of Cemetery Hill and at the coveted Culp's Hill behind it, the area's highest salient, and most advantageous. They watch Lee trot back and forth shouting directives; then he points at Big and Little Round Tops, two strategic rises south of Cemetery Hill.

"Our generals anticipate Lee will try to deliver a smashing blow against our south end at Big and Little Round Tops, while another of his corps will simultaneously attack Cemetery and Culp's Hills. If they take those north and south strategic points…we've lost this battle."

He calms his horse, then continues in a voice ominous and loud. "By now, you know those Rebs hate taking prisoners. Their only objective is to *kill* you. You lose this battle, your mothers and sisters, the whole damned North, will be owned by *slavers!*"

He trots off to consult with senior officers, then trots back again.

"As men of the Third Corps, we are now under the command of General Daniel Sickles, who's been assigned to protect the lower front of Cemetery Hill and to occupy Big and Little Round Tops to the south."

Word passes frantically up and down the ranks.

"We're done for, boys. Sickles is loony as a cuckoo bird!"

"Word is, he shot and killed his wife's lover, then pleaded temporary insanity. He's unpredictable as hell…"

Their first sergeant shouts them back to order, and Johnny checks that his canteen is full, his cap box hanging from his belt, and his cartridge box with fifty rounds of cartridges. His musket is at the ready, pressed against his thigh. Troops come to attention as General Sickles rides across their division front, acknowledging the salutes of officers. Regiments of infantry salute, but no one cheers as they once cheered for other generals who bled their hearts dry.

Their ranks slowly proceed up the rear of Cemetery Hill, where they are suddenly commanded to pause along the crest. Surveying the land with field glasses, Sickles sees that he is assigned the most vulnerable part of the valley fronting Cemetery Hill—low ground, difficult to defend, with only a byway called Emmitsburg Road separating him from oncoming Confederate forces. He studies the two Round Top hills to the south and fears he cannot stretch his divisions to meet them.

He begins to panic. Half a mile west, Emmitsburg Road passes over a broad, flat hill on top of which is a peach orchard. He suspects that if the Rebels plant men in the orchard, they could drive his troops back. His aide also observes that an uneven fold of land runs off from the orchard in the direction of the Round Tops. On a map, it is marked as thickets, rocky ravines, and massive boulders. A place called Devil's Den.

"If those Rebs penetrate Devil's Den, they'll be lodged squarely on our left bank. A disaster."

Sickles trots his horse toward his commanding general, George Meade, and requests that he re-examine the situation. Meade adamantly shakes his head No! He will not change his orders. He turns his back on Sickles, a man he is rumored to despise, and canters off. Furious, Sickles rides back to his troops and orders a company down to Emmitsburg Road to scan for enemies. They heave down the valley toward the road and discover a solid mass of Rebel infantry moving around to their left. Again, Sickles panics. Fearing that the Rebels are about to smash his left flank, he commands his entire Third Corps—eight thousand men—to quickly move forward to Emmitsburg Road.

An astonishing mile-long line of cavalry and infantry now floods the valley, accompanied by waving flags, rumbling batteries, bugles sounding stirring blasts.

There is the call to "Shoulder arms!" To "Forward... quick time! March!" Lieutenants shouting, "Keep your dress! Keep your dress! Dress it up!"

As troops press forward, boys look back in horror. "Jesus and Mary. What has Sickles done? Meade's Army is just sitting on that ridge. We're out here all alone!"

Sickles's Third Corps is now half a mile out in front of the Army of the Potomac, leaving its left and right flanks tragically exposed. From the heights of Cemetery Hill, almost seventy thousand Union soldiers stare down, speechless, at Sickles's unprotected troops. In later years, George Meade will deny that he had shouted, "That witless son of a bitch! I hope they blow his head off."

Before Sickles can realign his troops, fifty Rebel guns aimed at his men fire simultaneously. With Meade's Army slow in rallying to support him, he is battered down and helpless and, caught in the open valley, men run for the rocks and ravines of Devil's Den. Johnny hugs the ground as everything explodes. A shell burst kills fifty men whose body parts will later amount to only twenty.

Praying aloud, troops watch the frantic effort of Union battalions dragging horses and massive artillery up Little Round Top, trying to position their deadly guns. Since no road runs up its rocky height, gunners are practically carrying their batteries, piece by piece, to the hilltop, key of the Union's left flank. If it is taken by the Confederates, all of Cemetery Hill will have to be abandoned. Boys stand and cheer them on as officers ride past shouting, "Fix...bayonets! Fix bayonets!"

The sound of thousands of bayonets rattling home on muzzles. Then the high, eerie quaver of the Rebel cry as they advance, ripping their way through thickets and ravines, driving straight for Devil's Den and Little Round Top. The order to "Charge!" And in an instant, lines are transformed into a forest of bayonets.

Running beside him, Casey cries out, "Oh, Jesus! I don't *want* to be killing..."

"Stay behind me," Johnny shouts. "Keep bayonet ready!"

As Rebels surge forward, yellow smoke blankets the hill so men cannot see where to thrust or fire. They stab blindly with bayonets, while others swing muskets viciously like clubs. Johnny dodges a man's blade, then stoves his bayonet straight through his skinny neck, and while he struggles to retrieve the blade, he looks left and right for his boys, but there is only chaos.

As the smoke begins to lift, Rebel cannons try to hit the batteries again, and in front of Little Round Top, everything explodes. Union cannons answer, and the valley becomes a pall of smoke. Half-blinded, men grope their way forward into the peach orchard, where more Rebel troops are waiting. They fight till there seems nothing left but random flesh and, utterly exhausted, they go down in fruit and gore.

At first they lie stunned, then slowly crawl out from under their dead. Rebel and Yank, they stand there disbelieving the carnage, the blood flowing incarnadine in gullies. Feeling a large, humid object in his hand, Johnny lies still, afraid it is a human head. He finally turns and sees he is holding an immense, plump peach. He stares at it. *How fortunate this peach. It does not have a conscience.*

Rising unsteadily to his feet, he calls out the names of his squad, but in the keening of the wounded, no one hears him. As smoke begins to lift, he sees Casey kneeling beside a dead boy, his hands full of shiny blue intestines. He is trying to push the boy's stomach back inside him, trying to give him back his life.

Seeing Johnny, he holds up the intestines like an offer-ing. "Can you help me? They won't stay in…"

Johnny slaps the intestines from his hands, lifts him to his feet, and shakes him.

The boy's eyes wander. "I didn't want to…But he came at me. Why in Mother Mary's name did he come at me?"

Johnny shakes him again. "No thinking! No *moong cha cha!*"

His angry voice brings Casey to his senses. He kneels and closes the Rebel's eyelids, the face pale and beautiful, hair through the filth all golden ringlets like his own.

He picks up his rifle and turns to Johnny. "I ain't a cow-ard…I ain't! It's just…why, he was younger than me."

Johnny takes his hand like a child's, and together, they walk to where officers are forming up troops again. Amongst his company, he finds his squad, filthy, blood-soaked, but each miraculously alive. Zebedee and Virgil, Rudi the Italian boy, Andy with a face like a hunting dog, half a dozen others, their eyes now fathomless so they look both present and absent.

In the lull, men turn to watch General Meade's troops spread across the valley in the distance. Over seventy thou-sand strong, they are battling to keep Cemetery Hill from the Confederates. With no rallying support here at Little Round Top, men understand that, thanks to Sickles, they have been essentially abandoned.

Now there are charges and countercharges as Rebel troops spring out of the ground around them, until they are pushed back against the base of Little Round Top. The battle surges back and forth for hours. Five times Confederate forces drive the Federals from their positions and attempt to mount the hill, and five times the Federals drive them back.

Trying to keep Casey near him at all times, Johnny sees that, once the fighting starts, the boy jumps into the thick of it, swinging his musket left and right, yelling unholy curses as he thrusts his bayonet. It is only after the slaughter that his conscience overwhelms him. Johnny has heard it said of the Irish: "Warriors in battle. Poets at heart. And a passionate affinity for guilt."

And so he relaxes his vigil as the two armies clash, Rebels sometimes so close the muzzles of their guns touch. By the time Little Round Top is finally secured, its slopes and summit are blanketed with thousands of corpses. Blood stands in deep puddles, the earth so soaked it cannot absorb it. Clumps of it sit on rocks like big, black steaks. The rocks themselves are flesh.

* * *

Trying to clear his head and bring life back to his limbs, Johnny staggers along with the others, trying to rendezvous with their main divisional body. Yellow smoke lifts in patches here and there, and they see soldiers clearing Little Round Top of corpses, Yank and Rebel, rolling them down the hill like logs, even pushing them over the edge, to quickly clear the way for gunners. Boys cry out at the inhumanity of it, refusing to accept that the dead do not care.

The still-smoldering devastation across the land imparts to survivors a listless, offhand manner so that they wander blank-eyed, their mouths hung open, speechless. Still, Johnny welcomes the foul, sweaty smell of his comrades pressing around him, the feel of their arms as they lean against him and each other. Men who have survived earlier battles with him, and prison camps, thus they share an unspoken love as they wait in the lull between attacks.

From Seminary Ridge, Rebel guns begin firing on them again. Reverberations of their cannons rock the earth. Once more, officers shout at men to "Come to order arms!" To "Lock and prime!" To "Fix bayonets!" A fresh Rebel division has sneaked up on them, and Sickles is nowhere to be seen. Exhausted and confounded, Johnny's brigade backs up until they are hugging the base of Little Round Top from the top of which Union gunners are now inadvertently shooting their own.

His men try frantically to break away, zigzagging across open ground to a stand of woods called Plum Run. From Cemetery Hill, Meade's cannoneers answer the big guns of the Rebels, and now the sky is transmogrified into a carnival of bursting shells, cartwheeling human limbs, so gaudily entrancing boys stop and stare. In response, the Confederates score a direct hit on a Union artillery battery, and with all its stock of ammunition, a caisson explodes.

Johnny sees Casey up ahead, pointing in astonishment at giant bursts of color, brilliant greens and purples, like a child at a circus watching gleaming ponies on a carousel. While he stands there, gaping, another massive shell bursts, and shards of glittering iron pour down like rain. Johnny starts running toward him, then suddenly sits down.

At first he is stunned, deafened by the shelling, but day is fading, and eventually, the shelling ceases. Gingerly, he touches a swelling above his eye, but finds there is no blood. He touches each part of his body. Everything intact. As his senses return, he hears water trickling from Plum Run, earlier a flowing creek, now an amassment of corpses surrounded by mud.

He struggles to his feet and moves forward, searching amongst bodies.

Everywhere, human innards lie about, and mixed in with fecal stench is the winey smell of cherries. Its homey smell permeates the fields. He places his feet carefully and calls out and, after an hour, is astonished to find Casey sitting on the ground, holding his hand against his head.

Seeing Johnny, he cries out, "You're alive! Mother Mary, you're alive!"

Johnny takes the boy's hand from the back of his head, and blood gushes out. Shocked by the size of the hole, he quickly covers it with his own hand.

The boy winces. "Shrapnel...I pulled it out; it wasn't much. Does it look bad?"

"Not too bad," Johnny lies. "You feel pain?"

"Truth is... I don't feel much of anything. Even in my arms."

Johnny's heart convulses. He suspects the ragged hole was caused not so much by the size of the iron missile as by its explosive impact on the skull. He rips part of a shirt from a corpse and wraps the cloth repeatedly round Casey's head.

"Must find medic." He tries not to sound frantic.

Then he remembers the creek and, carefully placing their feet between the faces of the dead, guides Casey back to Plum Run. Pushing corpses from the creek, Johnny packs the head cloth with mud until it is the thickness of a steak. He then directs Casey to sit up against the pull of gravity, so blood will stop flowing; air will harden the mud and seal the wound till they find help. He pours water from his canteen and makes him drink.

"Now...I go find medic. You stay put."

Casey grabs his hand. "Johnny, I'm scared. It's a big hole, isn't it?"

"Yes. Good size."

"Then please don't leave me here alone. We'll wait till morning. *Please.*"

He sits down and takes his hand. "OK, brave lad. I promise. But longer we wait...not good for you."

The boy essays a weak smile. "I know. It's just...you might get lost. I wouldn't want to die without you. We have so many memories now."

"Yes. Many. But you will heal, have many *years* of memories. Now, rest."

The day's fighting has ended. Now a brilliant moon looks down on them, flooding the battlefield with light. Even corpses in the stream gaze soulfully. The boy dozes, lulled by the cool beneficence of mud packed round his skull, the weight of it like a turban. From across the fields, Johnny hears the voices of men scavenging canteens, then other voices crying out.

"Sickles has lost his leg! Our general is down!"

The message is shouted up and down the valley, men fearing their battle is lost as, once again, they are leaderless. *But now battle is here*, Johnny thinks. *Reduced to this beautiful boy.* He moves slightly, adjusting his shoulder against which Casey's head is lightly resting. Finally, he gives in to exhaustion and dozes.

When he wakes, he hears distant ambu-wagons clattering up and down the battlefields, stretcher-bearers cursing as they slip in gore. He calls out, but they seem miles away. Somewhere, guns are still firing, the crackle and sputter of small arms. Above it all, the whispers of the dying in private conversations. So many thousands it seems the earth itself is whispering.

He sits up with a start. His shoulder is soaking wet. In the semidarkness he touches Casey's head. The packed mud round the head cloth is sticky and dripping, making his heart pound.

"Casey!" Johnny shakes him.

The boy groans. His head lolls to one side, and Johnny sees he is covered in blood, his face, his shoulders; only his flickering eyes show whites. Johnny claws furiously at the sopping mud and unwraps the head cloth. A passing cloud, a moment of semidarkness, then the light. He stares at the hole in Casey's head through which a lewd, wet mass is protruding. His brain is seeping out of his skull. Johnny's bowels go cold. He cries out in a woman's voice.

"Brave lad! Brave son! I am here!"

Whatever is left of his consciousness acknowledges this man who has loved him. Casey hums. His head lolls, and he hums. Johnny pulls him close and grasps his hands, and by some supernatural effort, the boy responds by squeezing back. Then, with mineral slowness, the squeezing stops and he falls still. In shock, Johnny tries pushing the brain back inside the skull. The gray mass slides between his fingers. *This will not be memory. This part will be forgetting.*

He gathers up the bloody boy and sobs. "You were true warrior! I was your witness!"

He rocks him and he sobs, thinking how he had filled Johnny's emptiness with his wild-hearted love. How he had reminded him that, after all, there was still youth and beauty in the world.

He carefully wraps Casey's head again and thinks how he will carry him. Across his back like rice sacks as he had carried his brother, Ah Fat, when he was weak from hunger. He will carry him until he finds a place of rich, dark soil in which to bury him, then will let the fire dragons take him home.

Johnny Tom

Gettysburg, July 3, 1863

At dawn, a fine rain blows soft and cool; fog hangs in the treetops. Behind stone walls and breastworks and on the summits of hills they have defended, Union troops sit at campfires, filthy and exhausted. Through field glasses, their commanders watch Lee and his officers ride back and forth along Seminary Ridge, behind them scores of guns with their muzzles pointed at the dead center of Cemetery Hill.

All night, Johnny's Third Corps has limped up and down the fields, trying to find their men and reassemble. Careful where he steps, he calls out to them, the boy's body so light he feels he is carrying a child across his shoulders as he moves toward the central valley of the battlefield. A landscape of exploded gun carriages and horses, and mangled bodies as far as he can see.

He stands in abject wonder. And it is like a flashback to his youth: a yellow, pigtailed boy in rags carrying his starving brother on his back through war, through famine. People had even carried their dead for fear they would be eaten. And he wonders, *What since my youth has changed? It is all the same! This becomes that, and it is all the same.*

Still, he soldiers on, searching for those whom he had vowed to honor and protect. He thinks especially of Zebedee and Virgil, who are not experienced in battle, and looks for their dark faces. As straggling soldiers pass, he sees that *every* face is black from dirt, gunpowder, smoke. He staggers, then rights himself, unable to remember when he last ate or slept. *Must ignore quicksand of fatigue. Move exhalations forward!*

From Seminary Ridge, a ripple of movement as hundreds of gunners spring to their feet. For a few minutes, only eerie silence, then every Confederate gun in line is fired in one rolling crash—the loudest noise he has ever heard. Johnny collapses, covers Casey with his body, and claps his hands over his ears. Three hundred and fifty Rebel guns now hit the Federals, the worst massed cannonade they have ever seen or heard, rendering some men deaf forever. Whole caissons explode, projecting shot and shell, and there are shouts of exultation from Confederate lines.

He lies still, not knowing where to run, for he seems to be in the direct line of fire as shells whistle and burst into the ground.

"Third Corps, Third Corps!" he shouts.

Above him, the long snake of Cemetery Ridge is ablaze with fires as Federal guns come alive. The sheer scale of the shelling lets loose a terror within him that leaves him curiously detached. He pats Casey's chest consolingly. *Maybe now is my turn, but first will find good soil for this boy.* The shelling seems to go back and forth forever. Then, almost imperceptibly, it ceases, leaving the central valley a pall of smoke that lifts like a curtain.

There is such an astonishing number of Union dead that, in places where shelling was intense, they lie in stark, tidy rows as if whole regiments had made their bivouac there and gone to sleep. Here Johnny finds some of his own. A boy who had read him letters from his family in Maine. One who had given him warm socks and carried a tintype of his hunting dog.

And here is Rudi, the Italian boy who had taught him the beautiful word *primavera*. Spring. And though it was r-full and hard to pronounce, Johnny had bested it. He stares at the handsome, swarthy lad, remembering him and Casey as "best pards," always ragging each other, larking and waltzing together round the campfire. He carefully lays Casey beside him so they are touching.

"Here is your pard to keep you safe," he tells him. "When battle is over, I come back to bury you both honorably."

He picks up two pebbles and covers Casey's eyes. One pebble falls away. The eye stares at him and through him.

Now he moves on, calling out for Zebedee and Virgil. A dozen voices answer, telling him, "Get down! Get ready! Fix bayonet!" A line of Confederates has broken across Emmitsburg Road, and as they advance up the hill, Johnny sees he will soon be in the thick of it. He sighs with exhaustion, or maybe the weariness of killing, and that quick, Rebels are upon him. Johnny swings wildly with his knife; it catches flesh. He jerks it back and lashes left and right with the odd sensation of swimming. Men fall beside him or rush on.

Then one charges him with that eerie Rebel yell. He hesitates because it is a child and he is so tired of slaughtering children. In that moment, a projectile hits the ground; shell fragments take the youngster's jaw. Johnny cries out and kneels to comfort him, and another projectile hits the ground. He stands as if electrified, his arms and legs lit, then falls backward with a sense of falling in slow motion.

He is halfway up the heights of Cemetery Hill. Lying in a semi-recline against the upslope of the earth, he seems to float upward, and he is with his troops again.

"Dress it up! Dress it up!" a captain yells. The sound of hoofs pawing the ground, the jangle of cavalry accoutrements. His regiment moving stately through green fields, advancing in a long, blue wave...Rifles shouldered and gleaming, colors bobbing, officers leading on high-stepping horses, a beautiful thing! They wave to farmers as they pass...The corn is high, the cherries ripe...The captain shouts, "All right, boys! At route step forward, ho!"

Johnny wakes, and it seems he is transported from a dream into a dream. The smoke has lifted and all of the valley, like a great amphitheater, lies before him. He looks across at Seminary Ridge, and it is a painting that takes his breath. What will be known as Pickett's Charge presents itself to him. Fifteen thousand Confederates marching elbow to elbow, their line over a mile wide. Flank to flank, tattered flags waving, they gallantly advance, mounted officers with their swords drawn, their lines dressed as if for a parade.

In that moment, even the Union guns are still, men paralyzed by the beauty and drama unfolding as perfectly aligned Rebel troops descend the far slopes and commence to cross the valley—fifteen hundred feet of open ground— to reach the Union lines and try to take Cemetery Hill. It is an extraordinary thing to see and will not be seen again in this War, or ever again in any war. The color and pageantry of battle in the grandest style—noble, magisterial, utterly sacrificial.

The long gray lines come swinging up the rise until they are at the fence at Emmitsburg Road, two hundred yards away. Then over the fence and up the slope to Cemetery Hill, drummers drumming, bayonets agleam, their cavalry galloping beside them. As they surge forward, Federal cannons open up, and Rebel cannons answer, so that, for a time, nothing can be seen but dense coiling smoke. Then it lifts and Johnny watches them approach in magnificent order, their lines closing doggedly as shells knock out huge segments of their forces.

Over ridge and slope, orchard and meadow, they come, their movements so perfectly aligned it seems a kind of hymn. He cries out feebly, wanting to warn his comrades as the enemy advances, but wanting to warn the Rebels too. Wanting to tell these half-starved Southern boys that they will be outnumbered and outgunned. He wants to tell them he does not hate them, that he wants them to go home and live to be old men. He wants everything to stop, to finally stop.

There is the sickening Rebel yell as they move closer and Federal troops rush down from the ridge, pounding the earth. Johnny hears their curses as armies collide and go berserk. In the clash of over fifty thousand men, order is lost, commands ignored; they fight with rifles, bayonets, bare fists, their teeth. They fire into each other's faces and die with arms entwined like lovers. He waits to be trampled. His heart crouches in a wrestler's stance, but then it lifts above the battle like a phoenix. Through clattering bayonets, he hears the bony click of dice.

...*O, I remember! Worn mah-jongg tiles the color of duck fat...The sound of strummed lutes in that perfumed town Po Lin. Painted fingernails and toenails of magistrates, the almond fragrance of their sleeves...*

His recollections become a mixed-up tapestry of locust plagues, and guillotines, and eunuchs decoding the secret life of chopsticks.

...*And Raindance with her deer-hoof scent, and O, the boy with flaming hair galloping through snow on a snow-colored horse...And father saying, "Run!" So we not become "worm dumplings"...O, I remember!...*

He floats through archipelagoes of memories while the battle rages around him. Eventually, Confederate guns die down, exhausted. Union artillery continues ripping at their flanks as, barefoot and starving, Southern boys fall apart in human bits and pieces until the last of them go down. Dusk approaches, the battle blurs, the air turns soft and still.

* * *

Like a half-reclining spectator, Johnny moves his head left to right and sees the tens of thousands lying unattended, bodies flung into the crevices of rocks, and up in trees, and in deep thickets, entangled in gun carriages and exploded caissons. Survivors stumble from shelters and breastworks and gaze across the land in silence. The sound of horses snorting, a cavalry patrol picking its way, searching for their own. He calls out; they trot away. Night falls. Lanterns chisel the darkness as men move amongst the dead. Relays with stretchers touch a body, then pass on. He calls again, but no one hears.

Now a full, bright moon that sheds a soft, forgiving luster. From the rear of Cemetery Hill, someone plays a violin, and across the valleys and hills, across the fields and into the hearts of the wounded and dying, the strains of "Home Sweet Home" is borne on the soft, night breeze. Johnny does not know the song, but its sound is so plaintive he understands the sobbing that rises from the ranks of both armies as it is played over and over to exhaustion.

And it is in the silence after that the rains come, first as a whisper, then growing heavier, presaging a storm. The sky opens along Cemetery Ridge drowning campfires, flooding crimson creeks and streams. He parts his lips and swallows, letting the rain run over him. In the dark, he cannot see his body; he feels nothing of his limbs. His heart pounds. That is all he knows.

The rain soaks in, adding to his weight, causing him to sink down and down until his arms and legs are buried. *Whatever is injured, mud will heal.* During the night, he hears screams on the slopes below him. Rains are flooding the low ground; wounded men are drowning. In flashes of lightning, he sees an arm reach up above the deluge. He sees a face go under. It rains all night, a hard, forbidding rain. By dawn, the fields and valleys are a sea of mud.

He swims out of his dreams as stretcher crews lean over neighboring bodies. Johnny opens his mouth and calls, but no words come. Sliding and cursing, the crews move on. There is only the rain. And it is so cool and forgiving he slips back into dreams again.

...Wistful sounds of temple bells...Sages in blue robes the color of immortality gliding through grass the green of stop-horse jade...Ancient ears pressed to the pages of my history... Parables of my many shames...

When he wakes, a man is bending over him, trying to comprehend what he is looking at: a strange yellow face with a body virtually buried in mud. Johnny moves his lips, blinks rapidly. In the rain, his blinks are not discernable, his voice not heard. The man shakes his head, moves on.

The rains continue, a wretched and dismal July Fourth. Federal troops sit and stare, not knowing when the next Rebel charge will come. They spend the day caring for their wounded, collecting their dead, and waiting. That night, in pounding rains, Lee leads his dismally defeated Confederate Army in its retreat to the Cumberland Valley, slowed by a wagon train seventeen miles long carrying his wounded and dying.

At dawn the next day, the Union Army learns of Lee's retreat, and all through the fields and valleys there is shouting and rejoicing. Then men gaze out at the land, at the human cost, and their cries abruptly die out.

* * *

The rains have stopped, and now flies moon sedulously over the landscape. They have settled on his face like a mask, yet he does not feel their bite. Across the fields, men half-eaten alive by them cry out like infants. In dawning light there is movement again, stretcher-bearers gathering the wounded. Thousands of soldiers roam the field, stepping gingerly, in search of a brother, a comrade. Near Johnny, a young boy tries to wake his friend. He lifts his head and screams as the spongy mass rolls down the hill.

"Leave it. Leave it." Someone walks the boy away.

Johnny calls out, "Please…over here…"

He thinks he is calling. When he opens his mouth, it is full of flies. He dozes again, and when he wakes someone is leaning over him, trying to brush the flies away. He thinks he sees Virgil peering down, his puppy eyes lit with terror. Johnny blinks rapidly.

"It him," Virgil cries. "He alive!" With bare hands he begins digging and flinging the mud away.

Stretcher-bearers approach, resembling bandits with kerchiefs covering their noses and mouths. They silently look down.

"Corporal John Tom!" Virgil cries. "He with our company."

Johnny tries to speak again. He tries to move. Men lean closer, look down at his body, then look at each other and shake their heads.

"You got to! He alive! Alive!"

Virgil's cries unsettle them. One of them lowers his kerchief from his mouth and speaks to Johnny. "Corporal, we're going to try to move you now."

And he is charged with lightning that momentarily blinds him. Bolts shoot through him, rendering him senseless. When he comes back to consciousness, there is the creak and jolt of wheels beneath him. Rags of sentences float to him from the ambu-drivers.

"…surgeons at the rear collapsing…some gone insane. They're even running out of saws…"

He rolls back and forth in the dank smell of his own blood. Hours pass, maybe days. He wakes again to new smells. Chloroform. Tobacco. The breath of a smoker leaning close, his voice incredulous.

"Oh, sweet Jesus…Look at this." The voice grows fainter as if, in shock, the man has stepped away. "I say this with a Christian conscience. Why bother?"

Comprehension seeps in, and Johnny considers the question. *Why bother?* For something in his deepest core longs for peace, a quiet glade.

The smoker's breath again, so close. "All right. If we must, let us proceed."

He opens his eyes. As if through a scrim, he sees the blood-spattered apron, the surgeon's eyes, glassy and gummy with exhaustion. Something hovers and comes down on his face, the bitter, etherish smell of chloroform. He breathes in and out, and time collapses. The War grows soft and distant.

And they drift past…Laughter, Raindance. Tropic jungles. Steamy bayous. It all drifts past. Only the musty emanations of a book remain…Its pages turning right to left, its Scriptures reading left to right…A yin and yang that comforts him as he scribbles on…telling and telling…

Lightning comes again. Great bolts of it that harness him and rein him in. Years seem to pass; the feel of scored flesh grows tighter. The reins in his mouth grow shorter, so his neck arches back, rendering his mouth useless. One day the reins are slackened, and slowly, almost grudgingly, Johnny reinhabits his body, each moment bringing new realization of what it will mean to be alive.

* * *

With great effort, he turns his head and sees Zebedee approaching at a dreamlike pace. He leans on a crutch, moving forward awkwardly, his midriff and stomach bound in bandages. He sits in a chair beside Johnny's cot in a large tent with rows upon rows of such cots. There is the sound of strangled breathing, a neighbor slowly expiring. The boy suddenly babbles, as if trying out a prayer appropriate to the end of his life.

Zebedee's eyes are red, the palms of his hands dead white. His skin looks dusty, and he seems to be talking to himself.

"...I jest kept rubbing tobacco in my eyes to stay awake. Eyes be like two balls of fire when they found me...But, praise Jesus, I still alive! Plugging my finger where that bullet went clean through me..."

He stares at the floor and shakes his head. "...weeks now, details burying the dead...thousands and thousands. Long, wide trenches, boys laid side by side...no gravestones, nothing. Jest headboards giving count of bodies. It ain't right..."

He wipes his eyes. "...still finding wounded. Can't believe they alive, half-drowning in they own blood...Devil wagons moving day and night...full of arms and legs, look like they waving. Devil surgeons sharpening they knives... try get me on the table. Can't wait to scoop out this old nigra, throw me in the dead pile..."

He stands up and waves a fist. "'Uh! Uh!' I said. 'Not this nigra!' Be throwing such a fit they toss me out, told me go die alone. And I still here! Old Zebedee still here!"

Hearing the rustle of sheets, he stares, then moves to Johnny's side. "Oh, Lord! You back. John Tom, you back!"

Eyes overflowing, he presses his lips to Johnny's cheek. He has come every day, determined to talk his friend back to life.

"Been conversating 'bout everything I know. Been praying and sleeping with your Bible so nobody steal your life. Now you back and going heal! Hear me, John Tom? You going heal!"

He feels strangely constricted; he can only blink his eyes. Zebedee presses a cup of water to his lips, telling how a nursing sister had washed the mud from Johnny's hair, then carefully braided it back into a queue. He moves his head, able to feel it still attached, lying beside his shoulder on the pillow. He tries to reach up and touch it, but his arms are bound.

Zebedee picks up the queue and gently waves it before Johnny's face, telling him how Gettysburg is now an immense field hospital—the town and its surroundings engorged with over twenty thousand wounded men laid out in people's homes, their living rooms, and bedrooms.

"Me and Virgil seen it with our own eyes, going in, out the houses searching for you. Rugs so fat with blood they be squishing. Books used for pillows so soaked they be floating."

For miles around, the wounded are being tended in barns, haystacks, churches, even in fields and ditches where they fell.

"But we won, John Tom. The Union won! Vicksburg 'bout to surrender in the West. This War near finished!"

What he does not tell him is that the Army of the Potomac has already marched south in expectation of the next engagement and has left behind shockingly few doctors and nurses in attendance. So appalling is the number of wounded waiting for attention doctors have begun the gruesome job of *triage*, separating men who are bound to die from those who might be saved.

In their search for Johnny, Zebedee and Virgil had discovered, in a nearby glade, hundreds of unattended, semiconscious men moaning and twitching fitfully. Partly incinerated, or with their skulls near gone, they had been put aside on the ground to die as slowly or as quickly as they might. Coming upon them, the two had frozen in horror.

Crawling up and down those rows in search of Johnny, Virgil had wept and turned aside to retch as he looked into the faces of boys whose brains were puddling in the dirt.

Some had bayonets still protruding from their skulls, their eyes dancing round in their sockets. As Zebedee made the sign of the cross over each of them, he had felt his testicles withdraw.

* * *

A nursing sister approaches, asking softly, "Is he awake?"

Zebedee nods. "I believe so, Sister."

She leans over him. "Hello, Corporal Tom. I'm Sister Ruth. Are you in pain?"

He wonders how to answer. *Is there a right way? And a wrong way?*

She wears flowing black robes beneath a colossal white structure balanced on her head like a cathedral. Her face is pale and kind, and he wants to ask her to unbind his arms and legs. Instead, he only nods his head. She returns with a needle, gently pulls back the sheet, finds a space midst all the bandages, and administers morphine meant for boys for whom there is still hope.

Then she straightens up and studies him. "Such a beautiful face. So stoic."

"He my best friend," Zebedee whispers.

"Does he understand where he is?"

"I be trying to explain to him."

Zebedee watches him nod off, knowing he will never tell Johnny where he is. "The Hopeless Compound," that is what they call it. A tent of forty or fifty patients tended by volunteer nursing sisters. There are almost two hundred such tents, set off away from hundreds of other tents where the wounded are expected to survive. By the end of July, eleven thousand men have been transported to city hospitals. What is left here are those too severely wounded to move, and they have been divided into those who *might* survive, and those not expected to live at all. Johnny is one of the "hopeless."

In a further declension, he has been put in one of the tents set aside for soldiers whom orderlies whimsically call "skins." Black skins, red skins, yellow skins. The soldiers brought in last from the battlefields whom surgeons administer to halfheartedly. They will not recover in this tent: their skin color has already pronounced them dead. Zebedee thinks on this at night when Sister Ruth lets down great gauzy veils of mosquito nets around each cot. He watches the white nets shiver in the breeze, and they appear to him as angels hovering over each man, spreading their wings to shelter and enfold them until they take them home.

A month passes, and he lingers. Sister Ruth, with her soft white wrists, brings him shots of brandy, and when his pain is too intense, she injects him with stolen morphine. And in the arms of Morpheus, Johnny euphorically divines that, because it is America, the great country he has fought for, America will fix him. He will be repaired.

When he comes back to consciousness, there is Zebedee dozing, and sometimes Virgil is there with his youthful, bounding gestures. In his shrill voice, he describes the immense harvest of discarded weapons left after the battle. Burial crews had attached bayonets to rifles lying in the fields and stuck them in the ground for later collection.

"You shoulda' seen, John Tom. Whole damn acres a rifles be standin' thick as treelin's. They sayin' thirty, forty thousand muskets left still loaded!"

In the madness of combat, boys had forgotten to fix their percussion caps or forgotten to pull their trigger, reloading repeatedly without ever firing.

Day after day they talk to him, praying for a response, even one word. Mostly, Johnny stares and, now and then, blinks. Zebedee comes to depend on those blinks. Two blinks approximate a sentence. One day, he stands close to Johnny's cot in his unbuttoned shirt and pants. His bandages have been removed, so it is possible, as he turns front to back and back to front, to show his gunshot wound to the abdomen and where the bullet exited through his back hip.

"See, John Tom? This here's my 'through and through!'"

A linen cord has been passed through the wound to drain it. Zebedee turns sideways, his right hand holding the thread in front, his left hand holding it in back. He slowly pulls the cord back and forth through his abdomen.

"Got to do this every day of my life. Else it be closing and turning infectious."

He leans close and whispers, "They be giving me a pension for this. You going get one too. We rich! Two rich boys."

"...Hurt?" His first clear word after weeks of silence.

Zebedee gasps with pleasure. "Oh, yeah. Hurt like hell. Smell bad too. But I'm alive. You alive! We going get better."

He does up his shirt and pants, near-breathless with plans. "We going take our pensions, build a house. Then we going find your girl and bring her home."

He pulls out Johnny's Bible that he has been keeping for him. "Meanwhile, I'm a read to you. Every day we be reading from the Good Book, till they put us on a train for one a them big city hospitals."

He reads slowly for effect, his rich baritone filling the silence, and one evening he jumps up from his chair. "What's that you say?"

"Write..." Johnny whispers. "Write me...my life..."

He endeavors to speak, but so softly Zebedee has to lean down, his ear to Johnny's lips. And in that way, hour after hour, day after day, he slowly tells and Zebedee writes, continuing his story, expanding and enriching the Scriptures of the Bible. Some nights Zebedee reads silently, piecing together Johnny's life. The starveling in China. The auction blocks in New Orleans. Raindance. The War. The aftermath.

He looks at his sleeping friend and smiles. "Such a life truly belong here. In the pages of the Good Book."

* * *

It has been eight weeks since the Battle of Gettysburg. Each day he drags himself from pain to pain from the bindings of his arms and legs. Some days he feels an urge, not to talk but just to listen and imagine.

He turns his head, his voice small like a child's. "Tell me...about...house we build..."

Zebedee slides his crutch aside and drags his chair closer. "Well...our house be on a slope, John Tom, so's we can see all the way to the river. Virgil going help us plant corn and beans. He got the touch..."

His voice takes on a dreaminess, envisioning his first house as a freeman. "Thas a white fence afront the house, a curving road with trees and shrubs so's no one can come calling without we seeing them arrive..."

He thinks of his future, life with a hole straight through his stomach that he will need to drain each day. And each day will be filled with the terror of gangrene. Then he thinks of Virgil, his manumitted slave-now-son who will take care of him. And of Johnny, his best friend, who will bless the house just by his being there to gaze upon it. Because that is all he will ever be able to do.

"...And horses, John Tom. They's going be horses tossing they heads and being beautiful. We going sit on the porch and watch they backs shining in moonlight. We won't never be hearing screams of dying horses no more."

The image is so peaceful and longed for he puts his hands to his eyes and weeps, knowing there will never be a house, never be a fence or horses, though he will live a long, long time.

Johnny whispers, "No...no cry..."

Only his head moves like a small, round-faced doll with the snake of his queue lying beside him. When Sister Ruth comes with his bedpan, Zebedee steps outside. Under her gothic wimple, she is small and rather frail, but has no trouble lifting him. The pain when she shifts his loins is so blinding he faints. His waste in the bedpan is that of a small pet, and each day there is less.

One day he asks her, "When...they unbandage my arms and legs? So tight... cannot move. Cannot breathe."

"Soon. Soon." She smoothes his brow and quickly walks away.

It is late afternoon when Virgil struggles with a man holding a camera, and pushes him along a path between the tents. "Git now! Jest git, you devil wit your devil eye..."

He runs to Zebedee with his fists balled up. "Them camera men be everywhere, crawlin' through these tents like lice. Takin' pictures of dyin' boys. Pictures of they wounds!"

Like crows, photographers have gathered, camping out in their wagons in the woods. They slip into the tents, posing as relatives, then quickly set up their equipment and record the unspeakable, the hardly believable. In cities, they will sell their pictures to collectors of "grotesqueries."

Late September now, and as nerve ends slowly come alive, Johnny has more sensation, more howling pain. Sister Ruth comes with her morphine, gently inserting the needle, watching his body relax. Under the sheet, his form is a small indentation. One evening she comes with a doctor, who leans down and studies him, for he is somewhat of a curiosity, having survived long past their expectations. The man is young and inexperienced, even in the shape of his moustache that he has shaved too much on one side.

"Does he understand?" the doctor asks.

Johnny feels a dull disquiet, not yet recognized as fear. He is suddenly beside himself, literally beside himself, as if a hidden calmness in him stands apart and watches his body take up attitudes of pleading. Then, in a moment of conscience he remembers that his actions will sum up his race's character forever. He therefore attempts a smile. With no means of comparison, the young doctor assumes that this is characteristic of Chinese. To smile in their dying.

He gathers his fading strength and asks, "Take off...bandages...please. Not want to die with...arms, legs...wrapped like...mummy."

The doctor looks at Sister Ruth, then leans down. "There are no bandages, Corporal Tom. They were removed weeks ago."

"Why...then..." he whispers, "...I cannot move?"

The man steps back and silently withdraws. Only Sister Ruth remains, her fingers stroking Johnny's face.

* * *

A quiet day. With great effort, he turns his head and, through lungs that are drowning, whispers, "Zeb..."

He moves quickly to his side. "I here. I always here."

"The War...is over?"

"Yes!" he lies.

"We...won?"

"Praise God...We won!"

"I am...American citizen now?"

"That's right! They got a medal for you too."

He smiles. How privileged, how rich he feels. *To die an American citizen.*

"What day...is now?"

"A beautiful October day...what we be calling Indian summer."

Raindance season. He lifts his head and smiles. "Zebedee...most cherished friend..."

He holds him for hours, feeling his body grow cold. He looks at that beautiful, ageless face and strokes his golden cheek. "I going find her for you, John Tom, I swear! Going hand your life in the Good Book to your girl."

They walk across grass thick with dew and Virgil fights back tears. "What we going do now?"

"Going bury him proper. Then we going go and find his girl."

"She prob'bly dead. Everybody dead."

"Well, then...we going know."

"But, Papa...What about our house? Our *freeman* house?"

Zebedee turns and places his hands on Virgil's shoulders. "Listen, boy, they already blame us for this War; now they going try and massacre us for losing it. We ain't *never* going be free. Never be equal. Not in this lifetime."

"Well, what we going do? How we survive?"

"We jest keep moving, living mainly in the spirit. Never revealing what we be thinking. Thas so they can't never reduce us, never completely destroy us."

Virgil nods and, in deep meditation, follows him.

WARREN

Chickamauga, September 1863

For six long months, Federal gunships and ground forces had besieged Vicksburg, Mississippi, until it was completely ringed by fire. In thousands of caves outside the town, women and children huddled and starved. While bombs leveled their city, they ate rat and snake and placed their dead in shrouds outside the caves they had dug out of yellow clay.

On July Fourth, over thirty thousand Confederate soldiers defending the city surrendered, crawling skeletal and ravaged from burning buildings. Shocked at their condition, Federal soldiers had drawn food from their haversacks, then knelt and fed the half-dead boys.

With Union forces now controlling the Mississippi, and with the Confederacy cut in two, Northern commanders now turn their gaze to Chattanooga. Lying just north of the Georgia border and considered the "Gateway to the Deep South," it stands on a bend of the Tennessee River at the meeting of two major railroads and guards the entrance to Rebel war industries in Georgia.

Undeterred by mounting defeats, General Braxton Bragg now leads his troops toward Chattanooga. "It is all that can save Tennessee. We must keep those crucial railroads in operation!"

For months, Union general William Rosecrans has held his Army near the town, aiming to cut the Chattanooga-Atlanta Railroad. Once reinforcements arrive from Vicksburg, he begins moving closer and by early September has established his headquarters there. Bragg's troops arrive and lure several divisions of Federals outside of Chattanooga, into the countryside just south of the Georgia border, near a creek called Chickamauga. With reinforcements flooding in, on the eve of their confrontation, each Army will have almost sixty thousand men.

The Battle of Chickamauga will be what Warren remembers most indelibly of the War. It will surpass Shiloh in horror and human loss, but he will ever recall it as his final reckoning, one that will challenge his honor, his loyalties.

* * *

September 19. Having lost the Mississippi River and the Battle of Gettysburg, Rebels now take on a blinding need to kill. Hollow-eyed, heartbroken, their Southland nearly taken, their divisions rush blindly forward. Many are barefoot, dressed in rags, yet each man's eyes reflect the terrible and divine calling—to die defending his homeland. They move at the quickstep, thousands upon thousands in serried ranks, gunstocks and bayonets shimmering in sunlight that, in broken arpeggios, runs up and down their lines.

Joe Wheeler urges his cavaliers forward. "Press on! Press on! The 'War Child' rides again!"

As battalions of cavalry join their troops, Warren tenses, squeezes his stump against his side, pulls tight on his reins, and fleetingly thinks how not one amongst them is more than one and twenty years, yet their faces and bodies are old, their smell abominable. Filthy and bloodthirsty, they fill the day with the promise of slaughter, for it has become their life. There is not one part of it they do not love, its multiple nostalgias, its fugitive perfumes—hot metal, exploding earth, the gore.

With untoward calm, the Confederate infantry advances, steady in their step, perfect in their alignment. For a moment, all is silent, then the fiendish Rebel yell, "Hey-Yeh-Yeh!

Hey-Yeh-Yeh!" And they have started on the double-quick, the half-trot as Federal troops open fire. In ragged, suicidal line, Warren and his troops ride toward the roar. Beyond caring, youth and memories gone, they toss down plugs of bull's eyes and ride on. He feels the tightening in his buttocks and his testicles as war brings him into its full scrutiny.

The "Forward" order is given, and he charges blindly, his horse leaping already fallen comrades. In the *hsss!* of shot and shell, he takes aim and shoots a Federal dead center in the forehead, then aims at another and takes him down. Ahead, four wounded *bluecoats* hold each other up like a barbershop quartet. He gallops right through them, then swerves his mount and shoots two of them in passing.

Pressing on, he feels no fear, no concern for his mortal life. Not since the Battle of Shiloh has he felt such total loss of being. What is gone now is the memory of what made him human. He has come to understand the word *bloodthirsty*—in his mouth the taste of blood, in his heart the thirst for more. Life has no other purpose now.

Backward and forward surge the lines, one hundred twenty thousand soldiers taking and losing the offensive, and it goes on for hours. A sudden impact, and Warren's horse goes down. Something bites him in the neck. He sits stunned, in blinding smoke and overwhelming stench. Men stagger as it rises above their ankles. They are awash in a valley of blood.

To avoid complete annihilation, troops are now recalled by their generals and fall back on both sides. Thousands of Confederates had gone into battle with strips of cloth wound round their hands in place of gloves, and round their feet in place of shoes. Many had newspapers stuffed inside their shirts and pants for warmth. Now bits of cloth and paper float through the air like scorched and wandering souls, and land on the shoulders and upturned faces of the dead.

* * *

His back is wet with blood. He feels enormous thirst and thinks if he must die, he would like a sip of water first. He turns his head and sees a wounded Federal struggling to retrieve a canteen from a dead man. Warren lies very still. The Federal's left leg and hip are gone. He has mashed a jacket against the gaping hole below his waist through which his blood flows copiously. He falls back clutching the canteen and drinks his fill, then, watching his life pour out of him, he sighs and places his revolver in his mouth. Warren cries out.

The man turns his head, takes the gun from his mouth, and thoughtfully points it at Warren.

"Water..." Warren whispers.

The man just stares.

"...Water, please. Then you can kill me."

Moments pass. Then, with great effort, the Federal holds the canteen out to Warren. "Drink...slow, Johnny Reb...else you...might could...choke..."

He drinks greedily, then slides the canteen back.

"Naw...just you...keep it..." The man collapses on his back.

The night is cold, and comes a chill from congealing blood that he is lying in, and from lifeless bodies all around. Shivering uncontrollably, Warren watches corpses turn a soft lavender and seem to become strangely aquatic, mingling their flesh with the colors of sunset. Finally, he dozes. The shot awakens him, the Yankee dead beside him.

Warren cries out, a childlike wail of abysmal loneliness, then edges forward and presses his body up against the dead man. The bullet has turned most of his face inside out. Still, Warren takes his hand and clasps it tightly in his own, as if through the force of desire he can bring him back to life. Through the long hours of the night, he clutches the hand and presses his body against the corpse, and intermittently he weeps, he begs for an end to it. But life is not through with him; it merely steps back and grants him respite.

And in that time, he dreams. Pale, slanted eyes. The smile with which she captivated him. But when she thought she was alone, that cold, remote expression that had puzzled him. Since her death he no longer sketches. Still, the War has continued to provide him with daily lessons in human anatomy. He has studied the major organs of men, has knelt over open skulls and stared at fluid brains. He has eaten his hardtack beside Union officers lying in random pieces. A torso here, a pelvis there.

After skirmishes, he has often knelt and studied hearts, stomachs, layers of muscle, things that held a man together. He has witnessed all that could be committed upon the human body, and wondered, *Where is an example of what could be done to the human mind?* In churches throughout the South, they had removed precious, stained glass windows, wrapped them in blankets to protect them, and carefully hidden them away.

If only they had done that with our minds.

* * *

Early dawn. His hand is empty, the Federal carried off by a burial detachment. Fog comes up from the warm waters of Chickamauga Creek and hangs over the battlefield so that litter-bearers appear as apparitions. He watches a nurse wring blood from her sodden skirt, her eyes completely wild as she stares across the landscape. Then he smells the greasy canvas litter as they lift him onto it.

At a field tent in the rear, he is swabbed and stitched where a bullet had passed through the flesh at the base of his neck. The surgeon studies the old, bunched-up shrapnel scars on his back and chest, the useless stump of arm. The leathery face, ancient eyes. He has heard this is a first-class cavalryman, a crack shot riding with Joe Wheeler. He wonders what Warren would be called in peacetime. Killer? Assassin? But that is what the Confederacy needs most now.

He leans close and speaks in soft, Southern tones. "That bullet wound is nothing. But, son…you are devitalized. I can see your mind's exhausted."

Warren sighs. "Yes, sir, I guess I am mightily tired. Aren't you?"

The surgeon's apron is filthy. Blood is matted in his hair, even in his eyebrows. His body trembles like a living nerve end.

"I believe I am mostly…tired of the truth." He holds a syringe to the light. "This will give you a few hours' rest. That battlefield will soon be but an abattoir."

He wakes to church bells tolling in the distance. Their peacefulness is soon made dissonant by the roar of Confederate artillery that commences the second day of Chickamauga. He begs several bull's eyes from a nurse, then makes his way to a paddock for a fresh mount and gallops back to what awaits him.

* * *

By midmorning, the battle is raging uncontrolled through fields, ravines, and heavily wooded areas. The generals of both North and South have lost all control of their armies as troops exultingly go berserk. By midafternoon, six miles of fields will be completely carpeted with corpses.

A trooper rides past Warren waving a human scalp. Union boys fresh from recruiting camps scramble backward, screaming as Rebel infantry pursue them. One of them bites off a boy's ear, stuffs it into his hatband and, whooping, rushes on. A second line of Union infantry advances, older, seasoned men who match the savagery of the Rebels, gleefully taking ears and noses with their Bowies. They go at each other until their weapons are exhausted and, in the carnage left by grape and canister, begin fighting with rocks, knives, bare hands, their teeth.

By four o'clock, Warren has shot twenty-seven men. He no longer knows what he is shooting at. He thinks he has shot several of his own. He steadies his mount as someone shouts his name.

"Petticomb! Wheeler's got a mess of Yanks behind that yonder breastwork...Yeee-Hahhh! The 'War Child' rides again!"

The mention of Wheeler brings him up sane. For he is still the symbol of all that is left of honor and gallantry. But as Warren nears the breastworks, it is not Joe Wheeler's regiment he sees but that of another cavalry commander, a clever strategist, but a man of such heinous vanity he constantly puts his troops at risk. It is said his men despise him. Now nearly a thousand of them press upon the breastworks, hemming in several hundred Federals.

Separated from Wheeler's corps, Warren and his troopers reluctantly urge their mounts forward to join the general's attack. Behind the breastworks, the enemy has run short of ammunition, and after two hours the Confederates have succeeded in surrounding them. As the sound of shooting dies, they appear through drifting smoke, waving white flags, their hands held high in surrender.

It is only when the smoke clears that Warren sees the Union soldiers are Negroes. At first, he is unsure. Then they step forward and light picks out their faces, the startling whites of their eyes. Silently, they line up, one hundred ninety men, as the cavalry troops prepare to take them prisoner.

Cold-eyed, self-consciously erect in his saddle, the Confederate general rides slowly back and forth before them. Back and forth. In the silence, Negro soldiers murmur, trying to keep their lines straight, hands held high, their white flags aloft. One of them steps forward and executes a perfect salute.

"Suh! We'uns surrendah! Suh!"

The general continues riding back and forth, studying each face as his horse engages in a kind of dance. Then, finally, he slows down and stops.

Thoughtfully, he strokes his beard, then theatrically shifts his saber in its skirt, turns back to his men, and shouts, "Shoot them!"

His troopers sit motionless and stunned.

Again, he shouts in a beautifully modulated Southern drawl, "Shoot them, I say! Every...last...one. I!...Am!...Youah!...Commanding Officah!"

The Negroes stare in disbelief. Their white flags flutter.

In the silence, the general shouts again, "Do you men heah me? Why...they don't even exist. There...ah...no *nigra* soldiers...fighting in this War. SHOOT THEM!"

Men from Wheeler's corps ride forward, shouting, but too late. They hear the shots, volley after volley. They see the Negro soldiers fall, line after line of them. Then, silence. The general lifts his hand, staying Wheeler's men, for this is his command, his corps. Still pompous and erect, he rides up close to the bodies, making sure each man is dead. If there is movement, he ceremoniously points his pistol and shoots.

Warren sits rigid on his mount, feeling blood bulging in the veins of his temples, the pumping of his heart. He sinks deep within himself, into the white-hot furnace of his rage where there is no logic or rationality. Only the voices of the dead men calling out for vengeance. And it is easy now, so easy. Everything fluid, all is known. The gloom of battle is lifted, and all the dying in him comes to life. He spurs his horse and gallops toward the general, while the man smiles down at the corpse of a Negro soldier. Still smiling, he lifts his head as Warren slows his mount and trots up close.

Returning the general's smile, he points his revolver. "You...Goddamned forsaken...bastard!"

He shoots him point-blank between the eyes, then another bullet to the heart. The man falls in slow motion to the ground. Warren turns his horse to face the troops, waiting to be shot. The general's troops do not react. Many shake their heads, staring at the ranks of dead and unarmed Negro soldiers. They do not even cast their eyes upon the general.

He flings his arms wide, *begging* them, wanting the impact of the bullet. In the silence, he finally turns to his own men, offering himself to them. Uneasy, they cast their glances back toward the still-raging battle, then spur their horses, motion for Warren to follow, and are gone. He looks back once at lines of Negro soldiers dead against the earth, then finally turns his horse and trots away.

Moving slowly through fog and smoke of battle, bituminous dust of shot and shell, he crosses a landscape lit by men on fire, hordes of blue and gray jackaling each other. Trotting more swiftly now, he leaves that world behind him, and drags his extinction out of the War.

* * *

Keeping to deep woods, he heads west toward the Mississippi River, passing burnt-out farmhouses whose still-
glowing frames assume a melancholy beauty like an artist's
rendering in embers. A rake hoards the moon in its curved
prongs, recalling for him the hardscrabble lives of toil and
simple joys for which he had been fighting. Gone now, forever gone.

Avoiding the shores of the Tennessee River plied by
Union convoys, he pushes deeper into sweet gum and
scrub-oak woods and slowly crosses Northern Alabama.
At the scene of a recent skirmish, he finds the corpse of a
Union officer, strips off his own ragged clothes and pulls on
the man's shirt and trousers, slouch hat, and frock coat with
the bars of a cavalry captain. He buries him and moves ever
west toward the Mississippi River, still hearing cannons,
deadly and distant.

He rests in caves, covering his horse's muzzle when Federal troops pass, then presses on through Mississippi, hardly
gazing north toward Corinth and Shiloh, just over the Tennessee border, where for him it all began. Somewhere near
the banks of the Mississippi River, he beds down and sleeps,
letting his horse graze on oat grass and fallen apples so it
fleshes out to look like a Union mount, not a half-starved
Confederate horse. It had served him well in battle, and he
speaks to it softly as he brushes its coat and combs its mane.

He grills three squirrels and eats till he is stuffed so he
won't have that desperate look, then cleans his teeth with
shredded twigs and scrubs his body in a stream, appalled by
the handfuls of lice that rinse off him. He washes and pats
down his hair, then brushes the frock coat and wipes and
shines his boots. Lastly, he counts Union coins he has found
in a pocket, and exclaims at a gold watch and chain tucked
inside an inner pocket.

Smelling the moldy odor of ancient silt and alluvial sands, he knows he is nearing the river. Gradually, deep woods step back, the sky grows huge, and he beholds the great Mississippi, its currents moving swiftly in places, gently in others. He trots along a rise until he sees a narrow bend in the river where a barge landing has been carved out of the levee. Warren dismounts, walks his horse down to the landing and rings a bell repeatedly until, from the opposite shore, the bargeman rings an answering bell.

He has neatly pinned up the sleeve of his coat, showing the bars of a Union cavalry captain. Now he remounts and sits high in his saddle, on his face the expression of an officer on the winning side of the War. The bargeman approaches, an old redneck whose eagerness and mercenary smile broadcast that he has gone over to the Union side to ensure his source of income. He poles closer, throws a looped rope round a stake in the earth, and grins.

"Hidy, Cap'n...Whar ya bound?"

Warren nods and wordlessly points to the opposite shore.

"Oh, a man of frugal words! Wal...guess ya be wantin' to cross. That's ten dollars silver. Union currency, o'course."

He hesitates, then hands forth all his coins.

"Wal, hell, Cap'n...That wouldn't even get ya horse across! Say, how come ya riding out alone?"

He whispers hoarsely, pointing to his bandaged neck.

"Oh...ya headed for that floating hospital on t'other side. Wal, this ain't near enough silver. I'd take ya brass buttons, but they'd string me up for that."

He gapes as Warren dangles the watch and chain before him.

"Lawd! That's simon-pure gold. I do know Yankee gold."

Gleefully, he examines the watch and pockets it as Warren dismounts, leads his horse onto the barge, and secures the reins to the railing. The horse prances with timorous steps until he quiets him, readjusts his haversack, and checks his revolver in its pommel holster. The bargeman frees the anchor rope and shoves off with his pole. Beneath his shirt, his muscles bulge from years of working the river. Warren eyes him, keeping his hand close to his holster.

As they work their way across, he stands erect, saluting when a Federal gunboat passes. Then another. There is so much activity on the river he is hardly noticed. If he is stopped and challenged, he will shoot his way out, or they will shoot him dead—it does not seem to matter. He squints hard against the sun, the weight of desertion on his mind.

Soon, as easily as a side step, he will be in Arkansas, then the Midwest and the far West of America—mysterious, unknown terrain toward which hundreds of thousands of deserters, homesteaders, and adventurers are already heading. He vows to avoid them, to strike out far from anything resembling civilization. He will instead head north, maybe all the way up to the wild Canadian territories. Saskatchewan, Manitoba. Names that suggest the end of all human habitation.

His hand on the railing feels sunburned. The barge creaks as it tips on the surface of waves. His horse snorts and shifts to rebalance itself, and the far shore draws closer. A hospital ship looms into view, the wounded on stretchers lined up for miles. Cavalry escorts trot to and fro, a blur of *bluecoats*. Through clouds of mosquitoes, Warren urges his horse up the levee, then looks back across the Mississippi at his homeland. For a moment, he feels run through, knowing he will not see it again.

The hospital ship is huge, thousands of wounded being carried up its ramps from ambu-wagons and trains. There is so much traffic back and forth no one acknowledges him but for an occasional rank and file who salute him. He walks his horse through crowds, then spurs him to a trot.

* * *

Since the Battle of Pea Ridge, the Confederate state of Arkansas is now pretty much in Union hands. Rebel guerrillas roam the woods, skirmishing with Federals, and after several hours Warren comes upon fresh corpses, finds suitable homespuns, and trades his uniform for them. He is now a civilian, his stump of arm and bandaged neck proof of having served honorably. Still, he lacks discharge papers, so for weeks he rides by night and by day dozes in hollows and bush shelters, a halt and infirm progress drifting ever north.

Some nights, from the paltry cache of his tired mind she rises unbidden, and he thinks of what had been done to her, things she told him at the end. Things she had shouted. Sometimes his stump aches. He presses it with his fingers to intensify the pain, recalling the sight of her fleeing on his horse. Recalling the shot, Era losing hold of the reins and falling from the saddle. In his mind he sees her dragged by the galloping horse, jagged rocks tearing her apart. He sits in a stupor of loss and recrimination.

Other times, when he thinks of her, his horse rears up, feeling the rage inside him that makes his body vibrate. She had deceived him in a way that had nothing to do with war. He had been used, not loved. Not loved at all. Each word, each gesture, even her eager passion, had been born of connivance and strategy. Memories seize him till he cannot rest, cannot sleep.

Entering Missouri, he cautiously approaches civilization, taking odd jobs with blacksmiths and tanners at trading posts. He purchases forged discharge papers and decent clothes, then hires on with small ranchers who stand amazed at how excellently he rides and ropes. He fleshes out and begins to look normal, a rangy, ruggedly handsome man prematurely aged by war. He glimpses old headlines that tell how Ulysses S. Grant defeated Braxton Bragg at the Battle of Chattanooga, effectively ending Bragg's field command forever.

Still bound for the wild Canadian territories, Warren drifts farther north, but then is drawn to the boomtown of Chicago, its stockyards and rodeos. And he begins to work the rodeos, drawing crowds as a one-armed buckaroo—calf roper, bull rider, anything they offer him. And it is here in this city of large human congregations that he sees the homecoming of soldiers from enemy prisons and hospitals—the starved, the grievously wounded, their minds completely gone.

Brass bands pipe them home, brief moments of celebration as they are handed down in wheelchairs and stretchers. Most are addicted to opium and morphine, the "soldiers' disease," identified by leather pouches worn round their necks containing morphine tablets, or leather bags containing syringes and needles issued to them on discharge. They are legless or blind. And some are faceless boys behind tin masks, to whom mirrors will forever be forbidden.

* * *

Months pass as the War ravels to its end. He no longer looks at headlines. Union victories, cities in flames. Finally, Robert E. Lee surrenders. For days Warren sits in his rented room, staring at a wall. The wall has lungs, it palpitates, and everything comes back to him. Each battle fought, each friend killed. And a girl, barely a woman, galloping through sun-dappled leaves, across her back a spreading crimson. *Era, woman of lightning, forever falling.*

One day, he rouses himself. Everything is dead but him, and he wonders Why? Why he is still alive? He thinks to pack, move on, but where? To what purpose? He tries to leave, but something holds him back. Something in this city is not through with him. He goes back to working the rodeos, and when they are slow, he works the stockyards where longhorns are driven up from Texas.

By now, cattle life has turned him tanned and sinewy. His aged, lined face is still rather handsome, his hair still blond though shot with gray. There is his leanness and his height, and the long, loping stride of a horseman. Only his eyes give strangers pause, eyes that have lost their civilization. And there is a certain way he looks at folks, distilling them down, as though seeing them for what they are.

Still, a cattleman befriends him, a transplanted Virginian who had stood firmly *against* his state's secession, thus had been forced to flee. Out of nostalgia and curiosity, he invites Warren to his home. He comes with trepidation, for it has been five long years since he entered a house not under attack. Gothic mirrors that reflect his haunted eyes. Antimacassars that recall decaying bones protruding from the earth like rotting crochet. He stares at heavy cutlery lined up like weapons as a servant slides onto his plate a slab of red beef not unlike a torn-open belly. Warren clutches the table and flees the room. His hosts apologize and calm him with whiskey, avoiding all discussion of the War.

Wanting to show off her orchids, the hostess guides him out to her garden, telling in mournful tones how she misses Virginia, how the winters here are cold and raw, as are the people. Inside a greenhouse, the air is uncommonly thick and damp. The orchids repulse him, looking carnivorous and famished.

She pridefully names each one for him: "*Vanda Sanderiana, Phalaenopsis, Cypripediums, Dendrobiums, Oncidiums.*"

Row upon row with open, waiting mouths. Even their names sound carnivorous.

Warren catches his breath as if he will faint. "Forgive me. I am not yet accustomed to…civilized things."

She speaks in soft Virginia tones. "Yes. Perhaps it is too much. Chicago is so verily uncivilized I feah I am trying to recreate something of home…for we can nevah go back. Nevah!"

She throws her head back, fighting tears, and the motion draws his gaze upward. Through the glass roof of the greenhouse, the sun comes out and filters through the panes, and before Warren's eyes, a thousand ghosts take shape. Phantom boys in Confederate uniforms forever young and smiling. He cries out and lifts his arm as if warding off a blow.

The woman looks up. "Oh, yes…photographic plates from the battlefields. Hundreds of thousands discarded. There was no demand for additional prints since their subjects, those poor boys, had all been slaughtered…"

She glances at his pinned-up sleeve. "My deah man! Forgive me if it brings back memories. I did not think. These negatives are fading, as you see, but one can still make out the images…"

She explains that, long before the War had ended, Southern photographers went bankrupt and were forced to sell their glass plates that had been used for negatives. Many were shipped North and purchased for greenhouse panes. While she talks, thousands of boys with their sunshot smiles and strong, young limbs hover over him like angels. The sun has already begun to fade their faces.

He imagines hundreds of thousands of glass panes like these shimmering in greenhouses across the land, lit with the smiles of youths who will slowly turn to phantoms, then fade and burn away. He shakes his head, his cheeks wet, and he does not care.

Finally, he pulls himself together. "I wonder if you could tell me…where did you find these plates?"

"Why, downtown," she tells him. "Where all the daguerrean galleries are, those three or four blocks they call Photographer's Row. Every window filled with pictures from the
War."

* * *

For weeks, he circles Photographer's Row the way an addict
might circle a drug, knowing it can harm him. He comes at
night when shops are closed, when he can stand before images in the windows and feel their gaze upon him. Memories overwhelm him, and he walks away. But days later he
returns, glancing sideways at their faces, angelic in death,
and those fresh from battle, looking as though they will
never be sane again.

When it grows late, the streets empty, he speaks aloud
to them, telling them he is lost without them, that he does
not know what to do with time. He avoids that district for a
while; it draws him back repeatedly, and he sees other veterans haunting the shops, drawn beyond their will. They
pass in the dark and stop and stare, as if finally grasping
the full mystery and terror and holiness of what they had
experienced. It was urgently *their* War, *their* story, and it has
reached in a thousand ways into their hearts. Thus, a part
of them will forever remain in those fields, in the declension of the valleys and ravines, in the small, earthly dips and
pauses. The preludes and afterludes.

One window displays photographs of men dressed like
raving women in fezes, bloomers, and gaiters—Confederate
regiments of Louisiana's Fire Zouaves. Another offers "Confederate Humor"—a Negro's head fitted onto the shoulders
of a headless Federal corpse. Some pictures are unspeakable, partial faces staring out as if importuning the viewer to
abhor them. Warren quickly walks away.

But one night, in the corner of a window he glimpses a picture of two Chinese with long queues wearing Federal uniforms. He leans close and stares, and returns to that window repeatedly. One day he steps into the shop, glancing at pictures of Europeans, American Indians, an Inuit Eskimo, in Confederate and Union uniforms. Not sure of his intentions, he asks the dealer if he has ever seen a picture of a Chinese soldier identified as Johnny Tom. The man consults a file and shakes his head. He enters other shops, and dealers pause, trying to conjure an image to match the name. They rifle through photographs and shrug their shoulders.

But one man thoughtfully sucks his pipe. "There are shops over on Evans Street that specialize in 'Orientalia and Exotica.'"

He tries several Evans shops until he comes upon one advertising "Rare and Unbelievable Grotesqueries. Enquire Within." The sound of a tinkling bell as he enters. On an easel, a photograph of a bare-chested woman with another miniature woman emerging from her side, the caption reading, *Attached at Birth*. On another, a gibbon-faced boy clandestinely half turning, exposing a taillike appendage. Instantly repulsed, Warren turns to leave, but a dapper little man appears.

"Good day. How may I serve you?"

He turns back. "I'm looking for…that is, I wonder… Have you ever seen a picture of a Chinese soldier named Johnny Tom?"

The man fingers his stickpin. "I have thousands of photographs of Chinese. Children, lotus-foot women—yes, even soldiers. Unfortunately, they are not available for viewing…unless you are a collector."

"I have money," Warren tells him. "Gold coins."

"Well…let us see…"

He steps into a back room, and for a while there is only the sound of his humming. When he returns, he looks immensely pleased. "I may have found your man. Was he a Union soldier?"

"Yes. I believe."

He ceremoniously opens a folder, then steps back and smiles. A Chinese man, eyes open wide, his black queue lying alongside his naked torso. Warren cannot at first register what he sees, or does not see.

The dealer reads notations on a card accompanying the photograph. "'Union soldier. Wounded at Battle of Gettysburg, July 1863.' Then I suppose hack surgeons did the rest. Says it took him three months to die."

Warren looks down in shock. "Was he…alive in this picture?"

"Oh, heavens, no! The photographer paid someone from a burial crew to open his eyes. They did that with thousands of corpses. Sometimes they slipped into hospital tents and positioned the dying men themselves. But this one…you see why it's a collector's dream!"

He braces himself and looks again. A human without arms or legs. Only a head and torso, and little stubs. The caption is written in elegant cursive: *Johnny Tom, The Chinese Human Pillow!*

The dealer leans close and smiles. "A steal at fifty dollars."

When Warren's vision clears, he is hoisting the man in the air by his throat.

"Listen closely, you little *ghoul*, or I will verily snap your windpipe. I want the negative and all the prints of this."

Gasping, he cries out, "I have only this print, I swear! From an itinerant photographer passing through the city…"

Warren drops him to the floor, tucks the folder with the portrait under his arm, and throws coins on the counter.

"Should I see another such print from your shop, God's truth, I will come back and shoot you *dead*."

In his rented room, he stares at the image for hours, trying to understand why he had purchased it. Perhaps out of decency. Or out of the need to know that her story had been true, that a father did exist. That *she* had really existed. Sometimes he thinks he has imagined her.

Yet while he sleeps, the portrait of Johnny Tom burns into his mind, his features recalling a passion and strength that had been loosed in the daughter in all its fury. He wakes with a quavering all through him and moves to tear the photograph to shreds. But the suffering, the imagined heroism of the man, forbids him. His image conjures up not just the horror of the War, but magnanimous valor and gallantry.

ERA

Washington, DC, 1864–1865

It is the hour of *aperitifs*. She has come to know the word
from wounded noblemen in their secluded ward, who had
journeyed from Europe to fight in America's Civil War. An
Italian count. A Bourbon prince. A Swedish baron with re-
current bowel infections. Russians, Hungarians. Titled Eng-
lishmen.

Pale, slender men with archetypal weak chins who spend
their days discussing the Peloponnesian War and various
approaches to theodicy, they are adored by the nursing sisters, for they seem to personify what noblemen should be.
With their aromatic colognes and privileged airs, they make
war look stylish and reasonable. A few are so nonchalant
about the gravity of their wounds they die utterly surprised.

She rarely ventures into their ward except when called
upon to read. When she enters, they tactfully lower their
eyes in deference to her limp, yet curiosity about the limp
attracts them. That and her exotic eyes, the golden skin, her
implacable indifference to them. As she sits reading to a patient, she feels their eyes on her back and on her neck, exposed beneath the ugly bun and hairnet.

One glance of hers takes in their hand-lasted boots and
signet rings bearing family crests. Some have arrived with
retinues of personal physicians, tailors, even chefs. During their meals, there is the delicate *ping!* of a finger tapping crystal, which will forever resurrect for her their silver
trays, their meticulous utensils holding delicate fruits, the
prismatic reflection of things called "finger bowls," which
they dab at after their little fruit bowls have been cleared,

and she is struck dumb by the dazzling miniatures of their improbable lives.

In her absence, they discuss her with the incautious intimacy of the privileged. "A comely form, but such strangely hued yellow skin…"

"Yet, have you noticed? In certain light, a reddish tone, rather like apricots."

"The eyes, though! As if she had outstared the devil."

A monocled Hungarian speaks in halting English. "Nonetheless, heart-takingly beautiful. For such a woman, we fight duels."

She is more relaxed with the rank and file, broken and dying boys consigned to thousands of tents across the hospital grounds. Here in the open she can breathe, feel human again, for there had been a period of darkness that consumed her, and in that time she was kept apart. Doctors diagnosed it as nerves.

Eventually, she began to recall the shouts of Confederates on a picket line, the galloping horse, and being half-dragged alongside it, clinging to the reins. Then the timbre of shouting voices had changed as scouts reined in the mount, which had run itself to exhaustion behind Federal lines. When they pulled her from the horse, its withers and back were covered with her blood.

At first, there was such pain it had seemed easier to die. But doctors whispered over her that there was something else, something alive, and they marveled at how it had survived, that it was yet thriving. In her delirium, Era had thought they were discussing the bullet.

When she regained full consciousness, a surgeon had informed her, "We had to take one of your lungs. Miraculously, the fetus seems fine."

He gave her the bullet for a keepsake. "Now, why don't you tell us who you are. Where you came from."

Eventually, she had asked to speak to a commanding officer. A colonel would not do, nor a brigadier general. She mentioned certain names, and the aide to a major general came. Then the general, and with him members of a Federal Intelligence team. They recorded everything she told them. Messages, couriers, the sutler named Wickett with the crimson hat.

When her information was confirmed, Era asked about her father, Corporal Johnny Tom. The Army had no ready information. She then asked to be transferred to a hospital in Washington, DC, as close as she could get to Falmouth, Virginia, from where he had last written. Nurses were desperately needed in the East, and when she was well enough she was sent to Washington by train.

* * *

Harewood Hospital is one of the largest and best equipped in the East. Its grounds are spread over several miles, and transportable cripples are sent here from as far west as Mississippi. Each day, Era watches trains bring boys who have had one or both legs amputated and have not yet been fitted with prosthetic limbs. On station platforms, the sheer numbers of their litters stretch beyond a mile and dominate the landscape.

Beside the main hospital, there is a kind of natatorium built into the calm tributary of a river. The water is clear and only shoulder-deep. On warm days she and other nurses and orderlies wheel out amputees and guide them down long, wooden ramps, at the end of which they are lifted into the water. There they lie floating and paddling while the staff at the water's edge watch over them.

Some have been amputated below the knees, others have no legs at all, merely stumps. As they splash about, only their heads show, and occasionally a young boy smiles. There is enough of him left to smile, for in those moments he is whole again. Then they swim to the water's edge, pull themselves up with their arms, and crawl upon the bank to bask in sunlight. Later, they are wrapped in blankets, lifted into wheelchairs, and guided back across the lawns.

There are others, with severed spinal cords, whose lower bodies are intact but have been rendered useless. In the water, their young faces and perfect torsos gleam as they stroke eloquently with their arms while their lower bodies, like giant tails, float aimlessly behind them. Era closes her eyes, envisioning mermen. At night, when she thinks of these boys, she weeps.

Now one of them pulls himself from the water and asks her to read to him. Something in his face makes her want to read William Blake, and she goes to the ward of noblemen to retrieve her book. A nursing sister intercepts her.

"It is their hour of *aperitifs*. Just now they will be flirtatious. I will bring your book."

Later, she reads to the boy, a poem she had long ago favored.

> *Let us agree to give up love/*
> *And root up the Infernal Grove,*
> *Then shall we return and see/*
> *The worlds of happy Eternity...*
> *And throughout all Eternity/*
> *I forgive you and you forgive me...*

He does not ask her what it means. He has lost interest in meanings. Still later, she helps him turn over on his stomach to sleep, flopping his lower body like a fish. She smooths his sheet and touches his hair and walks into the darkness. In a distant ward, the howling of the lost ones, those who will never return from the War. They have completely detached; their existence now appalls them.

The European ward is quiet, except for light snores. In the dimness, Era stares at noble profiles, men with their titles and their retinues who, in her eyes, had come to the War for mere diversion. She imagines draughts of costly liquors racing along subterranean channels of their privileged minds. In that moment, she wishes them legless and armless. Wishes them an eternal howling.

* * *

In her tent, a Negro girl watches over the infant. He has become a fixed point, a place where reality takes hold. A kind of twin to her wound, the thick welt on her back she can feel with her hand. Lung shot, heart missed by a filament, but the fetus intact. A *miracle*, the surgeon had said. She was never really shocked by the fact of the child inside her. She was so far beyond being shocked by then.

Not having named him, she calls the infant "He." It is Thespia, the Negro girl, who holds him all day and nurses him. But sometimes Era whispers certain words to him, and he burbles as if he understands. When she falls silent, he stares at her with a blankness suggesting idiocy, or the abiding shock of a creature lately brushed by death.

Some nights she holds the bullet in her palm, wondering at how close it brushed the womb. Had he felt the tremors? The jarring intrusion? That it had nearly killed them both is perhaps a tension they share, an invisible thread connecting them. Yet, as time passes, she acknowledges that it is something deeper, more elemental, that connects them. This perfect creature, this wholeness, has come forth from her.

Perhaps this is all I will be given in life. All I will be given of life. With infinite tact, she traces the outline of the child's face, and each of his limbs, and feels momentary surrender, a nobleness of the heart. At the same time, she is convulsed with the urge to protect him, to keep the world away from him. His existence now renders *her* existence plausible, and somehow deeply moral.

It is rumored amongst the nurses that she had served as a spy behind enemy lines, and then was wounded. They hear the mewling of the infant and see the dark girl rocking it, a pale-faced, sallow little thing, but with its mother's slanted eyes. No one conjectures about the father. Rebel? Yank? No one cares. The War has fathered so much death a thousand such infants seem meager compensation.

Some nights Era slips into the river and swims, recalling the child's birth. How, as her time drew near, she left the hospital grounds and nested in the woods. How, alone, she had squatted and grunted until it dropped out, then ate the placenta as her mother had eaten hers. Lips stained like a wolf's, she had stared at the newborn, and in that moment, it looked alien, not of her species. She had slid her fingers round its throat and slowly squeezed. But then she had heard its heartbeat, a tiny sledgehammer banging, a plea for clemency.

Occasionally, she walks beside the river with a short, stocky Russian, Ivan Golgoff, who is busy documenting the wounded at Harewood. He has seen both sides of the War, having spent months in Mississippi and Tennessee. A spy for the Federals, he had set up a photography shop in Nashville where he forged traveling papers for couriers. He had forged papers for her.

In the past several months she has allowed him to photograph her, for which he has paid her generous sums. She is saving the money for her future, she tells him, allowing herself to imagine a future tending her father and her child.

"And where your father is now?" he asks.

Era shakes her head. "So much chaos they are not sure. After the Battle of Gettysburg, his division was dispersed, transferred to other corps. I have enquired at the newspapers for casualty lists, the Sanitary Commission, the Christian Commission, who search for missing soldiers. So far, there is nothing…"

One day, Ivan tells her he is leaving. "War is winding down; Union has no more use for me. After four years I am tired, will go somewhere new, make my fortune."

He has been her only friend and she implores him to stay. "Washington is a big, thriving city…"

"Washington is exhausted! Here people want to forget. I will go West, somewhere not so touched by war. They will be fascinated by my photographs. Many collectors for such things."

He asks her to go with him, to marry him.

Era smiles and shakes her head. "You Russians are beguiled by all things American, even our War…even our broken women. I will never marry. But I will not forget you."

She limps away, a woman whose life has tilted sideways. Yet, when she turns to wave, there is still the beautiful and haunting face.

* * *

The big battles in the Western Theater are nearly over now, and Ulysses S. Grant has turned his armies to the East, heading toward Richmond, capital of the Confederacy. His general, William Tecumseh Sherman, now leads Federal troops in his "March to the Sea," leaving whole cities leveled and in flames. Atlanta, Columbia, Charleston. Era thinks of her little town, Shisan, which no longer exists. The War is her only home now. It has marked her in a thousand ways, and its passing threatens to take her with it. All that can save her is her father.

At night she tosses and rubs the smooth bone of her mother's knuckle. And here is a bull's eye to help her sleep. She breaks off a portion of it for Thespia, whose dreams are haunted by kinfolk perishing in flames. She thinks of slipping a bit of opium into the mouth of the whimpering child, but something inside her forbids it. She associates its well-being with her father's survival. It is only when she thinks of the *child's* father that she wants to bite down hard on its soft, infant skull. For she had loved him, and he had tried to destroy her.

The day Ivan departs, she feels very old. The child seems old too, pale and listless, as if knowing it is not his mother who tends him and sings to him. But some nights Era lifts him up, peers into his face, and whispers words her father taught her. "*San fui! San Lau! Chow wan!*" And she honors her mother's memory, telling the child how he is descended from eagle and bear.

She seldom thinks of the one who shot her. She will not allow such thoughts. But some nights, rogue images press in. An Army campground under snow, a human warmth beside her. Blue dawns, when waking she loved the world. One night she calls out his name in sleep, then wakes feeling terrified, runs to the river and swims to exhaustion.

The War moves closer. The Battle of Petersburg, the Battle of Five Forks, twelve miles from Richmond. When Grant's victorious Army enters Richmond, the city erupts in flames, parts of it leveled to the ground. Almost as an afterthought, Robert E. Lee surrenders, and before folks can fully react, the president is shot dead. For weeks people move about in shock, wondering what is left for them, what can be salvaged from this torn-apart land.

And it is now, the battles finally ended, that they begin to understand the price, as wounded and dying boys pour in across the East. Week after week, month after month, trains roll in, casualties flooding hospitals, pouring out onto surrounding grounds until it seems that all the green fields of Washington and Maryland and Virginia are covered with ghostly white hospital tents.

Each week Era appears at the offices of the Federal Secret Service, begging for news of Corporal Johnny Tom. In the chaos of victory, national mourning, and reassigning troops to guard defeated Southern cities, the Army has no news of him.

They ask her to be patient. In May, the victorious Army of the Potomac marches in Grand Review down Washington's Pennsylvania Avenue. For two days Era stands amongst the crowds, searching for her father in the ranks of hundreds of thousands of soldiers on parade.

* * *

It is late August when a tall, soft-spoken Negro and his son enter Harewood Hospital grounds, asking for medical assistance. For two years they have been shifted around, part of the diaspora of Colored Troop Units, many of whom, like Zebedee, have ended up working as burial crews.

He and Virgil have buried and reburied corpses and skeletons outside field hospitals, and hospital ships plying the Potomac and the Rappahannock, and everywhere, he has asked for a nurse named Era Tom. When his colored friends began to die of typhoid from handling corpses, he requested a medical discharge from the Army. Like many veterans now roaming the countryside, he has lived off his "freakish" wound by charging folks to watch him stick rags through his stomach while Virgil pulls them out the other side.

But lately Zebedee has grown feverish; rags of ribbons pulled out of his wounds are full of pus. Several times he has entered Colored Soldiers Hospitals, where attendants "patched" him up. Suspecting he needs more serious medical attention, he has worked his way to Harewood, largest and best-equipped hospital in the East.

For days he waits in the colored section of the grounds, lining up at the colored surgeon's tent for the ambulatory wounded, but there are thousands of men ahead of him. He and Virgil eat and sleep where they can, regaling soldiers with their adventures. And always, he mentions the name Era Tom. No one recognizes it, for there are hundreds of nurses ministering to these tens of thousands of wounded boys.

One day, blood and pus pour so profusely from his wound the smell of it knocks Zebedee off his feet. Days later, he wakes up inside the main hospital in a special ward for coloreds. A surgeon approaches, his white skin flushed, and speaks with unaccustomed candor.

"Mister, you nearly *expired* from blood poisoning. We've cleaned out your wound, but it's a curiosity—it won't be closed! We tried that, and it brings on infection. We have tried everything—sutured, unsutured—worked on you back to front, and front to back. It seems to have a mind of its own."

Zebedee frowns. "Well, does that signify I going die?"

"You might. Unless you thoroughly clean that wound with antiseptic twice a day, every day, for the rest of your life. Actually...we'd like to keep you here for observation. And to take photographs."

"You mean you be wanting to put me in your book of 'freaks.' I seen such books. You take pictures of these faceless, legless boys and be putting them out for the world to see."

"Well, such studies help advance medical research…"

"And what it be doing for all these broken boys? How you going advance them?"

He pats Zebedee's arm. "You think about it. Your photographs would be a real contribution to the medical profession."

He thinks about it for several days, then calls the surgeon back. "Doc, I might could sit for your pictures—on one condition. You help me find a nurse who might be here. Her papa died at Gettysburg. I promised him I'd find her."

The surgeon shakes his head. "There are over a thousand nurses at Harewood. And a hundred such hospitals all over the East. Why would you think she's here?"

"I'm not *sure* she's here. But I be searching near every hospital in Washington, Maryland, Virginia. Her papa once saved a brigadier general's life. I tracked him down, argued my way past his adjutants, appealed to his Christian conscience, you might say. Told him the corporal who saved his life done perished, and would he help me find his daughter who I feared be nursing soldiers in the South. I knew those Rebs probably hang me, but I was bound to go down there and find her…

"Corporal Johnny Tom was Chinese. 'Sides that, he was a hero, saved many lives. Well, this general, he goes to the higher-ups, and they get on them telegraph wires and track the daughter, Era Tom. For some reason, she be known to them. Seems she been transferred East, somewhere near Washington. Then all hell break loose, the War ends, and here I be. Can you help me, Doc?"

"Sounds impossible. So many displaced in this War. I'll see what I can do."

Virgil comes every day, wringing his hands. "You ain't goin' die on me, are you, Papa?"

"Hell, I'm a outlive you! You jest got to help me keep this wound antiseptical, and don't be fainting on me like you do."

One day when Virgil comes, he wears a dreamy expression that turns sly as he begins to talk.

"There's a real peaceful river nearby. I be sittin' there, thinkin' I might rig a line and catch me some fish. Tell you, Papa, it was passin' strange. Suddenly, I be seein' boys in this river, swimmin' without they *legs*. Scare me half to death. Then they pulled theyselfs out the river and up the bank, lookin' jest like frogs!"

His eyes grow narrow as he continues. "Then I see these nurses and orderlies with blankets, helpin' these frog-boys into wheelchairs. And I get me this...notion. I ask them orderlies they ever hear the name Era Tom. That she a nurse. That we carryin' a message from her papa. One a them orderlies kinda' frown, say, yeah, maybe he know of such a nurse. Say he stay clear of her cause she got evil eyes. Say she look after the frog-boys."

* * *

Late afternoon. She sits on the lawn beside the river. Not far away, a boy resolutely struggles with a newspaper. He has lost both hands and holds the paper with two devices made of metal and leather attached to his arms. Now and then, a small rustle is heard when, with glints of steel, he turns a page. Wanting to give him privacy, she concentrates on the book in her lap. Shadows grow long, and after a while she looks up.

A tall, rather dignified man stands before her, clearing his throat. "I do beg your pardon, ma'am."

She bends back a page and closes her book. "Yes? How can I help you?"

"I believe your name is Era Tom?"

"Yes. That's right…"

Tears cloud his eyes. Zebedee falters and holds a Bible to his chest.

"Ma'am, I be looking for you for two long years. I come to tell you of my friend…my best friend…"

They sit for hours as the river flows. The soft-spoken Negro and the pale young nurse. The boy with artificial hands watches as she bows her head and weeps, and the dark man takes her hand and goes on talking. Dusk brings a paler cast to her features so she seems childlike and vulnerable. Her shoulders cave in forward; still, she weeps.

Eventually—their shoulders touching, and their heads—the older man and the young nurse open the pages of a tattered Bible and trail their fingers over the small, earnest handwriting crosshatched over the Scriptures that then trails off into the margins, page after page, so that the Book seems swollen with his writing.

"It all here," Zebedee whispers. "His whole life written out for you. A brand-new story, over the old chronicles of Exodus, Leviticus…and Ruth, and Sam…"

They turn a page, and there is the tintype of them in uniform: the wiry, little Chinese with his long black queue and the tall, rather stately Negro.

"…and Psalms and Proverbs. Solomon and Amos and on and on…"

WARREN

The Great Plains, 1866–1867

Trains now crisscross the states and the New Territories. Nightmarish in scale, they ponderously drag themselves westward with their rumbling infinity of passenger and freight cars. Forsaking his dreams of the wilds of Canada, Warren lets the trains bear him away, going where they go, stopping where they stop.

Even in the remotest towns, he seeks out daguerrean galleries, little shops with their dusty windows displaying photos of the War. The images therein give him a sense of equilibrium and connectedness. They have become his touchstone in this alien, uncharted world. On through Kansas, then into the Great Plains of Indian and buffalo, thundering herds soon to be killed off by "sportsmen" shooting them from passing trains. He is in the geographical heart of America, nothing to break the distance but sod huts and the nightly fish spawn of stars.

Sometimes he stops at railroad camps and, displaying his one-armed agility, hires on as spike driver. Hammer to the iron rail, spike heads flashing out as he strikes them. The hot smell of cross ties, heat from the sun on his shoulders a balm. Still, there is continual seepage of blood through his long johns, sharp bits of shrapnel working their way out of his legs and back. Damp weather causes his stump to ache and throb from lack of circulation, and when he moves, his joints creak like an old man's. His bones, his very marrow, seem to retain the memory of war.

The railroad camps are honeycombs of illicit trade in humans, and he learns that buried beneath the railroad tracks are thousands of Chinese who had laid those tracks, then been sacrificed to the railroad—exhaustion, disease, all-out massacre—as whites began to fear their growing numbers. In one town, Warren sees Chinese corpses swinging from trees. Others are spread-eagled on planks for reveling, knife-throwing crowds.

"Why are they so hated?" he asks. "They've connected the country end to end."

An old-timer buys him a whiskey. "Problem is they're hardy little devils. 'Stead of going back to China, they stay and prosper. Now they're taking our mining and railroad jobs. More of a nuisance than the red man!"

Chinese women are led into railroad camps by ropes. Husbands and fathers murdered, they are auctioned off for the night by their "owners." Warren sees how slavery has never ended; its victims have merely changed colors. Suspecting it will ever be that way in this boundless, heartless country, he moves on.

Crossing into Texas, when railroad tracks run out, he joins one of thousands of wagon trains pushing west. Some men are War veterans like him, headed to Venezuela or Argentina to work vast cattle ranches. They speak of these plans without eagerness, almost without interest, and have few possessions or needs, except the need for motion. Still young, they look riven and old. Warren thinks of hooking up with them, for what does it matter where he goes? But something drives him westward.

One night they are joined by other wagoneers. Food is plentiful, but there are not enough utensils to go round. Men sit patiently, while others assiduously hack at their food, then grind away with their teeth and jaws, pulverizing each mouthful before passing on forks and spoons. Mid-meal, a woman appears, a hawk perched on her wrist. A fiddler strikes up a tune, and she locks arms with a cowboy as they two-step round and round, the hawk circling with them. Debauched on rum, she recklessly laughs and throws up her arms, her dress discolored at the armpits. From her body issues a stale reminder of female musk that excites imaginations, and produces a silence amongst the men.

Warren's neighbor whispers, "You believe it? She was a nursing sister in the War. Seen too much, I reckon. A lot of them nurses headed west, running from their nightmares."

Her scent makes him dizzy, makes his thoughts run wild. He reels off alone, swallows a bull's eye and lies back upon the ground. Era's voice speaks out in straight lines that come back to him in circles. ...*like her eyes that could seek, and could hide.* He remembers how she could cast them down and craftily blend into the background. Even her skin could blend, almost disappear.

As time passes, his memories of her seem to grow more, rather than less, profound. Her absence has become for him like his arm, a physical removal, irreparable and permanent. Yet, as he still feels the grip of missing fingers, an itching in the skin, so she is an amputation he cannot accept or comprehend. He wakes shouting her name into the desert.

Another year passes as he drifts through New Mexico Territory, surviving the winters in railroad camps. In spring, he comes out of the wilderness and enters California.

* * *

Los Angeles is a boomtown of gold miners and cattlemen, its streets thronged with the flotsam of a dozen countries. Midst the cacophony of foreign tongues, Warren moves cautiously through muddy streets lined with gambling houses and brothels from which outrageously painted women call to him wearing bustiers of hard, coiled wire padded with falsies made of elk hair. The fashion for ladies' hoopskirts has died; the metal-cage crinolines have been cut up and made into wire brushes that vendors sell for currycombing horses. Men trot up and down the streets on groomed mounts that leave in their wake the perfumed scent of ladies' underwear.

He finds a public bath, a room, and eats a proper meal in a steak house.

He visits a brothel offering whores of ornamental diversities, but chooses a pale, thin blonde whose face is pitted from smallpox. Their transaction is silent. He does not remove his shirt, although he tips her generously. Then he presses through shouting crowds as a fever sweeps the town, onslaught of a killing spree. Turning a corner, he sees Chinese, even women and children, hanging by their necks from balconies. Lynch mobs have flowered overnight, bent on purging the city of "pigtails" who are stealing their jobs and businesses. A horse gallops by, dragging a headless corpse.

With profound loathing for the town, Warren books passage on a freighter bound for San Francisco, a huge port city where he has heard ships dock from all over the world. He has no destination; he does not want a destination. Perhaps he will live at sea until his days are over, for he has reached the end of a country that offers him nothing, it seems, but hate.

Occasionally, War veterans try to engage him in conversation. Their words melt away in his inner ear. Curiosity, opinions, manners—all the conventional props that shore up a man's character—are rapidly deserting him. All the heart he has for living in this world begins to fade. He feels life slowly running down his chest and down his limbs.

With two days left to spare, he wanders the streets again. Inevitably, as is his wont, he seeks out small emporiums of souvenirs, shops offering portraits in ambrotypes, daguerreotypes. As if to attract humans of a more contemplative nature, they are set off by themselves on quiet streets, away from thoroughfares of greater commerce. On Sonora Street he finds shops whose pictures are devoted to the War. In sunlit windows, the images resonate—drilling troops, generals resplendent in full dress.

As he progresses down the street, the photographs turn grim—corpses, carnage, the broken men. He stops and stares, feeling the old, familiar grief. But as he approaches one shop, Warren feels his body lifted, feels momentarily blinded. He leans against the storefront, trying to catch his breath, to focus his eyes again.

There are other images displayed, but they recede, for centered in the window is a portrait of a nurse. The caption below it reads: *Harewood Hospital, Washington, DC, 1864.* She is crossing a lawn beside a river, her body half-turned so that her face is partially shaded, yet her golden, slanted eyes have caught the light.

* * *

He enters a shop smelling of lemon oil, a cozily furnished place with battlefield scenes framed in mahogany. A stocky man enters from a backroom.

"Hullo! You are first customer today."

Warren is suddenly aware of his pinned-up sleeve, his worn-out clothes.

"That picture in the window. The nurse. May I ask how you came to have it?"

The dealer smiles, pours from a bottle, and offers him a glass. "Sit. Have a whiskey. We make conversation."

Still in shock and struck by the foreign accent, the stress and cadence of his speech, Warren sits down and empties the glass. "I'm sorry. I was struck by that picture and wondered how you acquired it."

The man leans forward and pours another drink. "In my country, we make introductions first. I am Ivan Golgoff, photographer. I take that picture."

Warren tells him his name, then says he thinks he knew the woman in the photograph. "Her name was Era Tom."

"Yes. You knew her in the War, no doubt. You maybe were in love with her. We all were, a little."

He swallows the second drink and struggles for composure. "You seem a decent man. Please tell me…when did you last see her?"

"When I last saw her? Near end of War, when all was chaos."

"But, this Era Tom is dead!"

Ivan smiles. "Yes. Is possible we all died in the War."

"I assure you…I saw her body in a grave."

"So perhaps a miracle. The woman I speak of *was* Era Tom. We know each other from before, in city of Nashville, Tennessee…"

"Yes. She was there."

"She had since been injured, but was very much alive. Date of picture is accurate."

He covers his face and shakes his head as if trying to shake it loose from his body. His anguish calls out for compassion, and the Russian leans forward, touching his arm.

"Relax, my friend. I will tell you what I know."

He explains how, weeks before he encountered her, he was working on the grounds of Harewood Hospital.

"Tents of wounded stretched all the way to horizon. Many photographers shooting day and night for historical documentation. Then…one day, I see her."

He goes to the window, brings back her photograph, and sets it on an easel. Then he tells of nurses gathered on the shore of a river, tending boys who had lost their legs.

"They swim, splashing with their arms, trying still to be human."

One day Era broke from the others and moved across the lawn.

"I think I maybe never forget it. Around her hangs soft, green haze, one blue heron poised on river's shore. She turns her face. Pale yellow skin, strange Oriental eyes. wide apart and searching. I know then is Era Tom."

He relates how she had been wounded "in a skirmish" like so many nurses, and how in searching for her father she had ended up at Harewood.

"I was fatigued from seeing too much War. I want to escape, come west. I ask her to come with me, but she stay put, searching for father. When I am settled here, I write her. Maybe one year later she respond…"

He shakes his head, remembering. "Her father killed at Gettysburg. A man bring her his Bible with stories written of his life. She write she is going to his homelands, to China. Nothing in the South but death."

Warren has been straining at each word, and now he sits back. "Do you think she really went?"

"I think would be impossible. I write back saying China is all chaos with its own civil war, thirty million dead. She, a foreigner, would be killed."

Years of thinking she was dead. She *should* be dead. Yet something in him had never quite countenanced that breach. He had never witnessed that final consummation, her last breath.

Ivan pours himself another drink. "She once tell me her family history. Tragic. Like ten thousand others."

"Did she tell you she was a scout, a…Federal spy?"

"Ah, my friend, we were all spies one way or another. Sutlers, photographers, whores following the troops. We did what we believed in. Was it not the same for you?"

"I was too young to have beliefs. Then I was too old."

They gaze at her photograph, the slender neck, the small, straight cartilage of nose. Cheekbones like a pale, carved bowl upon whose rim the eyes are set.

"A beautiful portrait. Strange that no one buys, though many stop and stare. The face perhaps unsettling. I think were many scars she never spoke of."

"Are you sure she left Washington?"

"No. Am not sure. But why she would stay? After Sherman, everything destroyed. South nothing but a carcass. Buzzards. Widows tending graves. Who knows? It may be she sailed for China. May be the only place for her. You see what is happening in America, this hate for anyone not white."

They study her image again. She would now be twenty-one or twenty-two.

"A woman like that, so distant...She will always leave men feeling haunted. You agree?"

Warren shakes his head. "I gave up feelings years ago."

"Perhaps your mutilations have not gone deep enough! If you have no feelings, why you are here?"

"Maybe, out of disbelief."

Ivan laughs. "No, my friend. You entered my shop because you are hoping for a miracle. You want to *suffer*. To feel again."

Unconsciously, he rubs his stump. "You are...absolutely...wrong."

"But why? Be glad for pain. Without it, we are insects."

"Look, the woman was evil. She caused the death of innocent boys...maybe hundreds."

"And you, Mr. Warren Petticomb, you did not kill? You did not cause the death of many? And sometimes even... relish it?"

Warren falls silent, swept again by the full phantasma-
goria of war—the human descants, the bright, wet guns. "I
never deceived her."

"Ah! Then we are speaking of hurt pride."

"I have no pride. The war took care of that too. What
would I be proud of?"

Whiskey loosens his tongue, and the Russian speaks out
with a hectoring zeal.

"When man has nothing else, he is proud of his *scars*.
Scars of your youth obliterated by war, your manhood forever dwarfed by ghosts. This has left you full of rage, so
you look for a scapegoat in this woman who deceived you.
But think! What is a little deception in the face of massive
deaths?"

Warren slumps, no longer sure of what is true. "For
years, I have thought her dead. I *wished* her dead."

"Yet you cannot forget her. We have old saying in my
country: *When well is dry, we drink at the mirage.*"

He suddenly rises, extending his hand. "I've taken too
much of your time. I thank you for…your information, your
hospitality."

Ivan grips his hand. "You are in shock, my friend. Go
home, lie down. Is almost dusk, that hour when is hardest
to pretend."

"I thank you again."

"No need to thank. You will be back."

* * *

He moves with a sense of great fatigue, yet with the knowledge that something in him has been waiting, something
that knew instinctively she had survived. It has been quietly
waiting for proof. Now, wherever she is, she is his again; their
unfinished history makes her his alone. His meager belong-

ings—his boots, his gun—now acquire special meaning be-cause they will make the journey with him to find her, no matter where in this world she has gone to.

Warren calls out in his dreams. "I will find you! And finally, you will tell me the truth. That you never really loved me."

Yet he knows the truth, knew it in an instant the day he shot her. Or *was* it the truth? What he had known were merely facts. She had cold-bloodedly deceived him. She was responsible for acts that took the lives of Southern boys. But the War and life have taught him that facts are not the truth, merely part of it. Perhaps since the day she rode off he has been waiting for the full truth to present itself; it is what kept him alive while others died.

The ship he had booked passage on departs, and he walks dusty streets, thinking how his hate for her had burned through the years like a scorching beam. Yet, in weaker mo-ments, he concedes that betrayal and running were all that had been left to her, her world savaged, her parents gone. Perhaps betraying him had been the only way to keep her honor.

He thinks how she had lain in his arms and wittingly turned him into an accomplice. It is still incomprehensible that she had committed these acts against him personally. She could have turned away from him, chosen someone else. She did not have to kneel beside him—his stump raw and aching, his mind in shock—and let her fragrance enter him. She did not have to hold him, or give herself to him.

At night he tosses, remembers pointing his revolver, and he wonders if one is least guilty at that moment one aims a weapon at another human. For the guilt already exists; it is manifestly there in the *intention*. It may be that something in him suspected her early on, that all those nights they lay together he was, in fact, preparing.

He recalls the feel of the revolver, how he lifted the hammer with that quiet, cold click, the sound of perfectly tempered steel going about its fatal task—a gun being cocked for the kill. In that moment, he could not move; his fate was no longer his to control. The moment had come, the thing was going to happen of its own volition. Yet, at first, he had not fired.

"Your horse," she cried. "Give me your horse."

While Warren stood there she had, in one motion, mounted his horse and taken off. The gun had fired itself. That was a shame more painful than any other. The gun, not he, had been in control, and it had done a meager job. Yet when he saw her dragged off by the horse, thinking her dead, he had almost turned the gun upon himself. So here is another question he has never been able to answer: When he—or the gun—had shot her, was he trying to kill her? Or keep her from leaving.

Now great care is required. Life has beckoned him again. He thinks of all he has seen and learned: that the universe is indifferent to our human endeavors, that what gives our lives meaning is the passion that invades our hearts and burns in us, and maybe even destroys us. Without Era, there is nothing. He is nothing. He goes to the Russian's shop again.

"So, Warren Petticomb! You return to impale yourself on memory."

"I'm leaving town," he says, then carefully unwraps the photograph of Johnny Tom. "But first, I wanted to show you this. From the caption, I believe it was her father."

Ivan stares, then glances at the identifying card attached to the back. The reference to Johnny Tom at Gettysburg. "Where did you find this?"

"Chicago. A shop of 'Exotica and Human Grotesqueries.'"

Ivan picks up a pair of scissors and cuts the caption from the picture. *Johnny Tom, the Chinese Human Pillow!*

"It is not grotesque. Is a portrait of brave soldier. Such pictures were only made grotesque by dealers."

"Well, I would like you to have it. It should be framed and cared for."

Ivan shakes his head. "This is not for me. And not for you. Is for *her*, if you find her."

Warren steps back, shocked that his intention is so evident. "Why ever do you think I want to find her?"

"You are haunted by her. You are dying of that last disease called *hope!* Look, I make a gift for you. I have copies."

He takes Era's picture from the window, removes it from the frame, and carefully rolls it up together with that of Johnny Tom, then slides them into a cardboard cylinder. "Brave father and daughter together."

He motions for Warren to sit down and, once again, pours drinks.

"We have a talk before you go. My background...I, too, was fleeing slavery...of Imperial Russian tsars. For this, Era took pity on me, but pity mixed with envy, for I have traveled many places. Wild Territories of Oregon, Washington, Alaska."

He tells how, for years, huge trading ships had anchored there from Russia, China, the Pacific Islands, and how, in the Pacific Northwest, he had seen people of every race and color living together, intermarrying with Tlingits, Inuits, Athbascans.

He taps his finger on his lip. "I remember she was intrigued when I speak of these people of different skins, different tongues, living side by side. But I warn her was not a place for her. Pirates, outlaws, men who kill for gold. We seldom speak of it again."

He shakes his head. "Pacific Northwest. China. Is all the same. Not possible for such a woman to reach alone. She was frail, would not survive. And first, she would have to cross America!"

He studies Warren, whose eyes seem paler for their sadness. "How long it is since you have seen her?"

"More than five years."

"Ah, my friend. I think only a miracle could find her."

When he departs, Ivan embraces him and gives him his card. "One day you might write me in case I have more news of her."

* * *

He studies the photographs of Era and Johnny Tom. *Brave father and daughter together.* He thinks of his own family lost in the War and longs for them, for someone to confide in. Life has unexpectedly come at him, setting off reflexes he is not sure of. He sits thoughtful, then draws out pen and paper.

> *My dearest sister Annabelle,*
>
> *Having no kith or kin left in this world I feel the need to write you, though you are gone. Father's last letter said you had followed your sweetheart to Vicksburg. Sometime later with surpassing sadness I learned that his entire regiment had fallen there. Wanting to believe you survived and went home to Prattville, I have wrote you twice care of the Courthouse. Both letters came back marked DECEASED.*
>
> *You were always brave and headstrong, so I am disposed to think you would have stayed near your sweetheart in the conflagration of the city, maybe even fought beside him. If he was wounded you would have*

tended him, and if he perished I can depend you died fighting in his place. It excites my heart to know that you achieved what you were put upon this earth to do: to love with all your being, and then to stand and fall beside that loved one.

I do not calculate upon ever going South again. For years I have had no direction, no desire. The War did that though, honor bright, sometimes I miss it. I miss my Prattville pards to weeping. Life was simple then, all we had to do was kill or die. I lost an arm at Shiloh, and that is when I learned how a whole boyhood is contained in a body-part. Sometimes I stare at people's arms, not out of envy much as longing for that innocence. Still, I don't know why I lived and others died. It seems indecent.

Oh, Annabelle! You were always my good glue, my conscience. When I read how you rushed to join your sweetheart, in that moment I understood how the heart is an ethical thing. It makes choices. It tells us what it means to be alive, and what it means to be prepared to die. When he was called away to fight, you were not impaired by weak repining. Instead you followed him. And when he perished I warrant that grieving did not sanctify for you, so you picked up his gun and soldiered on. I mourn. I mourn for the fury of your passion and your youth...

Feeling a great fragility and weariness of spirit, Warren rests his head upon his arm, and for the first time in years, he weeps. He weeps as if there is no end to it. Finally, he pulls himself together and tries to make sense of his musings.

...but lately my grief has been jostled by hope. I feel a reawakening, a panicky resurrection. Someone

I thought had died is yet alive, someone I loved who deceived me to the core. My first reaction was to seek her out and kill her. But then I thought of you, your valor, and I began to feel there is still a part of me not blighted by the War. Forgiveness has been a thing my heart could never brook, but I am weary now of hating. And I wonder if in finding this woman, in forgiving her, I might begin to forgive myself. I might find a higher destiny than this worthless life of drift.

My beloved Annabelle, your brief life has by example led me to this knowledge that love comes first, no matter what. Before logic, before judgement, before right and wrong. Now, in your memory I will set out to find this woman and face whatever truth is left between us. And mayhap I will stand but a modest remove from being human once again. You are forever in my recollections and my heart.

Your devoted brother, Warren R. Petticomb

He reads the letter several times, then folds it carefully and slides it into his pocket next to his heart. In the coming weeks and months he will read it often.

WARREN

Pacific Northwest Coast, 1868–1872

He studies crude maps of America showing distances from the East Coast to the West, and he recalls women who had crossed those grueling distances in wagon trains, many of whom had perished. The hardier ones worked their passage as nurses, teachers, even prostitutes in mining and railroad camps, and some had settled in the camps too worn out to go on.

Most wagon trains still come through Texas into New Mexico Territory, so Warren wanders back into that land, stopping at camps, showing Era's photograph to itinerant doctors and nurses. After six months, he moves on to Utah Territory, where he hires on again as spike driver for the railroads. The city of Promontory is now a boomtown where, within a year, the last piece of track will be nailed into place, joining the West Coast of America to the East Coast. He approaches railroad crews and shows men her picture.

"I remember. She went that way." A man points north.

"That way." Another man points south.

He chooses Nevada next. If she is still in America, she would surely be traveling west, as far from the South as she can get. A year passes, then another. He sends Ivan Golgoff a picture postcard of two train engines facing each other. The railroads have finally connected the coasts of this vast continent.

He rounds up wild horses for the U.S. Army, not caring that they were once the enemy. He changes jobs, then repeats them, the spiral of seasons giving each year the sensation of brevity. Drifting through a dozen towns and camps,

Warren realizes that, in the swift current of weeks and months, they have entered a new decade. He begins to suspect he will never find her.

One day, he unrolls the photograph of Johnny Tom and studies the flatness of his face, the wide plains of cheekbones more pronounced in death. Yet the man seems alive, his face now oddly familiar. Ivan had told him fragments of what Era learned of her father's youth, and now Warren picks up pen and paper and tries to sketch him, not as a dead artifact, but as a boy running rickshaws at a dogtrot, thin shoulders bent under bamboo yokes. He imagines his gray lips from which all iron had been leached, imagines his starved expression. Pondering the sadness of his life—the appalling tragedy of his ending—Warren stares at his face for hours, contemplating the daughter's fate.

* * *

In San Francisco's Chinatown, he walks in and out of shops with Era's picture, knowing instinctively she is not there. She would not linger where hatred for Orientals resonates on every street, as whites continue driving them out of America. He sees a Chinese bakery blown up, bodies floating heavenward like floured angels. Appalled, he goes back to his room to his solitary bull's eye, the vivisection of his life into empty hours, minutes, seconds.

Having arrived at the edge of the continent, he admits he will never find her. The world is too large, the odds too small. His next choice must be north or south, perhaps the sea route to South America, vast unknowns that will swallow him. Finally, this is what he wants: to be swallowed, to disappear. He writes Ivan Golgoff of his plans, that he is relinquishing the search for Era. Even her photograph has begun to fade, the edges creased and stained.

He broods over his letter to Annabelle, whom he has dismally failed to honor. "...*You were my good glue, my conscience...You taught me by example that love comes first, before logic, before judgement...In your memory I will set out to find this woman...*"

He stands in crowds, hearing the *basso profundo* of a ship's horn, the shipping line giving notice that it is headed for Canton with the remains of Chinese workers: *BRING THE BONES OF YOUR DEAD. SEND THEM HOME IN LACQUERED JARS. FINANCES ARRANGED.* So many killed or worked to death, two thousand pounds of polished bones are going home. He imagines her bones are on that ship. He wonders what they weigh.

Finally, he books passage on a freighter bound for Valparaiso. The morning his ship departs, the landlady shakes his hand, calling him a quiet one, a gentleman. Then she taps her forehead, digs into her pocket, and hands him a letter.

"It came a week back, but I have missed your comings and goings."

Dear Warren Petticomb,

Should this find you may be is important. After many years I hear from Era Tom. She is living where I never think she would go. Pacific Northwest Coast, north even of Wild Territories. Worked her way up year by year as teacher, nurse, in gold camps, logging camps. I am chagrined to know she is so brave.

She sent no return address but mention Cisco Bay near where she was living. Her letter come one year back but I have no address for you. May be she already is gone from there. By now on ship, going all the way to China!

*I salute you in your travels, wishing you much
color and intoxication, help you forget the past. I now
have pretty Mexicali wife.*

Your friend, Ivan Golgoff

For two days, he stares at the letter, his heart hammering at his ribs, and he recalls that winter in Tullahoma, how their love had been like a dementia. Now he loves her more for all her suffering and how in spite of it, at the risk of her life, she had kept her self-respect. He thinks of the Battle of Chickamauga, how he deserted, turning his back on his comrades, on the whole of the dying Confederacy. He feels he is about to embark on a journey, not just to find her, but to confess that, in the end, *he* was the traitor. And finally, he understands that he must find her because she holds his heart; she has always held his heart. Without her, he can neither live nor die.

* * *

Within days, he is headed up the North Pacific Coast. Changing ships in Seattle, he sees how people begin to look different—round-faced like Orientals but with darker, copper-colored skin. Their hair is uniformly black, glossy, and pungent from fish oils, and he learns they are Inuits, Athabascans, Pacific Coast Indians of a dozen confederacies. Women pour down the streets arm in arm in twos and fours. Even prostitutes walk out in numbers, carrying pistols, armed against men abducting them for auctioning off in mining camps.

Weeks later, he is northbound on a trading ship. Taking the inside passage between Vancouver Island and Canada, they pass mythic forests of fir and pine surrounding gold-mining and fur-trading camps and fishing canneries, and thousands of settlements of Indians and mixed-bloods interbred with Europeans. With every mile he travels, Warren wonders how he will ever find her. And if he does, how will she behold him?

Each time the ship docks to off-load cargo, he walks through encampments with her picture. A tattooed Siberian remembers her as a Bible thumper traveling with a dwarf. A miner swears she is a prostitute and gold thief. A dozen versions in each port. But one day, an Athabascan woman points north.

"She with the limp. Headed that way."

Along the coast of British Columbia, they approach the booming grounds of Cisco Bay, big husky loggers engaged in the tricky dance of log sorting, hopping from one to the next with long pike poles as thousands of logs crash down from the river. Huge seabirds call and wheel over the cliffs, and under a cold, pinchbeck sun, the air bites Warren's cheeks like razors. Through drifting fog, the captain points out dancing curls of smoke.

"Mixed-blood settlements stretching all the way up to Ketchikan, Alaska. Every kind of squaw hitched up with Irish, Russians, French, Chinese."

Warren hesitates. "Do many white women venture here alone?"

"Only the used-ups. Women on the run."

From the stormy Hecate Straits, they travel up Cisco River, the ship's final destination. Ramshackle buildings huddle near the harbor, behind them tents of Indian encampments and salt-worn cabins of workers' camps. Warren disembarks, pressing cautiously through crowds. Knowing instinctively she would not be in a port settlement, with no clear direction, he sets off on horseback, moving slowly from camp to camp.

Lowering fog, primeval forests, fox all sense of perspective and seem to cancel out the centuries. He slips into timelessness, hearing only the crying out of prey, death in little hawk-blinks. And he ponders how such an otherworldly region may be the only place left for her. *A woman unprovided for, except in the provision of herself.*

After many days, he meets two Tlingit women who remember her. "Good nurse. Good teacher." They point vaguely north. "One-Blood Camp."

He moves on, asking at settlements for directions to One-Blood Camp. People shrug and turn away. One day, he encounters a trapper on his path. They gaze at each other with the wariness of loners reconnoitering away from the rigors of other humans. The man slowly tips his hat, his bald head girdled by ragged curls. Under a bearskin coat, he is tricked out at his neck and wrists in the chased bones of elk and deer.

Warren asks the way to One-Blood Camp, and the man's eyes quickly catalogue him: the wiry, condensed power of the shoulders, the slight repercussion of movement common to military men and lawmen.

His response flushes out a French accent. "So. You are a marshal? Bounty hunter? Be warned. Those types disappear up here."

Warren explains he is looking for a woman named Era Tom.

"And…what was her crime?"

With malign weariness, he slumps in his saddle. "I reckon you could say she…left me in unwarranted confusion."

The Frenchman smiles and relaxes as Warren describes her, and how many years he has been searching. When the man speaks again, there is pathos in his voice.

"Could be the yellow-eyed woman with a limp. I sometimes trade with mix-bloods who might know her."

They lay down sleeping bags and, through the hours, exchange a rough text of their lives, the War, and drifting, the good luck and bad. At dawn, they leave their horses with Tlingits and paddle upriver for hours, then portage their canoe to the clearing of One-Blood Camp.

"So many mixed-blood pairings and offspring they're all one," the Frenchman explains. "Be patient, *mon ami*. Here there is not much reliance on words. Nuance can take you a hundred miles."

They sit at a big campfire with others, eating and drinking. Warren does not look beyond the fire; he has a sense she is not near. He lets himself relax, observing the seedy magnetism of these raw, rugged mix-bloods, miners and trappers, as they whisper of gold finds, prices paid for cougar pelts. Evening auguring toward night, they break out concertinas, rachety violins. Deep in whiskey, they dance wildly, furiously, so even their bloodstreams seem to dance.

Later, there is the slow heartbeat of slapped drums as Indians chant pagan psalmodies, their plaintive voices stirring unnameable sorrows in the heart. Wolves howl from the forests. Shafts of moonlight pour through cathedral ceilings of fir and pine, and Warren feels he has been summoned to sit in abject wonder. He bows his head and something issues from his throat.

The Frenchman speaks softly. "Grief is common here. We have all run from something."

* * *

As days pass, he tries to mingle in the camp, but when he mentions Era's name, people stare, taking his measure, then turn away.

"They are wary," the Frenchman advises. "You have to *earn* their trust."

He sits outside his tent, surrounded by sheds poised at a trapezoid tilt from which sweet-faced, little half-breeds stare. Slop buckets hang from the boughs of trees, and rigged up between the trees are hammocks for elders with tuberculosis. Women in bright-colored shawls breast-feed their infants while holding outspread turkey wings, fanning the stricken elders hour after hour. The eternal human cycle—an elder's cough, the mewling of a newborn, the shifting nows of death and life.

Warren brings out pencil and paper and begins to sketch. But always, his eyes search here and there, seeing, not seeing her. Children lark in and out of the shadows and eventually approach, drawn by his missing arm and the swiftness of his pencil strokes. It is late summer out in the world, but here there is only a trace of sun, brisk air presaging autumn. He points to a great horned owl that has grown its double coat of feathers, and the children gather close as he begins to sketch the owl.

Nearby, elder women stretch pelts on wide, nailed planks, and one day they call out in merriment as older boys return from a nearby missionary school. They run through the woods, leaping and laughing with youths' abandon. Most are husky copper-skins and half-breeds, but one boy is light-skinned, with remarkably pale hair.

Each day, while children gather round Warren, the boy stands at a distance, offhandedly studying his blond, water-parted hair, pale gray eyes, the missing arm. The way he rubs his stump beneath the pinned-up sleeve brings on slight concern, a threatening compassion in the boy. He wonders if the man's stump hurts. Then he steps back, having learned to be wary of white-skins.

From a distance, the Frenchman watches too. His eyes move from Warren to the boy and back again, struck by the almost preternatural resemblance, except for the lad's almond-slanted eyes. He asks an elder the boy's name.

"We call him 'Shy Tongue.' Sometimes broods like old woman."

"And what is his English name?"

"John Warren...Mother is the yellow-eye who sits on distant cliffs."

* * *

One day, a little half-breed taps Warren's knee and speaks out with perfervid, boyish innocence.

"Say, mister...was you ever either-handed? Or was you born this way?"

Warren ruffles his hair and smiles. Then he looks up to see the Frenchman approaching, glancing over his shoulder so that he seems to be walking sideways. He shoos off the children, sits down with Warren, and points in the distance to the lad. He tells him what he has learned.

A breeze comes up, and for a moment the boy looks at Warren through a kelp of yellow hair. He is pale and long boned, a threatening gangliness, his shirt already shy at the wrists. The Frenchman waves him closer and, curious, he approaches, tossing back his hair and baring his face so that his eyes devour Warren. Seeing her likeness in a near replica of himself, the hair on Warren's arm stands up in a ghostly halo, his expression almost bestial in its shock.

ERA

The Cliffs of One-Blood

On an outcrop of cliffs dotted with swept-back pines, she sits in the crevice of a boulder sculpted by winds like the cupped palm of a giant. She sits unmoving, offering herself to the scenery. In her stoic serenity, she has *become* the scenery. Somewhere, she had stopped running, stopped reinventing; she had simply stepped out of her life. In this remote and rustic place, she has become refined to a pinpoint of reflection.

On rare, clement days, the sun brings a modicum of warmth —and with it, memories of the War. It is then she hears the dead boys whispering, and she is moved to whisper back. *For they, perforce, have entered me. Their battles have entered me.* She recalls their mutilations, their smells, resurrecting that pestilential dreamscape of her past, and in that time, her grief assembles. She sows the years of grief. But there are tender memories too.

…Women laboring in poppy-fields, their sunburned skin against gray pods…Light glistening on "gum" as it dripped from the pods, and after licking the "gum" from their hands, how the women drifted like dancers…

…And boys floating in a river, as if they were uninjured and intact. How they smiled! Then crawled up on shore, legless, sunning themselves like turtles…And the others, the ones with broken spines who swam with only their arms, lifeless legs floating behind them like mermen…

When finally she rises, she flows with a kind of bonelessness, her skin pale against brown, disabled furs. And sometimes a presence walks with her, the flash of pale, assassin eyes. She steps aside to let it pass. In her cabin, she broods over her father's Bible, her nightly way of honoring him. Amongst the tattered pages upon which is written the history of his life, is a red-ribbon bookmark that has lain in the Good Book's creases for decades, perhaps generations. Yet, it is still so bright it shimmers, throwing off musty perfumes.

When she turns a page, the ribbon flutters slightly, its liveliness and brightness comforting her, reminding her that some things outlast time. And somehow it tells her she is not alone, though she has felt very much alone. It compels her to believe that forces are gathering, that life is not finished with her. She begins to wake with the sense that something is approaching, that the end of a story will be known.

Throughout neighboring encampments, folks look upon her as something of a seer. They see it in the eyes, so bottomless. She has coaxed drowned Inuits back to life, delivered healthy infants from Metis women dying of tuberculosis, the ministrations of an experienced nurse rather than a seer. Still, only her students venture close, seeing Era as a ruined incarnation of a beauty in a fairy tale, for she is still beautiful in a fragile way. They bring her the veriest of trifles, gaudy corpses of giant moths, sea-carved driftwood.

Some days, from her outcrop on the cliffs, she watches them on the beach below, darting amongst rocks and shallows, her son amongst them. There is the Orient in his eyes, but the yellow in his skin sleeps. He is all pale and pale-haired. Still, she worries about his future. At ten, he is somewhat intractable, uncategorizable, beyond race or class, and burdened with inordinate pride. *How will he fare in life without a father's instructions?* Then she consoles herself that he has grown strong and tough in these mining camps, intimate with Tlingits and Athabascan, French and Irish trappers, Swedes and Russians singing Vladivostok love songs. *He can wield a knife, and bow and arrow. He can stalk and skin a wolf. He will be all right in the world.*

John Warren is quick and bright, but in the company of others conducts himself with modesty. Through the years, Era has taught him a gentleness, a shy generosity toward others that calls out to the goodness inherent in him. Still, their years on the run had fed into his consciousness the tendency to bear things in silence, to never register shock or pain, and a memory of the outside world as menacing.

She recalls his infancy when she refused to name him, but how eventually she came to love him. With that love, a task was imposed upon the boy: He would be her ally, her witness, in the terrible years of their fleeing. She remembers crossing the country in reeking wagon trains, nursing workers in filthy camps. Wherever they went, the gaze of white men fixed on her: a wrong-eyed woman, her wrong-eyed boy. They spat on him, called him *half-breed, mongrel,* and he knew they would have to flee again.

Town to town, state to state, then into the wilderness— territory to territory. In those years, he had learned to be silent, to turn his face to the wall, to even *become* that wall when whites ran the streets slaughtering "yellow dogs." Era remembers holding him, the pounding of his heart against her heart. His eyes trying to hide from his face.

By then, they had survived years on the run, the massacres in Nevada, San Francisco. Whites were even murdering Chinese women and children. One night, lynchers had come upon them unexpectedly and dragged them from a boardinghouse, but they were wily and got away. When they arrived half-starved in the Pacific Northwest camps, their clothes were so faded and threadbare they were the same color as their skin. As though they were wearing only dust.

She taught, nursed, saved her meager earnings. When she finally inquired about passage to China, ships' captains quickly disenthralled her. The Chinese were slaughtering all foreigners, trying to sweep their country clean.

The Pacific wilderness, this primordial outpost between hate and hate, proved the only safe place for her and her son.

Some nights, she watches him in sleep, remembering how he was born. How she had squatted, consuming the umbilical cord, how in her madness she nearly consumed all of him. At such times she wonders, *Was I finally a good mother? Did I minister well? To what good purpose did I minister? Was it with love? Was love enough?* She bows her head and weeps, understanding that in nurturing and protecting him, she has added to the sum of goodness. She has proven that, within her, goodness still exists.

Still, she wonders what kind of future this wilderness can offer him. Each week, desperate white women arrive on "bride ships" for loggers and miners. She watches as they sit dabbing their smallpox-pitted cheeks with beeswax under the yellow gaze of cougars. And each night, the sobbing of malemutes longing for deep snows. She pictures John Warren a grown man, longing for so much more. But then, the blind ruck of chance: a rumor in the camps, the one-armed stranger searching.

At first, shock, then the wondering if all these years she has been pulling the father across the continent, winding his life up between thumb and elbow like a fishing line, praying he would come. That he *must* come. For the boy. For her. Conjuring Warren's battle-weary face, the warm, tannic scent of him, she moves through the woods like a revenant. She hardly disturbs the air.

* * *

He stands in the empty classroom. No signs, no auguries, to give him hope. His Tlingit guide explains.

"School recessed for now. Children help prepare for winter. Crabs to be sorted. Salmon, herring, to be smoked."

"Then where is the teacher? The one who limps?" Warren feels hallucinatory with apprehension.

"Now she make rounds of camps, tending sick and wounded. Come. I lead you here and there."

They ride from camp to camp in search of her, and hour after hour, Warren espies the boy following, paralleling them through dense fir and pines, still not comprehending who this stranger is. Warren reflects on the beauty and austerity of him, still so shocked by his existence he touches his own face to see if it is there. He touches his heart, recalling the moment when John Warren first approached. The somber, questioning eyes. The wild, woodsy scent of him. His neck shadowed with a golden down, a strong neck forecasting the man to be. And finally, the touch of him when they shook hands. The shocking sense of connectedness.

He suspects it might take months, maybe years, for them to begin to ask and answer questions, to wander together down long mental trails with a nascent father-son contentment. Perhaps, in time, the boy might step closer to his side, as if fearing the flotsam of the great sea of life will carry Warren off again. He might begin to draw out words like his father, even imitate his penetrating gaze. And that will be the beginning.

But just now, the agonizing fear. *Will I be allowed to know him?*

* * *

It is late afternoon when they find her. An open-air clinic set up for wounded trappers and miners. Long plank boards upon which are set makeshift counters holding whiskey, ointments, medicaments. Jars holding scissors and knives.

In the posture of a surgeon, she leans over a man on a table, wrapping a homemade splint round his shattered leg. Her apron and her hands stained red.

Warren feels chills skate up his back, across his scalp, a sizzling in his brain. The eerie familiarity of the scene—Era in blood, tending the wounded—sweeps him violently back to the past. Suddenly he hears his pards, his cavaliers, galloping down a concourse, all jangling spurs and sabers. The sky alive with shot and shell. The call to glory. She washes her hands and moves away, triaging others of the wounded, and her calmness, her tender, nurturing movements, summon Warren back to the present.

She had not looked up when they rode into camp. He cannot see her face. But he discerns the familiar shape of her head, her long, dark hair gathered in a bun. She straightens up and turns away to wash her hands again. With measured slowness, Warren dismounts from his horse and stands in the shadows. From the back, her body looks so frail and slender he feels momentarily frightened.

Then she turns, and he sees her face, the still-enduring beauty. She dries her hands, exhaustedly rolls down her sleeves, and consoles the miner in the leg splint. The soft awe in his voice when he answers. She speaks quietly to a young nurse, then slips into a coat of ragged pelts and pats the heads of several children.

Warren steps from the shadows. At first she does not distinguish him, but as her eyes sweep past, the orbit of their light seems to fasten on him. A wind springs up, disturbing her furs so the end hairs quiver. Leaves rustle. She stands frozen in intricacies of sunlight.

Somewhere, the sun begins to set, the sky offering them its spillages, its brilliant running colors. He thinks how soon, dimly and hesitantly, the stars will step out, stronger and stronger in their radiance. Just as their son is stepping out from the forest to stand beside his mother. Era turns and takes his hand, murmuring reassuring words, then slowly leads him forward.

In that moment, Warren's senses drift, his body seems to fall away from him. He staggers, hand going to his eyes, hearing again the false rhapsody of War. The snort and dance of horses, his cavaliers calling out to him to follow. But Era stays him.

"Warren." Her hand soft upon his brow.

By sheer inveteracy of will, he struggles to steady himself, remembering how she had held him, two humans fused together in the War. How she had taken the dead husk of him and breathed it into flame again. Now, by some miracle, she holds him once more, and whispers softly, brief elliptic thoughts like clouds she has plucked from the ethers.

And he comes back to her, she to whom all his wounded catastrophes will run. He comes back because she is the only truth: that finally the world is irrelevant, that what matters is what obtains in the human heart. And in that affirmation, he feels the universe reveal itself, if only for a moment, as inexorably moral.

Acknowledgments

I would especially like to thank my cousins Polly Camp Kreitz and Charline Camp Smith for their years of research on our ancestor Warren Davenport of Prattville, Alabama. And my cousin Evelyn Kam Liu for her valuable insight into our Chinese family history. This book could not have been written without their guidance and encouragement.

I also thank Andy Bartlett, my editor, and the folks at Thomas & Mercer. Heartfelt thanks also to the intrepid Jan Constantine of the Author's Guild. And to my brilliant friend and author Kathrin Perutz, who painstakingly read this novel in its early drafts.

For their friendship and continuing support I also thank: Denise Davenport and Shaun McVay, Lorraine Dusky and Tony Brandt, Lis Harris and Marty Washburn, Tina Howe and Norman Levy, Cheryl and Victor James, Edith Konecky, John Livermore, Jan and Frank Morgan, Alix Kates Shulman and Scott York, Nani and Don Svendsen, Dr. Janet Talvacchia, Bill and Scotti Tomson, Kathleen Valentine, Anita and Robert Yantorno, and Becky Young.

And especially Alice Walker, whose Native American family history was the inspiration for my heroine, Era Tom.

Books that were especially helpful to me in my research included the excellent, groundbreaking memoirs in *Veterans of War, Veterans of Peace*, edited by Maxine Hong Kingston and Arnie Kotler, and also Maxine's enduring classic, *China Men*.

Also invaluable to me were two brilliant books about the role of Southern women in the U.S. Civil War: *Mothers of Invention: Women of the Slaveholding South in the American Civil War* and *This Republic of Suffering: Death and the American Civil War*. Both books were written by Dr. Drew Gilpin Faust, President, Harvard University.

Author's Note

Despite exclusionary laws preventing U.S. citizenship, many Chinese and Chinese-American soldiers served honorably in the Union and Confederate Armies and Navies of the U.S. Civil War. Still, they were denied citizenship after their services due to continuing anti-Asian sentiment, culminating in the Naturalization Act of 1870 and the Chinese Exclusion Act of 1882, which were enforced until 1943. Only in 1965 were all restrictions on national origin and race abolished.

In April 2003, the House Joint Resolution #45 was introduced to Congress to posthumously proclaim all U.S. Civil War soldiers of Chinese descent to be honorary citizens of the United States in recognition of their honorable services. But it denied pensions to their descendants.

About the Author

Kiana Davenport is the author of the bestselling novels *House of Many Gods*, *Song of the Exile*, and *Shark Dialogues*, and two story collections, *House of Skin* and *Cannibal Nights*. A Native Hawaiian, her novels and stories have won numerous awards and have been translated into twenty languages.